A sharp knock at the driver's side window startled a scream out of her, and she snapped her head in that direction only to find an amused-looking Carter peering in. Because of course. Think of the annoyingly perfect ex-boyfriend and he shall appear...Hoping he hadn't borne witness to her not-so-silent pep talk, she pressed the button to roll down her window.

"Hi." She smiled up at him, ignoring the chiseled cut of his scruffy jaw and how his piercing green eyes managed to get under her skin every time she was in his presence. Okay, so she *tried* to ignore those things. Trouble was, Carter and all his attributes were pretty damn hard to ignore.

"Hey," he said, resting his forearms on her open window. He cocked his head and studied her, his eyes raking over every part of her he could see, like an actual caress. Clearing his throat, he lifted his gaze to meet hers. "You about ready to come in, or did you still have more to discuss with yourself?"

Abby could feel the blush creeping up her neck, her embarrassment sure to flood her face at any moment. So she did the only thing she could think of—she scowled at him. Fortunately, red cheeks on her meant any number of things, including irritation and anger. And, okay, arousal, too, but she wasn't going there.

"A gentleman wouldn't have pointed that out, you jerk."

He grinned, just one side of his mouth tipping up, before stepping back and opening the door for her. "Never was very good at being one around you, was I?"

Flashes of heated memories they'd shared whipped through her mind before she shut them down.

Not. Going. There. Not tonight, and not with him.

The House on Sunshine Corner

A Sunshine Corner Novel

Phoebe Mills

FOREVER

New York   Boston

Copyright © 2021 by Grand Central Publishing

Excerpt from *Only for You* copyright © 2021 by Barbara Curtis

Cover design by Daniela Medina. Cover images © Shutterstock. Cover copyright © 2021 by Hachette Book Group, Inc.

Forever
Hachette Book Group
1290 Avenue of the Americas, New York, NY 10104
read-forever.com
twitter.com/readforeverpub

First Edition: August 2021

Forever is an imprint of Grand Central Publishing. The Forever name and logo are trademarks of Hachette Book Group, Inc.

The publisher is not responsible for websites (or their content) that are not owned by the publisher.

The Hachette Speakers Bureau provides a wide range of authors for speaking events. To find out more, go to www.hachettespeakersbureau.com or call (866) 376-6591.

ISBNs: 978-1-5387-5395-8 (mass market), 978-1-5387-5396-5 (ebook)

Printed in the United States of America

CW

10 9 8 7 6 5 4 3 2 1

The House on Sunshine Corner

Chapter One

Abby Engel understood the whole concept of needing to work her way through some frogs before finding her prince, but just exactly how many was she expected to kiss before she found The One? At twenty-nine, she wasn't old by any stretch of the imagination, but with her abysmal dating track record, she felt ancient. And in a town as quaint—read: small—as Heart's Hope Bay, Oregon, she feared she was running out of frogs *to* kiss.

After last night's doozy of a blind date—despite him being perfect on paper with a stable job and a love for his big family—her options felt exceptionally dreadful. If the selection of men she had to choose from didn't drastically improve, she might actually lose hope in finding that forever love she was searching for.

She sighed, looking over the day's schedule for the

Sunshine Corner, the day care she owned and ran out of the home she shared with her grandma. "Maybe I brought this on myself when I asked for a family man."

Savannah—one of her oldest and best girlfriends and fellow day-care cohort—laughed, blowing a strand of blond hair out of her face as she prepped the sand table for their nine o'clock texture time with the toddlers. "I'm pretty sure every deity in the world knows you didn't mean someone who was obsessed with their mom. I mean... *yuck*. What dude knows his mom even has a UTI let alone that she has chronic ones, and then decides they're appropriate first date dinner conversation? You have the *worst* luck in men, I swear. I don't understand. It's like you're cursed."

"She's right," Jenn said with a definitive nod, her shoulder-length black hair swinging with the motion. She bounced Amaya—one of their youngest charges—on a hip as the baby cooed and gnawed on her tiny fist. "Remember the guy who told you that you were pretty but that you'd be super hot if you lost ten pounds?"

Savannah made a disgusted sound in her throat. "I'd like to..." She trailed off so as not to be overheard by the children, but she mumbled what sounded an awful lot like *punch that guy in the junk*. "Remember the one who brought his own sandwich in a baggie to the restaurant to save a few bucks?"

"Oh! How about the guy who—"

"Okay!" Abby cut in, throwing her hands up. "I get it. My dating life sucks."

"It doesn't..." Savannah said, but the rebuttal was half-hearted at best.

"It does. And I can't even blame it on small-town selection. I've gone out with the most eligible bachelors in Heart's Hope Bay, and, yeah, a couple stuck for a while, but nothing more than six months. Now I'm in this drought, even though you guys talked me into setting up an account on that dating site. But they all turn out the same—a mediocre, if not horrible, first date and no signs of a second. Either the guys are completely weird or there's no chemistry." Abby dropped into one of the kiddie chairs and let loose a heavy sigh as her shoulders slumped. "I don't get it. Is it me? Am I awful?"

"No!" Savannah and Jenn said in unison, their heads shaking rapidly.

The corner of Abby's mouth ticked up, the only whisper of a smile she could manage right then. She might have atrocious luck in love, but her friendship pool was filled to bursting. She adored her girlfriends—both the ones who worked with her and her closest friends who didn't—but they couldn't give her the big family she'd always dreamed of.

A buzz sounded from the front door, and Abby stood to answer it, happy for a distraction from her thoughts.

"I got it," Jenn said, passing Amaya off to her along the way.

Fortunately, a baby to snuggle was an equally good

distraction. Abby looked down as Amaya kept up a constant string of babble and felt urgency tug her in gut as she stared into the baby's beautiful face. Her butterscotch eyes, surrounded by impossibly thick lashes, were set off by her warm sepia skin, her riot of tight black curls backlit by the sun coming in through the window. Amaya was a good baby—sweet and giggly and cuddly—but the truth was, even if she wasn't, Abby still would've felt that pull in her stomach. To have a child of her own. To have a *family* of her own.

"I see how you're looking at that baby right now," Savannah said.

"How am I looking at her?"

"Like you might stick her in your bag and take her upstairs with you tonight to keep her."

Abby gasped and snapped her head up to stare at her friend. "I would never!"

Savannah's peal of laughter caused a couple kids to turn and look at them with curious eyes before focusing back on their puzzle. "I was just joking. *Obviously* you wouldn't nab a child. Besides, there are easier ways to get a baby," she said dryly.

"Yeah, well, if I could get past the first date with one of these guys, that'd be a great step in the right direction."

"Who says you need to date, period? You can just have one on your own."

"Haha. So funny."

"What?"

Abby huffed out a disbelieving laugh. "Please tell me you're still joking."

"Why?" Savannah shrugged. "Women do it all the time. The only thing you need a guy for is his—"

"I don't think anyone needs to hear that before eight in the morning, Savannah." Abby's grandmother, Hilde, tutted as she breezed down the curved mahogany staircase from their living quarters upstairs. Her dark purple skirt swirled around her ankles like waves kissing the shore, and she wore her gray hair in a knot at the base of her head.

Savannah's only response was a tinkling laugh as she bent to help a few of the kids with their puzzle.

"What's so funny?" Jenn asked, being tugged in by one of their preschoolers.

"Nothing," Abby said.

But Savannah wasn't deterred and lifted her head. "I was just telling Abby she doesn't need a man if she wants a baby."

Jenn grinned. "Well, that's true. Lori and I are proof enough of that."

Abby understood where her friends were coming from, but they were forgetting one major, glaring detail—she didn't just want the baby. She wanted the whole big, happy family. "Yeah, but you and Lori have each other. It isn't just you raising Brayden by yourself. You have a partner."

Amaya started to fuss in Abby's arms, all the commotion of the day's drop-offs no doubt getting to her. Abby bounced and patted, rocked and shushed to no avail. As Abby tried to console the baby, the preschooler who'd tugged Jenn in released her hand and took off with a speed only seen in four-year-olds, her brother toddling behind her. Neither of them spared their mom, Norah, a backward glance.

"You're right," Jenn said, her dark brown eyes softening along with the rest of her as she met Abby's gaze. "But the option's there if you want it."

"And if you decide to go that route, just let me know," Norah said, easily sliding into the conversation. "I've got boxes upon boxes of baby clothes I could give you. I'd love to get them out of my house."

Hilde swooped in, plucking a crying Amaya from Abby's arms. Just like always, the child calmed within seconds of being in the Baby Whisperer's arms. "I wouldn't get rid of those just yet, Norah."

Norah laughed. "Believe me, we're done."

"Mmm-hmm..." Hilde said, her raised eyebrow and smirk speaking of secrets the mere mortal folk weren't yet privy to.

"Oh no," Norah said, shaking her finger at Abby's grandmother. "Don't you send any of those baby vibes my way, Hilde. I mean it! I'm outta here. Have a great day, ladies."

They all laughed at her quickly retreating form, even though there was truth in what she'd said. Hilde was known in Heart's Hope Bay as the Baby Whisperer for two reasons. First, she could calm any baby at any time, without fail—a handy person to have on call at a day care, no doubt. And second, she had the uncanny ability of knowing who was going to be the next person gracing the town with a precious little one. And she was never, ever wrong.

"Do you *have* to do that? You know she's going to be a wreck for the rest of the day," Abby said to her grandmother, waving to one of the dads dropping off his twins.

Hilde shrugged, her nose pressed to Amaya's curls as she swayed the baby side to side. "I can't control it, Abby. I only know what I know."

"Maybe you should try keeping that knowledge to yourself once in a while. Or focusing your powers on something else."

A grin tugged up the corner of her grandma's mouth, a mischievous spark in blue eyes the exact shade of her own. "Now, where's the fun in that? And as for your other suggestion, I'm working on it. Thought I might take a stab at your love life. How's that sound?"

"Like a horrible idea you absolutely should not attempt."

"Too late," her grandma said with zero remorse.

Abby's groan mixed with everyone else's laughter before they were interrupted by Sofia, one of their preschoolers, who was bursting with excitement. "Miss Abby! Look! Look who brought me today!"

"Who's that?" Abby asked, bending down and smiling at the little girl.

But before Sofia could respond, a deep, male voice said, "Hi, Abby."

Abby froze, every cell in her body sparking to life at the sound of those mere three syllables, goose bumps sweeping over her skin as her body hummed with a re-membered awareness. Before she even turned around, she knew who'd be standing there. There was only one person in the world who, by merely speaking, could send shivers racing down her spine, igniting long-forgotten memories in their wake. One person who could fill her up and wring her out in the same breath.

Carter Hayes, her high school sweetheart, the boy she'd given two years of her life—not to mention her heart—to, and the one who'd gotten away.

It may have been eleven years since she'd heard his voice, but she'd recognize it anywhere. Mostly because it'd haunted her dreams the entirety of the time he'd been gone, leaving her wondering more often than not about what might have been, if only...

If only he hadn't gone away to college.

If only they'd actually tried the long-distance thing.

If only he'd come home after graduation instead of setting up residence a thousand miles away.

If only she'd meant enough to him to stay. Or return.

Savannah stared at her with wide eyes, her eye-brows lifting in an *Oh shit* expression as a group of four kids with clasped hands played Ring Around the Rosie with her in the middle. Abby returned the stare before glancing down and silently cursing herself that she was meeting Carter for the first time in more than a decade when she had baby spit-up on her shirt.

Rolling her shoulders back, she pasted on a bright smile and turned to face him. "Carter. Hi."

"You know my uncle, Miss Abby?" Sofia asked, her head cocked to the side.

She broke eye contact with Carter and smiled down at his niece, grateful for the excuse to get her fluttery heart under control. "I do. We, um…" She flicked her gaze back to Carter's briefly before returning it to the little girl. "We went to high school together."

"I love playing school. It's my favorite!" With that, she sped off into the melee of fellow three-year-olds, locating her best friend in seconds.

Abby turned back to Carter only to find his gaze sweeping over her, another thing to be grateful for. She'd always gotten lost in his eyes, and she wasn't so sure this time would be any different. Since he was otherwise occupied, she returned the favor, drinking him in for the first time in too long—and, no, those times she stalked his social media accounts while inebriated absolutely did not count.

Holy *moly* had the years agreed with him. He was tall and broad, filling out since he'd been gone, though he still had the sleek, lithe body of a swimmer. His hair was longer than it'd been in high school, the dark strands a little shaggy and the perfect length to delve her fingers into.

But she wasn't thinking about that. Nor about how

broad his shoulders looked under his peacoat, or about that delicious shadow of scruff he'd never had when they'd been teenagers and the way it framed his kissable lips, or about—

Savannah cleared her throat, and Abby snapped her gaze up just in time to watch Carter do the same. At least she hadn't been the only one with roaming eyes.

"It's good to see you." His smile was a little stilted as he ran a hand through his hair, seeming unsure as to a proper greeting. Abby was right there with him—did exes hug? Did they shake hands? She wasn't quite ready to see if the spark that had always been charged between them still existed, and, it seemed, neither was he.

He shoved his hands in his jeans pockets. "My sister told me you worked here."

"She does more than work here," Jenn said a little defensively, clearly picking up on the weird vibes between him and Abby. As a transplant to Heart's Hope Bay, Jenn never knew Carter from years ago. Didn't know his and Abby's history either. "The Sunshine Corner is Abby's baby."

"That's right. Becca told me that, too," he said, his voice tinged with a note of something Abby couldn't quite place. "That's amazing. Congratulations."

"Thanks." Abby offered him a genuine smile. "What about you? What are you doing now?"

See? That sounded like a totally reasonable question and not at all like she already knew the answer.

"I'm an architect specializing in historic restoration

with a firm in Vegas. Just here working remotely for about six weeks to help with Sofia until Becca gets back up and running."

Abby cringed, recalling the details of the car wreck that'd happened just outside of town only a couple days ago. "I heard about your sister's accident. I'm glad it wasn't anything more serious than a broken ankle and that Sofia wasn't hurt."

"Me too." He glanced over at his niece, who was currently in an animated conversation with her best friend.

"It's nice of you to come back and help. Did your dad look after them until you could get up here?"

Carter and Rebecca's dad, though a lifelong Heart's Hope Bay resident, had become a bit of a recluse in recent years, rarely leaving his home on the outskirts of town. She had memories of him being more active in the community once upon a time, but then Carter's mom had passed away, and everything had seemed to change.

Carter's mouth tightened, his shoulders tensing. His words, when they came, were tinged with a hardness she'd forgotten he'd had whenever he spoke of his father. "No. I flew in the night Becca called me. I'll be the only one helping my sister and Sofia with what they need."

Abby nodded, folding her hands in front of herself, not wanting to pry into that family matter when it obviously made him uncomfortable. Never mind the fact that it wasn't her place anymore. They used to share their hopes and fears with each other, but they hadn't even shared hellos since he'd left.

"Well... I'm glad you're able to work remotely to be with them. I'm sure Becca appreciates it." She tucked her hair behind her ear as thoughts of Carter being in town for a month and a half finally caught up with her, her stomach somersaulting for no good reason. Offering him a smile, she said, "And it'll be nice to have you back in town, too."

He opened his mouth to respond, but Sofia ran over and tugged on his finger, pulling with all her might to drag him away. "Uncle Carter, come look!"

"Okay, all right. Give me just a sec." He chuckled, fondness replacing the animosity that'd been there moments before when he'd spoken of his father. Lifting his gaze back to Abby, he said, "Looks like I'm being summoned. It was good to see you, Abby."

"Yeah, you too."

With one final glance in Abby's direction, he let himself be led away by his niece. Abby didn't want to watch him walk away with that stupid swagger, and she *certainly* didn't want her heart pumping like she'd chugged a triple-shot espresso, leaving her hands trembling and her stomach unsettled.

"Need a bib?" Savannah asked with a wry lilt to her voice. "You've got a little drool..."

Abby snapped her gaze away from Carter and glared at her oldest friend. "Oh, shut up."

"I feel like I'm missing something here." Jenn divided a look between them. "Who's Carter, why are you giving him your you-know-what eyes, and why haven't you gotten all over that?"

"Oh, she's gotten all over it, all right."

"*Savannah!*" Abby hissed, shooting a glance around to make sure no little—or big—ears had picked up on what she'd said.

Her friend just shrugged. "What? It's the truth. Abby and Carter over there"—she jerked her head toward the tall, dark, and handsome man—"were high school sweethearts once upon a time."

"Oh *really?*" Jenn asked, her interest clear. "Tell me more."

"No. There will be absolutely no telling of more. At least not right now." Abby pointedly looked around to all the little people surrounding them.

Jenn heaved a deep sigh. "Fine. I guess you're right. I wouldn't be able to hear the good stuff anyway."

And there *had* been good stuff. Two years' worth. Her split with Carter had been pretty average for high school seniors who went to different colleges, but her feelings for him had been anything but. Hell, even after all this time—after countless misses with men and bad date after bad date—she knew that what they'd had was something special. She'd loved him with all her heart, and she'd thought they were perfect for one another.

Had thought, maybe, he'd be it for her. That they'd be one of those couples to make it last.

Maybe that was why she'd had such a hard time finding a connection with anyone else in the time since he'd been gone. Had she subconsciously been holding each and every guy up to Carter? To the memory of a love that no longer existed?

She glanced up only to find him already watching her, her eyes automatically connecting with his across the room, and Abby felt a zing from her head to her toes, struck by that disorienting sensation of not simply being looked at, but really *seen*—something that'd been lacking in her life for far too long.

This was going to be a long six weeks.

Chapter Two

✺

It was odd being back in a place that felt so familiar and so foreign all at once, but Carter couldn't deny the truth of both. Heart's Hope Bay was an idyllic small town nestled on the rocky Oregon coast, complete with a gorgeous beachfront and a downtown worthy of a postcard. This town, long as he'd been gone, would always be home to him...same as it would always be the place that held memories he'd spent more than a decade running from.

He'd been back a handful of times over the years, but whenever possible, he'd paid to fly his sister and niece out to Vegas to visit him instead of returning. He shouldn't have found it shocking how little the town had changed in the time he'd been gone. The ice cream parlor on Main Street still had a hand-drawn sign on the sidewalk proclaiming today's flavor, and Mr. Reyes still had his Christmas lights up despite it being February, and the *Daily Heart* was still delivered every day before dawn. It felt like stepping into a time warp, except *he'd* changed since he'd been gone.

His phone rang as he walked through the back door of his sister's house. He tossed his keys onto the checkered kitchen counter and pulled his phone from his pocket, glancing down to see his manager's name on the screen.

He swiped to answer. "Hey, Jake."

"Carter, hey, man. You get all settled in Heartful Bay?"

Chuckling, he dropped into one of the mismatched chairs at the small, round, red table set up in the eat-in kitchen. "Heart's Hope Bay, and yeah. I'm good. Though it's hard to catch up on sleep with a three-year-old belting out *Frozen* at six in the morning."

Jake made a gruff sound of commiseration. "Thanks for sticking around to take care of Redmond before you left. I know that put you on a late flight out of here."

"No problem." That had been Carter's motto the entirety of his career since the day he'd graduated college and started at his first entry-level job. He'd busted his ass, working his way up the ladder. Learning everything he could from the most intelligent people in the field...all with the goal to branch off and start his own firm at some point.

"Since you've had more than twenty-four hours of downtime, does that mean you're ready to dive in?"

The corner of Carter's mouth lifted. His boss—and friend—was a hard-ass, but at least he didn't pretend otherwise. "It's eight fifteen. Aren't you jumping on my case a little early?"

"Hey, not all of us got to sleep in. I've been at it for two hours already."

Carter snorted and rooted around in his messenger bag for his laptop. "It's not my fault no one's kept you company this week."

"Who says I haven't been kept company?" Jake asked wryly. "My late-night companions know the score."

The score being that Jake was a workaholic and didn't have time for a relationship or a family—much like Carter. He had enjoyed his job at Mosley & Associates for the past several years, but working for other people wasn't his end goal. He wanted the freedom and prestige that came from owning his own architecture firm.

He'd been well on his way toward seeing that come to fruition, with the last big promotion he wanted coming up for grabs at the end of this quarter. But he couldn't have anticipated Rebecca's accident, or his need to return to Heart's Hope Bay for the next six to eight weeks to help her take care of a high-energy three-year-old. Never mind that their father lived in town—Carter wouldn't trust the man to watch over a pet rock, let alone his flesh and blood. It put a wrench in Carter's plans, but he'd do anything for his sister and niece, even if that meant pushing back his goals a little.

And even if it meant interacting with Abby Engel while he was home.

In the time he'd been gone, he'd somehow managed to avoid seeing her, even on his few short trips back. Considering his current stay was more than a two-day stint, he figured he'd run into his high school sweetheart at some point while he was back, but he didn't think it'd get dumped on him right after his arrival. Seeing her had been a punch to the gut. The years had only made her more beautiful—something he hadn't thought possible, way back when. Her cheekbones had become more pronounced, her body filling out in ways that made his mouth water. She wore her red hair a little longer, a little sleeker, the waves more tamed than they'd once been. But one thing that hadn't changed was her eyes—still the same deep, soulful blue they'd always been.

Those eyes had had a way of seeing past every wall he'd erected and pinpointing the real him. Something he hadn't experienced with anyone else in the time since. Or ever.

He'd be lying to himself if he didn't acknowledge that he still had feelings for her, mostly of the *what could've been* variety. They'd split after high school because it'd made the most sense—four years at different colleges in different states made for a challenging relationship. And while that was certainly true, the real reason Carter called it off was because they wanted drastically different things in life—him, a prestigious career and the responsibilities that came with it. And her, a big family she could raise right here in Heart's Hope Bay.

Carter had zero desire for such a thing. Based on his history, he didn't think he had the whole family thing in him. Not to mention the idea of being tied down to a person—or persons—and a place that felt claustrophobic to him. He hadn't been able to fly the nest fast enough or get far enough away. He'd run from this tiny town with its too-painful memories that reminded him of everything he'd lost and the voice in his head that sounded an awful lot like his dad whispering that he'd never amount to anything.

"...get that sent off to Redmond this morning, that'd be great."

Carter zoned back into the conversation and shook his head to clear the thoughts he had no business thinking. He was here to help his sister, care for his niece, and do his job. Thinking about Abby—or his dad, for that matter—didn't factor in.

Luckily, he'd worked with Jake long enough to know exactly what he needed to send off to Redmond without having to admit to his boss that he'd been daydreaming about his ex-girlfriend instead of listening.

"No problem," Carter said, opening his laptop. "He'll have it by ten."

"See?" Jake's smile rang through the line. "That's exactly why you're my point person on our biggest projects. You get shit done."

That he did. He'd been a career-focused guy since

the day he'd graduated college, climbing the corporate ladder as fast as humanly possible. It meant long hours and an exhaustive travel schedule, but that was fine with him. He had time for Becca and Sofia and little else. What more did he need?

Being home was going to present a challenge he hadn't foreseen, but he wasn't planning on shying away from it. He just needed to figure out how he was going to progress his goals while he was stuck in Heart's Hope Bay and away from the connections he needed to be making.

And how he was going to do that without getting distracted by a certain redhead who had a way of turning him inside out.

* * *

That evening, after he'd picked up Sofia from the Sunshine Corner—thankfully avoiding another encounter with Abby—Carter was fixing dinner when his sister came in through the back door.

Normally, he'd rush to assist her as she was still getting her bearings with her crutches. She'd only broken her ankle a couple days ago, after all. But the truth was, he was a little pissed at her for blindsiding him with Abby this morning.

He knew he was being unreasonable—she'd probably had an exhausting first day back to work at her desk job at the bank, and she hadn't even taken off her coat yet. Yet he couldn't help but dig into her before the door even closed behind her. "You couldn't warn me I'd be seeing Abby today?" He glanced over at her in time to see her eye roll.

She dropped her purse on the floor, shrugged out of her coat, then fell into a dining chair, propping her crutches against the wall. Huffing out a deep breath, she blew her dark bangs out of her eyes. "I'm not sure why I'd need to. You knew the Sunshine Corner was hers—that's why I chose it for Sofia, remember?"

He turned back around, focusing his efforts on the oh-so-difficult task of scrambling eggs, if only to avoid her eyes. He *had* known that was why Becca had chosen that particular day care for Sofia. And that she and Abby had remained friends throughout the years. Somehow, in the commotion of the quick trip up here and in the sudden barrage of responsibilities he normally didn't contend with, it hadn't been in the forefront of his mind until he'd pulled up in front of the very same house he'd spent so many days at in high school.

"Anyway, did you guys have a chance to catch up?" she asked.

Glancing at her over his shoulder, he narrowed his eyes, picking up on the way-too-heavy-to-be-authentic nonchalance in her tone. Becca hadn't kept it a secret that she thought he and Abby were the perfect couple. She'd been nearly as devastated as Abby when the two of them had broken up right after graduation. And she'd taken every opportunity since he'd been gone to slip in any bit of information about Abby she could.

It was going to be really goddamn awkward when his ex realized he knew things about her life that he had no business knowing. Like how many boyfriends she'd had (two, though neither lasted more than six months), or that she and her grandmother took a trip each year just the two of them (renting a small cottage down the coast), or that she had bigger plans for her day care (to eventually add a preschool to her offerings). Not to mention the dozens of other tidbits he'd become aware of, thanks to his sister.

He'd often wondered if Becca had truly liked them together that much, or if it was simply the only way she could foresee tying him back to this town.

"What?" She lifted a single shoulder. "I'm just asking."

"Yeah, I bet." Carter returned to his task at the stove, feeling Becca's eyes on his back the entire time. "We spoke."

After several seconds of silence, she huffed out a breath. "*Aaaaand*?"

"And it was fine."

"You're such an ass."

"Why's he an ass?" Sofia asked, her ninja-like appearances, popping in without announcing herself, something he was going to have to get used to.

He barely managed to tamp down his smile at how his sister was going to handle this one. All he knew was he was damn glad it hadn't been him who'd slipped up with the swearing, because he'd never hear the end of it.

But all Becca did was wrap her arms around her daughter and pull her onto her lap, no mention of the swear word at all. "Hi, bug. I missed you today! Tell me your favorite thing you did while at the Sunshine Corner with Miss Abby."

Apparently, his sister's form of parenting meant a whole lot of avoidance. There was no way that was going to fly. His niece was like a dog with a bone when she wanted to know something.

But he'd underestimated just how much the three-year-old loved to talk about Miss Abby and her favorite things.

"Today was my most favorite day *ever!*"

"I knew it. I could just feel it when we got up this morning that it was going to be a good one," Becca said with a straight face.

Sofia nodded vigorously. "Me too! We read my favorite book and played my favorite games and had my favorite lunch."

Carter was beginning to realize that quite literally anything was Sofia's "favorite." But he couldn't help but smile at his niece's animated retelling of her day, spending five minutes on innocuous details—like the size and shape of the cheese she had at snack—while totally glossing over what most would consider to be the important items.

She was still talking when he dished up every-one's plates for their gourmet meal of scrambled eggs and toast.

"Hey, peanut, can you get the orange juice out of the fridge so your mommy doesn't have to get up?" Carter asked his niece when there was a half-second lull in the conversation.

"Oh yes!" She jumped up, then gently pressed her hands to Becca's cast, leaning down as if to hug it. "You sit here and rest, Mommy."

"I can do things," Becca protested, shifting to stand, but Carter pressed his hands on her shoulders and forced her back into the chair.

"Everyone is aware that you can *do things*." He rolled his eyes. "But how about for now, while I'm here and while we've got the best helper in the world around—"

"That's me!" Sofia interrupted. "*I'm* the best helper!"

Carter shot his niece a grin and a wink, then finished, "You let us do the work."

"I'm not going to have you do everything for me while you're here. Running Sofia around and doing the grocery shopping and other errands is enough."

"I think I can handle that, plus whatever else you have on your list. I'm not completely hopeless."

"You are *not* going to go through my to-do list while you're home, too. Besides, I'm perfectly capable of fixing the leaky faucet in here, broken ankle or not."

"Leaky faucet? Consider it done."

She made a noise of frustration in her throat, and

Sofia laughed, tossing her head back in glee. She loved how he and Becca goaded each other, arguing back and forth. Usually, his sister won—if only because it was exhausting to argue with her. But not this time. Besides the fact that it would make him some kind of supreme jerk to watch his incapacitated sister fumble her way on the ground doing something he was perfectly capable of doing himself, he'd actually...missed that sort of thing. It'd been a long time since he'd been in the thick of things, being more hands on and getting dirtier than his office job required.

Maybe while he was home, he could fulfill a little of that for himself. Besides, it'd give him something to focus on, and he'd desperately need that if he was going to have daily run-ins with Abby while he was back in Heart's Hope Bay.

Chapter Three

❋

Once upon a time, Abby spent her Saturday afternoons doing fun things. Like curling up and getting lost in a good book for a few hours. Or drawing out and decorating next week's spread in her bullet journal. Or grabbing lunch with a friend.

But on *this* particular Saturday afternoon, she was roaming the aisles of the hardware store, trying to figure out what crap she needed to strip the hideous wallpaper from their second-story landing—the future home to their preschool coatroom and cubbies.

The house she and her grandmother lived in—and the location where she ran the Sunshine Corner—was stunning, if a continual work in progress. Dating back to the late 1800s, the Victorian was a historic beast, vast and sprawling, with ornate woodwork and arches and more secrets than she'd yet to uncover. It'd been in their family for as long as she could remember, and she loved it as though it was an entity of its own.

Her best childhood memories had taken place in that home, considering it was where she and her mom always landed whenever things in the real world got a little tough, and thus the only real consistency in her life. It was the one place in the world she felt the safest.

With thousands more square feet than she and her grandma needed, it had only made sense to make it the base for the Sunshine Corner. That she was able to offer a safe space to other kids who might need it filled her heart to bursting. The trouble was, there was much work to be done on it before it was ready to house the preschool program that'd been in her goal planner for the past three years, and time was ticking down to her target date.

"*Hellooo*," her friend Gia said into the phone. "Are you even listening to me?"

Abby shook her head, breaking her stare-down with the overwhelming display of tools she'd been looking at. "Sorry. I spaced. What'd you say?"

"I asked if you wanted to hang out later. It's poker night for Marco—thankfully not at our place—so it'll just be me and Ollie at home. I contemplated leading a paint-and-sip thing over here…"

Gia was an amazing artist who filled her time as a traveling instructor, teaching weekly art classes for the kids at the Sunshine Corner, plus the nursing home in Heart's Hope Bay and the community center. She was well loved around town—both for her art and for her canine companion, Ollie, that she brought along. She also supplemented her income with paint-and-sip events at local bars and restaurants—obviously sans dog—but once in a while, she did a private event at her home for just a few girlfriends.

"Actually," Gia said before Abby could respond, "never mind. I don't want to be *on* tonight, you know? How about a couple bottles of wine and a marathon featuring one or more of the Chrises instead?"

Abby laughed, tucking her phone between her ear and shoulder as she pushed the cart into another aisle, hoping she'd somehow stumble upon what she needed. "Honestly, that sounds amazing. I was just thinking about how I used to spend my weekends doing fun things. Remember when we met at that bullet journaling class at the craft store? *That* was fun. And now I'm over here, roaming around the hardware store. Worse is that I don't even know what I'm looking for."

"What *are* you looking for?"

"I just said I had no idea."

Gia snorted. "I mean, why are you there? What is your purpose for stepping foot into Hank's domain?"

Hank—as in Hank's Hardware—was anywhere between eighty and a hundred twenty years old and had owned the hardware store ever since her grandma had been young. If you needed something, chances were he had it or could get it. The trouble was, Abby had no idea what it was she needed.

"I'm trying to get wallpaper down from the second-story landing. You have any experience removing wallpaper?"

"Not even a little."

"Damn." Abby blew out a long sigh. "I need to find Hank and ask him. I better run."

"Okay, but I'll see you tonight? Eight work for you?"

"Yep, I'll be there. You want me to invite Savannah?"

"Definitely."

"Will do." Abby ended the call, slipped her phone into her purse, and whipped her cart around to head to the front of the store, only to stop short when she crashed straight into another person. Or another person's cart, anyway.

"Oh my God, I'm so sor—" Abby's words died in her throat as soon as her eyes connected with who she'd run into.

Carter stood behind a cart, his long fingers gripping the handle, looking just as surprised to see her as she was to see him.

"Miss Abby!" Sofia twisted around where she sat in the cart, her eyes bright and smile wide.

Abby's shock at seeing Carter melted at the sight of her. "Hi, Sofia! I like your sweater."

The little girl's smile grew impossibly wide as she looked down at the pink sweater with a teal mermaid on the front, her tail curling around the side to the back. "Thanks, it's my favorite!"

Abby smirked, catching the subtle shake of Carter's

head and the fondness in his eyes when he looked down at his niece. He'd no doubt become familiar with the fact that the girl didn't play favorites, in that every single thing she touched, played with, wore, or ate took that spot at any given time.

"What are you guys doing here?" Abby directed the question at Sofia, but the little girl's attention had already been drawn back to what Abby assumed was Carter's phone and a game she was playing. Abby lifted her gaze to Carter and found him watching her, his eyes pinning her in place.

It was unsettling how much that stare affected her, even after all this time. How she felt it in all kinds of places that had no business perking up for him. But she couldn't deny the facts of both any more than she could deny her own name.

"We're just picking up a few things so I can fix a leaky faucet for Becca."

The corner of Abby's mouth lifted, her heart warming at that. "That's sweet of you."

He shrugged in a way that suggested he didn't think much of it at all. "No big deal. I help where I can. Speaking of…I didn't mean to eavesdrop, but I heard you say you need to remove some wallpaper?"

Abby's shoulders slumped. "Yeah, but I have no idea what I need. I was just headed up to ask Hank."

"I've done it more than should be allowed in a single lifetime. You want some tips?"

"Yes!"

He chuckled at her exuberance, and Abby found herself smiling in response. It'd been so long since she had heard his laugh, she'd forgotten the sound, all warm and inviting, like the sun peeking out after a long stretch of clouds.

"Okay, then. You'll need a scoring tool to perforate the paper, and then you just spray the sh—" He glanced down at his niece, then amended, "Crap out of it with some hot water. It's best if you use a compression sprayer and not just a spray bottle so the glue gets really saturated. Then just let it soak for a bit and scrape it off with a putty knife."

"That's it?"

Nodding once, he said, "That's it."

"Oh, thank God." Abby sagged against the cart. "I thought I was looking at hundreds of dollars just in equipment."

"Glad to be the bearer of good news, then. You guys finally getting rid of that wallpaper from the eighties upstairs?"

Abby had no idea why, but it made her go all gooey inside that he remembered an innocuous detail like that from her grandmother's house. What was wrong with her? "We're actually turning it into the coatroom and cubbies for the preschool I'm planning to open."

"Oh yeah? That's great. Becca told me you were expanding."

"That's the plan—but I need to get in gear if I have any hope of it being ready by the fall."

"Mommy says that's the preschool *I'm* gonna go to!" Sofia chimed in. "The Sunshine Corner is my favorite."

Abby's and Carter's laughter mixed together, and their eyes locked, electricity sparking between them despite their distance. More than ten years and a lingering heartbreak hadn't changed how the whole world seemed to disappear when he was around. Her breathing went shallow, her throat dry as she got lost in the depth of his gaze and memories that had no place in mixed company.

Carter broke eye contact first, glancing away as he cleared his throat. "Well, I'll let you get to it. See you on Monday."

Abby blinked, struggling to snap out of her trance. "Yeah, see you."

"Bye, Miss Abby!"

She returned Sofia's wave as the little girl and Carter strolled off. She pretended as if she was suddenly very interested in the ant traps she'd been standing in front of and not flustered by the spark she still felt every time she and Carter got close.

* * *

Abby didn't like to show up anywhere empty-handed, and since Gia's wine fridge was a thing of beauty and always well stocked, Abby figured she'd swing by on her way over and grab some snacks at the grocery store. She was a sucker for the brownie bites the bakery made. And she should probably also pick up a few bags of her favorite salt-and-vinegar chips to munch on during the movie. Who was she to discriminate between salty and sweet snacks?

After tossing the chip bags in her cart, she plowed out of the aisle with a single-minded focus, intent on hitting the bakery and seeing what kind of goodies they'd cooked up today. But she stopped short as another cart passed in the main aisle, narrowly avoiding another collision today.

"Sorry!" She glanced up only to meet the amused eyes of none other than Carter, Sofia grinning widely from her perch in the cart.

"If I didn't know better, I'd think you were dead set on running me over today," Carter said.

Abby breathed out a laugh and gripped the cart handle, preemptively giving a silent but stern lecture to her body to just calm the hell down. None of the fawning and tingling that had happened at the hardware store would be happening here. None. At. All.

"Maybe I am." She shrugged, then winked at Sofia to let her know she was teasing. The little girl pressed her hands over her mouth and giggled, tipping her head back as if what Abby had said was the funniest thing she'd ever heard.

"I better watch my back, then." Carter shot her a smile, then seemed to realize what he was doing and wiped the expression from his face.

Apparently she wasn't the only one falling back into old habits.

He glanced into her cart before meeting her eyes with a raised brow. "Quite the spread you've got there."

Abby peered down at the copious amounts of junk food stashed in her basket—so she'd gotten more than a few bags of chips... A girl had needs. "Hey, no cart judging."

Raising his hands in surrender, Carter shook his head. "I would never. Besides, I'm a fine one to judge." He gestured into his own cart, which consisted of... absolutely nothing.

"You guys just get here?"

After Carter and Sofia had left the hardware store, Abby had spent a fair amount of time discussing with Hank what she needed and picking out the best options for her project. It'd been at least an hour since they'd gone their separate ways.

"You'd think so, wouldn't you? But nope. We've been here for a while."

"Can we go, Uncle Carter? I'm hungry."

He snorted and looked down at his niece. "You've had four donut holes and every sample they have out today, including a piece of pizza, some cheese, and two mini corn dogs."

"Uh-huh."

"And you're still hungry?"

"Yes." She nodded vigorously.

"Okay, we'll hurry. Just tell me what you like to eat for lunches and we can go."

Sofia shrugged, her attention already back on an image-matching game on Carter's phone. "I don't know."

Carter blew out a defeated breath and ran a hand through his hair. "It's been like that the whole time. How can a kid who's eaten lunch every day of her life have no idea what she actually eats? I don't get it. And Becca's working, so I'm not going to bother her with something as simple as this. Maybe I'll just get a bunch of boxes of mac and cheese and call it a day."

Abby grimaced. "Um... actually, she hates mac and cheese."

"Excuse me?"

"I know, right?" she said through a laugh. "Only kid I've ever met who doesn't eat the stuff. We always make her something different when we're having that at day care."

Carter's eyes brightened. "Like what kinds of things?"

With a shrug, she said, "I don't know... quesadillas, munchable lunches like cheese, veggies, crackers, and fruit. Let's see... pasta salad or turkey roll-ups. And then of course there's the old standby: PB and J."

"Right, right." He nodded, then held out his hand to Sofia. "Peanut, can I use my phone real quick, please?"

"No, thank you," Sofia said without even glancing up at him.

He chuckled under his breath. "That's very polite of

you, but I need it to type Miss Abby's suggestions so I don't forget them."

"But *I* need my matching game. See?" She turned the phone around to face Carter before cradling it to her chest as if he might swoop in and steal it at any moment.

Abby's grin only widened as she watched him interact with his niece. It was a side of him she'd never seen before, and she needed to pretend it didn't turn her insides to mush or she might not survive the next several weeks while he was home. "Would you like some help?"

"God, yes," he said, his voice a low rumble. Almost a groan.

She valiantly attempted to ignore the other circumstances in which he'd say those same words, in that same timbre.

She valiantly failed.

Unwanted and unwelcome memories from their past together popped into her head, and Abby was helpless to stop them. That'd been happening more and more this week since her first encounter with Carter, and they showed no signs of stopping now.

What was she supposed to do, though? They had so much history—and not just of the *God, yes* variety.

His gaze, so focused and intent, reminded her of the way he'd looked at her when she'd come down the steps the night of prom. His muscular arms reminded her of the way he used to hold her. One smile on his full lips and she was reliving their first kiss like it was yesterday, toe-curling tingles and all.

Those lips quirked up now, and Abby jerked her eyes away from the sight, tucking her hair behind her ear as she looked everywhere but at him. "Right. Okay. Lunch food. Off we go!" Her voice was high-pitched, too chipper for the location or the circumstances, but she rolled with it because what else was she going to do? Admit to her ex-boyfriend that she still thought about the two of them and everything they'd shared together? She'd pass, thanks.

Half an hour later, Carter's cart was full of healthy options—and a couple questionable ones because life was all about balance—for meals for the next several days.

"You do this a couple times a week?" he asked, sounding exhausted at the thought.

She shrugged. "Not usually. I have a menu planner at home and at the Sunshine Corner, so I only do my major shopping once a week. The produce is what gets tricky, so I might swing by and pick up the fresh stuff more than once."

"A menu planner, huh?" He slid her a look out of the corner of his eye, his full lips tipping up in a smirk. "Why doesn't that surprise me?"

She cracked a grin. "It's laminated and everything."

He held a hand to his chest and bit his lip. "Better watch your mouth, Abby. There are children around."

The laugh burst out of her, pure and carefree, and

she didn't try to stifle it in the least as she tossed her head back.

"What's funny, Miss Abby?" Sofia leaned out of the cart, her mouth curved in a smile as she extended her little hand out to pat Abby's arm. "Why are you laughing?"

She bit her lip to stop from chuckling again. "Your uncle said something funny."

Sofia nodded. "He's silly. Last night, he dressed up like a ballerina!"

"You're not supposed to tell anyone that," Carter mock-whispered, and his niece fell into a fit of giggles at the stern look on his face.

"Is that so?" Abby asked. "I would've liked to see that."

"I'll check if Sofia's dance teacher has any room for me in the recital."

As the three of them strode toward the checkout lanes, easy conversation passing between them, it felt like Abby's smile was permanently etched on her face. She couldn't remember the last time she'd had so much fun with a man—and she'd been *grocery shopping*. It'd been a lifetime since she'd seen Carter, and in the time he'd been gone, she'd forgotten just how easy things were between them . . . how well they meshed together.

Why couldn't she find someone like *him* in Heart's Hope Bay?

Chapter Four

✳

If Carter had thought he'd only have to interact with Abby during drop-offs and pickups at the Sunshine Corner, he was sorely mistaken. Since he'd been home, they'd run into each other nearly every time he'd left the house. Post office, bakery, the brand-new—to him, anyway—Indian restaurant that was surprisingly good, the hardware store again...and he'd only been back in town for a little more than a week. They'd managed to go more than ten years without seeing each other, and now it seemed like they couldn't manage ten hours.

It'd be a lot easier to ignore her and all the feelings she stirred up if she wasn't thrown in his face every day—some days more than once. It would also be a lot easier if his sister would stop with her petty meddling in an attempt to encourage some kind of romance between him and Abby because there was no way that was happening.

Thankfully, he had willpower. And he had willpower when it came to Abby, specifically—as proven when he'd been nothing but a ball of teenage hormones. He hadn't had a problem waiting to sleep together until she was ready, because it'd been what she'd needed. Well, what *he* needed now was to keep his distance, so his willpower was just going to have to buck up and take one for the team again.

"Can I get 'ubble gum, Uncle Carter?" Sofia asked as they walked, hand in hand, to Dream Cream, the ice cream parlor on Main Street, situated between the flower shop and the bakery.

"If that's what you want…" Carter couldn't think of a less appealing ice cream flavor, but he'd realized his tastes skewed quite a bit from his three-year-old niece's.

She brought her other hand to their clasped ones and tugged while jumping up and down. "I do, I do!"

With a chuckle, he opened the door and led her into the shop. "Then that's what you'll get."

Three scoops later—one bubble gum for her and two butter pecan for him—they sat down at one of the small tables set up inside since it was too chilly to eat on the patio, despite the heat lamps and strings of lights set up to welcome customers.

"Mommy doesn't like ice cream in the winter. She says it's only for hot days."

Normally, he didn't like to speak ill of his sister to his niece—he didn't want any of his inevitable frustrations with his sibling to influence Sofia—but he felt pretty justified in calling Becca out for this. "Yeah, well, your mommy's wrong. Ice cream is for *any* time."

Sofia giggled and nodded enthusiastically, shoveling as much into her mouth as she could. She'd only been eating for two minutes, and she already had a ring of blue around her face, the creamy concoction dribbling down her chin.

"You're getting awful messy over there, peanut. Maybe that's why your mom says ice cream is only for the summer."

Sofia lifted her arm as if to swipe it across her mouth and use her sweater sleeve as a napkin, but Carter's reflexes had been getting better since he'd come home, and he snapped his hand out to stop her before she could.

"Were you about to wipe your mouth on your sleeve?"

"No," Sofia said, but her eyes flitted everywhere but at Carter.

With a laugh, he plucked a few napkins out of the dispenser and wiped her mouth, Sofia still trying valiantly to look anywhere but at him. As she was peering off to the left, her eyes suddenly lit up and she pulled away from his cleanup efforts.

"Miss Abby!" she yelled, then waved, her hand fluttering faster than a hummingbird's wings. "Uncle Carter, it's Miss Abby!"

At the mention of Abby's name, Carter glanced over his shoulder, and sure enough, there she stood in a bright red coat wearing a deep yellow knit hat complete with a giant puff on the top, her long red hair spilling out beneath it. Her cheeks were pink from the cold, her eyes sparkling, and the sight of her hit him square in the gut.

Of *course* she'd be eating ice cream in February on a random Monday night, just like they were. He needed to figure out what he did to piss off the universe and rectify it immediately because this couldn't go on. Sure, he had willpower, but there was no need to taunt it every waking minute.

Abby smiled and waved, holding up a finger to them before collecting her ice cream and paying. She grabbed a napkin, wrapped it around her dish, and made her way toward them. "Hi, guys. Got a craving for ice cream like I did?"

"I got ubble gum!" Sofia lifted her dish toward Abby before cradling it close to her chest and taking another too-big bite.

"Your favorite," Abby said with a smile.

"Uh-huh." Sofia nodded and stuffed another bite in her mouth before she'd finished swallowing the first.

With a chuckle, Carter said, "Slow down, peanut. I don't think Abby's here to take it from you."

She turned to Abby with suspicion written on every inch of her face, and Abby laughed, holding up a hand in surrender. "It's all yours, promise."

Sofia smiled then, all blue teeth and excitement, before patting the chair next to her. "I saved this for you."

"Oh—" Abby flicked her eyes to Carter for only a brief moment before focusing once again on Sofia. "That's okay. I don't want to impose on your time together."

Yeah, he'd definitely pissed off one god or another. How exactly was he supposed to say no to this when his niece was practically bursting at the thought of Abby joining them? There was really only one clear answer to that: He wasn't.

"It's no imposition. We've got plenty of room." Carter jerked his chin to the chair, using the toe of his boot to push the seat back from the table and toward her.

Abby paused for only a second, her eyes locked with his, before she gave a small nod and settled into the chair. She shrugged out of her coat, leaving her in a fitted, pale pink sweater that showcased all her soft curves in a way that definitely wasn't helping his willpower cause.

"Sofia got her favorite, but what about you?" She turned to Carter and eyed his ice cream. "Have you ventured beyond butter pecan?"

He froze with his spoon an inch from his mouth, his eyebrows shooting up. "You remember that?"

Her laugh tinkled out of her, filling the small shop— not to mention a space in his chest he had no idea had been hollow—and she offered a small shrug. "Kind of hard to forget when we used to come here every weekend."

They had done that... Snippets of every time they'd come in flipped through his mind—the kind of memories that weren't forgotten but rather just misplaced for a while. The kind that got a little rusty with disuse. She used to offer him a bite of every flavor she'd get—a rotating variation he could never pinpoint the pattern of—but his favorite was always butter pecan. Unless he was tasting it from her lips, in which case any and all of them took first place.

He shook his head and adjusted in his seat, his blood thrumming at the thought of swiping his tongue across her lips for a taste. If he didn't get himself under control, his reaction would be all too apparent to everyone in the vicinity.

Clearing his throat, he tipped his dish toward her. "Still butter pecan." He lifted his chin to hers. "How about you? Still playing the flavor field?"

She raised an eyebrow as if to say, *See? I'm not the only one who remembers...* And then she shrugged while scooping a bite out from her bowl. "I don't want to be tied down to one flavor. I like to see what's out there, you know?"

Basically, she approached ice cream the exact opposite of how she approached life. It was what had caused their split in the first place—at least on his end. Yes, they'd gone to different colleges, and it'd been an easy excuse to cop to, but the truth was, her desire

and yearning for permanence in Heart's Hope Bay—
complete with a husband, two-point-five kids, and a
white picket fence—scared the hell out of him. He'd
made it his life's mission to get as far away from here
and the awful memories this small town contained as
he could. Didn't matter that he'd loved her. Didn't
matter that he hadn't found anyone with whom he'd
connected as well in the years since.

What mattered was that he wasn't the kind of man
who could settle down. Who *should* settle down. His
worthless father was proof enough of that.

"Did you get ubble gum?" Sofia asked, pulling Carter
out of his thoughts.

"Not today." Abby smiled down at his niece. "I got
today's flavor—double fudge brownie. Have you ever
tried it? Can't go wrong with chocolate."

"Chocolate's my favorite!" Sofia said, even as she
licked the remnants of her bubble gum ice cream from
the dish like a dog.

"Hey," Carter said on a laugh he was trying desperately to tamp down. He reached out and grabbed the
bowl from her. "Are you seriously licking that? Would
you do that if your mom was here?"

Sofia looked properly chastised and lowered her eyes,
once again looking everywhere but at him. Uh-huh,
that's what he thought. He had no problem being the
fun one—he loved it, actually—but apparently allowing her to eat like an animal in public was where he
drew the line.

After wetting a few napkins, he handed them over and let her try her hardest to clean up the mess herself before he'd get whatever remained. Satisfied she wasn't going to face-dive into her ice cream again as soon as he turned his back, he lifted his gaze to find Abby staring at them, a small smile tugging up the side of her mouth.

"What?" he asked.

She shook her head and glanced down at her dish, scooping up a small bite. "Nothing. I'm just not used to seeing you with kids." Looking up, she met his stare. "You're good with her."

He shrugged, not sure what else to do or say. Sure, he was good with her, but he wasn't her primary caregiver. He got to hand her back at the end of the day when things got too serious or too hard. Or too permanent. "She's a good kid, so she makes it easy."

"Even the best kids are difficult sometimes." And she'd probably know that more than anyone, considering her line of work and that she saw a dozen kids every day at their best *and* worst.

"Hey, I've been meaning to ask you," Carter said. "Did you get your wallpaper situation taken care of?"

Abby blew out a breath and sank back in her chair. "Definitely not taken care of, but getting there. Hank got me all set up with what I need, so it's just a matter of finding a whole day to do it. Those are my big plans this weekend."

"Well, you always were one to party hard."

She laughed and their eyes connected, a hundred shared memories sparking between them. Was she remembering that bonfire they'd been to on the beach? The last party before they'd each gone their separate ways? There'd been tears—on both their parts—and some ill-advised naked time. He'd found sand in places it should never go, but he'd never regretted that night. It'd been the last time they'd been together.

Abby licked her lips, drawing his gaze to her mouth, and he shifted in his seat. When did eating ice cream become so damn erotic? "You're right—I do like it hard."

Carter choked on his own spit as he snapped his attention up to her eyes. "You what?" he managed through his coughs.

Her brows were drawn down, and she split a glance between him and Sofia as if she were missing something. "I like to party hard, like you said. Me and my bullet journal really get up to a lot of craziness."

"Right. Of course."

She tipped her head to the side, studying him intently. "What'd you think I said?"

Jesus, he definitely couldn't tell her the dirty places his brain had been heading.

He opened his mouth to say something—what, he had no goddamn clue—when his sister hobbled in on her crutches, still not completely comfortable with the added encumbrance.

"Hey, sorry I'm late. I—Oh, Abby! I didn't know you'd be here."

Abby lifted a single shoulder in a shrug. "I sort of crashed their date."

Becca's smile widened as she continued toward them. "Well I'm glad you did. It's good to see you. I'd give you a hug, but, well..." She lifted one of her crutches before bending to press a kiss to Sofia's hair. "Hi, bug. I missed you today."

"Me too, Mommy. Can I have ice cream now?"

Carter's mouth dropped as he huffed out a disbelieving laugh. "Sofia."

Becca chuckled as she shuffled to the chair opposite her daughter and sat. "By your uncle's response, I take it you've already had your ice cream, Little Miss Con Artist."

"She did," he confirmed. "Licked the dish like a dog and everything."

"Sounds about right." Becca turned her attention to Abby. "Do *all* kids do that or just mine?"

"Haven't met one yet who didn't. On ice cream days, hair cleaning is pretty much a guaranteed."

"How're things going over there? Are you still on track to open the preschool in the fall?"

Abby shifted, her eyes flicking down for only a moment before connecting back with Becca's. It wasn't much—and most people probably wouldn't have even noticed. But he wasn't most people, at least not when it came to Abby. He'd spent the sum total of entire days looking at her, studying her features and expressions. And there was no denying she was uncertain, maybe even nervous.

"They're going. And I hope so. We've got a lot to get done, and getting the timing of everything to line up is tricky."

"Well, I'd love to hear about it. You should come over for dinner soon. It's been too long since we've gotten together."

"Oh, I'm not sure..." Abby looked over at him, as if questioning if she should accept the invitation.

Hell no, was what he wanted to say. Nothing good would come from spending even more time with Abby. Hell, his mind had been in the gutter while sitting next to his niece in an ice cream shop while townsfolk strolled by. There was no telling what would happen when the two of them were alone in his temporary home. But it wasn't his place to interfere with his sister's friendships, and it sure as hell wasn't his place to tell Abby what to do, so he kept his mouth shut.

"I'm not going to take no for an answer," Becca said. "You can tell us all about your plans. Maybe Carter can even help with some things. Give you a few suggestions to make the renovation easier."

At Becca's kick under the table—thankfully with her shoed foot and not her cast—he coughed. "Sure, no problem."

"What do you think, bug? Should Miss Abby come have dinner with us?"

"Yes! Yes! Yes!"

Abby finally dropped her eyes from Carter's and smiled down at his niece. She lifted her gaze once more to his as if giving him one last chance to put a stop to it. When he didn't, she said, "Well, okay, then. I'd love to have dinner with you guys."

Chapter Five

Ever since Abby had accepted Becca's invitation to dinner, she'd been a ball of nervous energy, and no amount of pro/con lists in her bullet journal were helping to calm her. With her and Carter's history, she knew spending time together was a recipe for disaster. Especially because he hadn't miraculously turned into an ugly, dumb troll since he'd been gone. No, instead the jerk had gotten *more* handsome and intelligent in their years apart. And, quite frankly, she wasn't sure how she was supposed to resist that.

"I ran into Becca at the bank, and she told me you guys have dinner plans this weekend at her place," Savannah said with a cocked eyebrow.

Gia whipped her head in their direction, her dark hair flying behind her, hands frozen in midair as she worked to clean up the art supplies from today's class. Ollie, her golden retriever and the Sunshine Corner's adopted dog, was off receiving lots of love from the kids. "Oh *really*."

Blowing out a deep breath, Abby shrugged. "Yeah."

Savannah laughed and bumped her hip into Abby's as she carried an armful of building blocks to put them away. "Don't sound so excited about it."

Abby's shoulders slumped as she collapsed in a chair, splitting a glance between her friends. "I'm just not sure it's a good idea. Maybe I should cancel."

"Why would you do that?" Gia asked. "You've had dinner with Becca before. Lots of times."

"Yeah, but this time it's not going to be just Becca. There's the tiny problem of my ex-boyfriend who will also be there."

"From what I've seen, he's anything but tiny..." Jenn said under her breath.

Abby gasped, whipping her head toward her friend. "Jenn!"

"What?" she asked, all wide eyes and innocence. "I meant he's *tall*. Is he not? Get your mind out of the gutter, girl."

Cheeks burning with embarrassment, Abby cleared her throat and tried to steer the conversation back on track and away from Carter's...erm...size. "It's just been a lot since he's been back, you know? I feel like I can't go anywhere in town without running into him. If I didn't know better, I'd think fate was working over-time to throw us together as much as humanly possible while he's home."

"What do you mean, if you didn't know better?" Jenn asked. "Maybe that's exactly what's happening."

"But fate wouldn't be that cruel, would she? She wouldn't throw me together with the one and only guy I've clicked with in years after sending me dozens of duds, just to take him away at the end of it all. Right?"

"Well, I don't know about all *that*," Savannah said with a dismissive wave. "It doesn't always have to be forever, Abby. If you like him, I don't see what the big deal is with having a little fun while he's here."

The big deal was Abby wasn't into just fun. She didn't knock those who preferred flings—as long as it was consensual and enjoyable, she was totally on board...for *other* people. She'd never been a one-and-done kind of girl, and she couldn't see herself suddenly shaking things up now when she was almost thirty. Not only that, but she also wasn't so sure her heart wouldn't try to jump in on the *fun*, too. It'd be all too easy with Carter, given their history.

Fortunately, she was saved from having to divulge all that by the buzz of the front door.

She didn't give anyone else the option of grabbing it as she practically leaped to her feet. Tossing an "I got it," over her shoulder, she strode toward the entryway, a dutiful Ollie trotting along by her side.

Reaching down to offer him a pet, she said, "You're such a good boy, making sure to greet everyone at the door."

Ollie looked up at her, his mouth parted and tongue lolling out, looking for all the world as if he were smiling at her compliment. She grinned right back.

After verifying on the camera system who was outside, she opened the giant front door—the inlaid leaded glass against the bright yellow paint one of her favorite features of their home—and welcomed Norah inside.

"Hey, you're here early. Skip out on work?" Abby asked as they headed toward the back of the house where the kids were stationed for the afternoon, Ollie seeking Norah's attention the entire way.

"Yeah, but it wasn't quite as fun as it could've been," she said, mindlessly patting the dog's head. "I had a doctor's appointment."

Abby lifted her eyebrows. "Oh? I hope everything's okay..." She didn't want to pry, but this way the door was open if Norah wanted to discuss it on her own terms.

Norah breathed out a laugh and shook her head as they stepped foot into the great room, her eyes locking on Abby's grandmother who sat cradling one of the babies to her chest. "I'm not sure if *okay* is the word I'd use. But Hilde was right." She pressed a hand to her stomach and exhaled a long breath. "Baby number three will be making their debut in October."

Abby gasped, along with Savannah, Jenn, and Gia. Hilde, however, only had a knowing smile on her face.

"Oh my God!" Abby said, then read the look on Norah's face, which was a mix of excitement, apprehension, and nerves. "Um...congratulations?"

Norah laughed and accepted the hug Abby offered. "Thank you. We certainly weren't planning it, but Mike and I are happy. We won't tell the kids for a while, though, so please don't spill the beans."

Abby mimed zipping her lips and tossing away the key, and the rest of the girls nodded their acknowledgment.

"And *you*." Norah pointed an accusatory finger at Hilde. "I don't know what kind of crazy mojo you do, but this is *it*, all right? No more kids! I better not show up here in two years and have you telling me I should keep my baby clothes again. I'll triple up on birth control if I have to, considering this one was the one percent to sneak past the pill."

Hilde chuckled softly as she lifted a single brow. "Well, my dear, *I* certainly wasn't the one who put that baby in you...I merely said it was so."

"Wait," Gia cut in, her hands outstretched as if to pause time, her voice slightly higher pitched than usual, piquing Ollie's interest. "Hilde predicted this?"

When Hilde only offered a shrug in response, Norah said, "I'm not sure if *predicted* is the right word. You know how she is. When I was trying to offload our old baby clothes, she mentioned I shouldn't get rid of them just yet."

Gia spun on Hilde, her eyes narrowed. "Hold on... You told me I should rethink setting up my paint studio in our extra bedroom because we might need it for something else. Is this what you meant?"

"Eh." Hilde waved a hand through the air as if brushing aside Gia's concern. "Whoever really knows what I mean?" Then she stood and strolled out of the room without a backward glance, rocking the baby she held as she went.

With her mouth agape, Gia turned back to them. "Do you think...I mean, why would she...Does that mean—"

"Whoa, sister, calm down." Savannah rested her hands on Gia's shoulders, smoothing them back and forth in a calming gesture. "Hilde makes comments like that all the time. I wouldn't get too worked up about it."

Savannah glanced in Abby's direction, their eyes connecting over Gia's head, both silently saying the same thing. It seemed like their little trio was about to become a foursome.

* * *

A couple days later, after dropping Sofia off at the Sunshine Corner and narrowly avoiding another encounter with Abby, Carter made his way to his friend Marco Alvarez's office. It wasn't that he was avoiding Abby so much as...intentionally staggering Sofia's drop-off and pickup times to when history had proven that Abby would be busy with other things.

So yeah, okay, maybe he was avoiding her.

But, hell, a man could only take so much. And

the upcoming dinner tomorrow was about all he could handle for one week. It was bad enough to run into Abby while out and about in public. Public was good. Safe. He wasn't going to forget himself and kiss her breathless when there were dozens of townsfolk to bear witness. But in the place he was calling home for several more weeks? When he'd bet his collection of Montblanc pens that Becca would make some excuse to run off, thus leaving him and Abby alone? He wasn't so sure he could trust himself to be on his best behavior then.

Not when he'd been dreaming about Abby nonstop since he'd been home. And his subconscious showed no signs of stopping anytime soon, the bastard.

He cut off that line of thinking as he strode up the front walk to Alvarez Architecture, not needing to greet one of his oldest friends while fantasizing about Abby. The bell over the front door chimed as he pulled it open and stepped inside the quaint space.

Instead of being set in a commercial building, Alvarez Architecture had made its home in an older Craftsman just a block east of downtown. Historic restoration wasn't their specialty, but they'd done a fantastic job renovating this space to showcase the talents they could offer their clients. And if there were things Carter would've done differently…well, he'd keep that to himself. He knew better than to look a gift horse in the mouth, and today, that gift horse was Marco and his scanner.

"Be right out!" Marco yelled from down the hall just as the phone rang, and Carter could barely make out the grumbled cursing of his friend before he answered the call.

A sign propped up on the front reception desk read *Be right back*, and the office chair behind it sat empty with nothing but a white cardigan draped over the back, the workspace scattered with stacks of project folders.

This section of the home had obviously, at one time, been the living room, but they'd done well reworking it into the receiving area of the business. They'd opened it up without sacrificing the character found in homes from the early 1900s, the pale blue wall color making the built-ins pop. Two archways led to different areas of the business, though it'd been too long since Carter had been here to remember where they went.

Through one of those arches came a frazzled-looking man, his black hair askew. His sleeves were rolled up, showcasing bronze forearms, his tie loosened and dress shirt already unbuttoned at the top despite it being barely noon.

"What can I—Oh, hey, man!" Marco extended his hand before pulling Carter into a back-slapping hug. "How the hell are you?"

Carter grinned at his friend's exuberance and returned the embrace. "I'm doing okay. How about you? It's been a while."

"No shit. And I can't complain." Marco leaned back

against the reception desk and crossed his arms over his chest. "Sorry we haven't been able to get together since you've been back. Things are crazy around here." No more had the words left his mouth than the phone rang again, and this time Carter could make out each and every one of the swear words Marco mumbled. He held up a finger before walking around the reception desk. "One sec."

As Marco snatched up the phone to take the call, Carter made himself busy, walking around the space and taking in the before and after photos of previous jobs they had framed on the walls. Marco's family's business did a wide range of projects—or they had, anyway. Last the two of them had talked, it was just Marco and his brother trying to hold down the shop after their dad had retired the year before, thus minimizing the jobs they'd been able to take on.

"Sorry about that." Marco hung up and gestured for Carter to follow him down the hall. "Come on back. You can fill me in on everything while you use me for my equipment." He glanced back at Carter, a smirk on his face. "Not the first time I've been used in that way. Gia can attest to that."

Carter snorted but followed, shaking his head. "As much as I'm sure your wife is *thrilled* with your equipment," Carter said dryly, "it's not anything I want to discuss, so let's leave that out of all convos between us."

Marco laughed outright, boisterous and contagious—the same as it'd been back in high school—and Carter found his own lips lifting at the sound. "Well, if you want any tips, you know where to find me."

Yeah, Carter wasn't touching that one with a ten-foot pole.

"I appreciate you letting me borrow this," Carter said as he scanned in the drawings he'd created for the Redmond project. He still needed to organize them into a presentation in InDesign with labels and arranged imagery this week before his video chat with the client on Monday, but this, at least, was one item off his to do list.

"No problem. What's mine is yours." Marco leaned back in his chair, his hands folded across his stomach as he swiveled from side to side. "Could quite literally be yours if you'd finally take me up on my offer."

Carter laughed, shaking his head. Ever since the two of them had graduated college, Marco had been trying to lure Carter back home, dangling a job at Alvarez Architecture in front of his nose as bait. Reminding him that he wouldn't have even looked into this career if it hadn't been for Marco's family's business piquing his interest. Unfortunately for Marco, Carter's endgame wasn't working for another firm—family owned or not. Also unfortunately for Marco, his family's firm was located in the one place in the world Carter never wanted to permanently return to.

"When are you going to let up on that?"

"When you finally come and work with me." Marco

lifted a hand as if to encompass the entire house. "In case you haven't noticed, we're drowning over here."

"I did notice, actually. Where is everyone?"

"If by everyone you mean Carlos and Dotty, they're out. My brother's on a job site all day, and our lovely receptionist is at lunch—also known as visiting her grandkids. If she's back before three, I'll eat my tie. We've got so many projects, we're going to be busy for the next two years even without taking on another soul."

"Sounds to me like you need to hire some more people."

Just then the phone rang, and Marco hung his head, swearing under his breath. Before picking up the receiver, he said, "What the hell do you think I've been trying to do? Pay attention, man."

Carter breathed out a laugh and turned back to the scanner. He couldn't lie and say he wouldn't have a blast working with one of his oldest and closest friends. They'd been inseparable as teens, and though they'd gone their separate ways after high school, they'd stayed in touch as best they could over the years. But as fun as it would be—not to mention how perfect considering their skill sets complemented each other— it wasn't what Carter had dreamed of. Wasn't what he'd been working his ass off for the entirety of his career. He wanted a firm of his own. Something with *his* name on it. Something he could call his and his alone.

Something that would prove to his dad once and for all that he'd amounted to something.

Besides that, he was in Heart's Hope Bay only as long as Becca and Sofia needed him, and then he was gone. Back to his life in Vegas where he was working steadily toward his dreams, where he didn't run into his ex-girlfriend every day, and where things in his life actually made sense.

Chapter Six

※

Abby couldn't remember the last time she'd been this nervous, and she'd been out on dozens of first dates over the past several years. She knew her nerves were ridiculous and one hundred percent unwarranted. But that didn't stop the butterflies from fluttering around in her stomach as if they were in a hurry to get somewhere important and were already late.

After pulling up to the curb in front of Becca's cute Cape Cod for their dinner, Abby put her car in park, gripped the steering wheel, and took three deep, calming breaths, slowly blowing out each exhalation.

"You're being ridiculous," she muttered to her empty car. "*He* didn't ask you over. This isn't a date. This is barely a hangout. Chill out."

All of those things might've been true, but with as often as she and Carter had been running into each other since he'd been home, she couldn't help but be hit over the head with what-could've-beens day in and day out.

How different could her life have been if he'd come back to Heart's Hope Bay after college? If they'd stayed together through the distance? If anyone could've made it work, it was them.

She tried to pretend it didn't, but the fact that he hadn't even wanted to try to keep their relationship intact through college still ate at her.

A sharp knock at the driver's side window startled a scream out of her, and she snapped her head in that direction only to find an amused-looking Carter peering in. Because of course. Think of the annoyingly perfect ex-boyfriend, and he shall appear...Hoping he hadn't borne witness to her not-so-silent pep talk, she pressed the button to roll down her window.

"Hi." She smiled up at him, ignoring the chiseled cut of his scruffy jaw and how his piercing green eyes managed to get under her skin every time she was in his presence. Okay, so she *tried* to ignore those things. Trouble was, Carter and all his attributes were pretty damn hard to ignore.

"Hey," he said, resting his forearms on her open window. He cocked his head and studied her, his eyes raking over every part of her he could see like an actual caress. Clearing his throat, he lifted his gaze to meet hers. "You about ready to come in, or did you still have more to discuss with yourself?"

Abby could feel the blush creeping up her neck, her embarrassment sure to flood her face at any moment. So she did the only thing she could think of—she scowled at him. Fortunately, red cheeks on her meant any number of things, including irritation and anger. And, okay, arousal, too, but she wasn't going there.

"A gentleman wouldn't have pointed that out, you jerk."

He grinned, just one side of his mouth tipping up, before stepping back and opening the door for her. "Never was very good at being one around you, was I?"

Flashes of heated memories they'd shared whipped through her mind before she shut them down. Not. Going. There. Not tonight, and not with him.

She busied herself with gathering her things, slinging her purse over her shoulder and grabbing the salad and bottle of wine she'd brought. "I don't know if I'd go that far. But you've definitely gotten worse."

She stepped out of her car, not realizing until it was too late just how close Carter was. His scent wafted over her—how was it possible that he still smelled the same and yet deliciously different?—as they stood near enough that his breath fanned over her parted lips, making her hungry for something more than just dinner.

The puffs of air he expelled in the chilly February evening drew her eyes to his mouth. It had always been a work of art—his lips soft and full without being pouty. The perpetual cast of scruff on his jaw, however, was altogether new. New and intriguing and daydream-inducing. But who could blame her for wondering what it'd feel like against her own lips…her neck…her—

"I better make up for my ungentlemanly behavior where I can, then," he said, pulling her out of her head. Without a word, he grabbed the salad and wine from her hands, stepped back as if she hadn't nearly face-planted straight into his mouth, and led them toward the house.

With his back turned, she shook her head of the thoughts that had no business invading her mind and gave herself a—this time silent—pep talk to tone it down a notch or twelve.

She caught up with him as he stepped onto the driveway along the side of the house, keeping pace with him. "Thanks for carrying those."

"No problem. Thanks for bringing them."

"Of course. What were you doing out here anyway? Besides spying on me."

He shot her a quick grin, the curve of his lips gone so fast she might've imagined it, and lifted a reusable bag. "Last-minute grocery store run. Apparently spaghetti isn't spaghetti without garlic bread, and I should've read Becca's mind that she wanted that, too, when I picked up the groceries this week."

Abby blew out a laugh and shook her head. "I see living together is going great for you guys."

Carter shrugged. "It's actually not that bad. Better than I'd been anticipating. We haven't spent this much time together since we both still lived at home, so I was a little worried. But it hasn't been awful."

"I heard that!" Becca called as Carter opened the back door.

He met Abby's stare and rolled his eyes, gesturing for her to enter ahead of him. "I wasn't whispering, so, yeah, I imagine so. Plus, I said it *wasn't* awful. I already spilled everything really bad out by Abby's car."

"I will kick you out on the street," Becca said without any heat, gliding toward them on her crutches. "Don't think I won't."

"Yeah, we'll see how long that lasts. Good luck," he said with a snort.

While Abby watched the verbal volley between the two siblings—which seemed to be as easy as breathing, Carter managing to unload his arms and hang up both their coats without missing a beat—she found herself smiling, a deep happiness and…yearning settling in her chest. They were giving each other grief, yes—had always as long as she'd been in their lives—but there was an undeniable affection between them, even in their teasing.

When Carter and Becca put down their verbal swords long enough for her to cut in, she said, "Well, even though the circumstances could've been better, I'm glad you guys have had this time together."

Even Abby could hear the wistfulness in her tone, and if the look Carter and Becca shot her was any indication, they did, too. She couldn't help it, though.

She'd longed for a big family—or, hell, even a medium-sized one—for as long as she could remember, and she hadn't kept that desire a secret. Definitely not one she'd kept from Carter.

Instead of the large family she'd craved, it'd been just her and her grandma most of her life. She hadn't even known her dad, and yeah, her mom had been present, but not *present*. And that had only solidified more as soon as Abby had turned eighteen and her mom had moved across the country to Florida. Being a teen mom, she'd harbored resentment toward Abby that she hadn't tried very hard to hide. Or at all, really. So, growing up, Abby had spent as much time as possible with her grandmother. With no siblings...no aunts, uncles, or cousins...no one else around but the two of them, was it any wonder she'd been called an old soul?

"Yeah, me too," Carter said. "We're lucky to have each other, even if I want to strangle her some days. And I'm glad I was able to get approval to work remotely so she didn't have to rely on our father to help her through." Gone was the lighthearted tone he'd used with his sister, and in its place was one that spoke of frustration and a whole lot of repressed—or maybe not so repressed—anger.

Abby didn't know what to do with the jarring change or the sudden tension in the room, so she filled the silence with small talk. "It's been a while since I've seen him in town. How's he doing?"

"Wouldn't know," Carter said at the same time Becca replied with, "He's okay."

Abby split a look between them, then focused her attention on Carter. "You haven't seen him since you've been back?"

"Nope," he said with zero remorse. "Don't plan to, either. I already know exactly how little he thinks of me. I don't need a refresher."

"Carter..." Becca said, her tone a mix of warning and placation.

"Why don't you guys catch up in the living room?" he said, turning his back to them to unpack the grocery bag he'd brought in. "I'll finish up in here and call when it's ready."

Abby stepped toward him, ready to help. "Oh, I can—"

Carter cut her off. "Nope, I got this."

"Come on." Becca tugged on Abby's sleeve and tipped her head toward the living room. "And grab that bottle of wine, will you? Maybe a couple glasses if you want some, too."

Abby chuckled, sparing Carter a quick glance as Becca left the room. His head was down as he stared intently at the pot of water on the stove, too much focus for what the task called for. She figured he needed some time to himself, so she did as Becca asked, grabbing the open bottle of wine sitting on the counter and two glasses from the under-counter rack, and followed her.

"Thank God you're here," Becca said. "I have no idea how I would've gotten that wine in here without you."

Abby laughed. "Glad I'm useful for something."

"I'm normally not a huge drinker—being the only one responsible for Sofia sort of zaps that freedom, you know?—but whenever Carter gets started on our dad, I need a glass or four."

"Yeah...," Abby said, settling back into the couch cushions. "I don't remember him being so..."

"Hostile?" Becca asked with a raised brow.

Abby winced and lifted a shoulder. "Has he always been like that toward your dad and I just didn't notice?"

"No...I think he hid a lot of it from you in high school. Didn't want to scare you off." Becca poured herself a healthy dose of wine before doing the same for Abby. "But they've always had a troubled relationship. Our dad was always worse on Carter."

Abby wasn't sure if she should be getting this information from Becca rather than the source himself, but she was desperate to know more about Carter's life since she hadn't been a part of it for so long. And if his sister was freely offering it, Abby wasn't going to turn it down.

"How so?" she asked.

Becca sighed. "It's your pretty standard dysfunctional family, I think. Wife dies of cancer, single dad is left to raise two kids on his own and instead buries himself in a bottle. And the only time he came up for air was to degrade Carter and tell him how worthless he was."

Abby gasped, bringing her hand up to cover her mouth. "Oh my God, that's awful."

"Yeah." Becca blew out a deep breath and sank back into the couch cushions. "Our dad was always...firm, I guess. But it got a lot worse after our mom died. I'm not making excuses for his behavior, but I think he saw a lot of himself in Carter. And Dad blamed himself for my mom's death, irrational as that is." She shrugged. "Probably why it was never as bad for me—Carter reminded him of himself, and I reminded him of the woman he lost."

Abby had always known there was something off about Carter and his dad's relationship, but she'd had no idea just how deep the wound ran. When she and Carter had been a couple, he'd never wanted to talk about his father. And any time they'd spent together had, more often than not, been at her grandmother's house or out and about in town.

Come to think of it, she could only remember visiting his childhood home once, when Carter had forgotten something. Even then, they'd just slipped in and out. He'd grabbed what he needed quickly and efficiently, and Abby had just figured it was because he was desperate to get out of a house where his little sister was. But now she wondered if he'd been hiding that part of himself from her.

"So you guys have cut off all contact with him?" Abby asked.

Becca sighed. "It's a long story. Yes and no. I still go to see him or call to make sure he's okay. But there's only so much I can do for a person who is desperate to self-destruct. Because of that, I won't allow him into Sofia's life. He knows about her, but he's never met her."

Abby's heart broke over that bit of information, but before she could respond, Sofia came bounding down the stairs, a superhero cape flying out behind her.

"Miss Abby!" Sofia yelled with the kind of exuberance only a three-year-old had. "You're at *my* house!"

"I sure am. Thank you for having me. Were you playing dress-up?"

Sofia tilted her head to the side and peered up at Abby. "No, why?"

Abby looked over Sofia's ensemble. She wore rainbow-striped tights, a bright blue tutu, an oversized vest that was clearly her mom's, a superhero cape, and a hat with earflaps.

Abby and Becca shared a smile over Sofia's head. "Just wondering. I really like what you're wearing."

"Thanks, it's my favorite!"

"I can see why. It's amazing."

Carter popped his head into the living room. "If you guys haven't drank your dinner already, spaghetti's on."

Abby laughed, picking up her still-full glass, as well as Becca's, before following her and Sofia into the kitchen. She'd been too engrossed in Becca's words to even pause to take a sip. Now, though, as she looked into Carter's eyes, questioning and wary, she wondered if Becca should have told her anything at all.

* * *

Dinner had gone surprisingly well. Abby hadn't felt out of place, and there'd been no awkward silences. Just lots of reminiscing and laughter. And though she'd tried to avoid staring at Carter, she couldn't help but be drawn to him. More often than not, she'd look at him only to find he was already watching her, at which time her stomach would flip-flop for absolutely no good reason.

This was the best date she'd had in forever. The only problem was, it wasn't a date at all, no matter how many looks Carter stole, or how many times he made her laugh, or how he'd rested his arm along the back of her chair after they'd finished eating. She swore she'd even felt his fingers whisper across the thin material of her sweater, sending her synapses into overdrive.

It was making all those could-have-been thoughts even more impossible to ignore.

After the plates had been cleared, Becca had whisked Sofia away for her nightly bath. That left Carter and Abby alone in the kitchen. They stood in front of the sink, him washing the dishes and her drying, as the conversation flowed easily between them. Granted, it was mostly surface level, but she didn't mind. She'd missed this with him. Had missed the easy way they had with one another, and she was content to soak in as much of it as she could while he was home.

"So...," Carter said as he passed her a dripping plate. "How much did she tell you?"

"What? Who?" Abby asked as she swiped at the dish with a towel.

Carter rolled his eyes. "My sister."

To Abby's credit, her movements stuttered only slightly. Okay...so maybe they were moving past surface level stuff now.

"Oh, well, she, um...She may have mentioned that you don't get along with your dad."

Carter laughed outright at that. "Now I know for a fact she didn't say that. Us *not getting along* is the biggest pile of bullshit I've ever heard. He hates me, and the feeling's mutual."

Abby's heart nearly broke in half at the matter-of-fact way Carter spoke. She knew what it was like to have a parent who wasn't all that interested in your life. One who'd rather be doing other things. One who saw you, at best, as an inconvenience, and, at worst, as a burden. What she didn't know was the level of dislike Carter was talking about. God knew she didn't have a great relationship with her mom, but she didn't hate her. Could never.

But that hate was something Carter had, apparently, been living with for a while. At least as long as she'd known him. His mom had died when they were sophomores, if she remembered correctly. They'd started dating the summer before junior year, so he'd been feeling this the entire time they'd been together. And she'd never, ever known.

She turned to face him, leaning her hip against the counter. "Why didn't you ever tell me?"

Carter braced his hands on the sink and blew out a deep breath, staring out the window into the inky black night. "I don't know. Because I was a teenager with a hot girlfriend, and I didn't want to jeopardize said hot girlfriend making out with me by unloading all that on her?"

She breathed out a laugh and shook her head. "But you knew about my mom—how she wanted to be anything *but* a mom. How she always made me feel unwanted." Abby's voice cracked at the last word, but she swallowed down the emotions that sometimes got the better of her and continued. "My life wasn't perfect, and my family certainly wasn't. I would have understood."

"Yeah, well." He shrugged. "I had him telling me how worthless I was. And at some point—especially when you're that young—you start to believe it."

Abby rested her hand on his forearm, feeling how tense he was. "Carter. You can't honestly believe that."

His mouth tipped up at the corner as he glanced over at her. "Twenty-nine-year-old Carter? No. I'm good. But sixteen-, seventeen-, eighteen-year-old Carter? Yeah. I believed it. Carried it with me for a lot of years, too. But since I've been gone, I've learned I'm more than what my father thinks of me."

He shrugged and passed another dish to Abby. "His words don't have power over me anymore. I'm going to do what I want, and I'm going to succeed while I'm at it. And if what I'm doing with my life happens to get back to him and makes him eat every last word he's ever said about me, then all the better."

"Does he know what you've been up to?"

"I'm honestly not sure. And I don't really care. I've got a great job that I love, and I'm doing exactly what he swore I never would—making something of myself. Like I said, if he had to eat his words, that'd just be karma, but if not, I don't care what he thinks anymore."

Abby studied his profile, reading the lines of frustration on his face, the stiff set of his shoulders, and knowing, with absolute certainty, that what he said wasn't the complete truth. Carter *did* care what his dad thought—at least enough to prove him wrong.

She cleared her throat. "Well, I'm glad you're in that place now... even if that means you're no longer a true resident of Heart's Hope Bay."

"I don't know, I think you're always a true resident here. No matter how long you've been gone, or how far away you've traveled."

Abby smiled. "Yeah, I guess that's true. I do know Mabel and Gladys were sure happy to have you back in town. Actually, I know *several* ladies who've been happy to have you back."

In fact, there'd been an uptick in her grandma's friends swinging by the Sunshine Corner to pop in and see their "grandchildren" or Hilde—conveniently during the times Carter usually dropped off or picked up Sofia. Abby didn't blame them in the least—he was definitely a treat for the eyes.

"Oh yeah?" he asked, turning to face her and mirroring her stance as he rested against the counter, his arms folded over his broad chest. "Are you one of these people?"

"Well...yes, but I didn't mean me."

"No? Who, then?"

"The Bridge Bunch."

"The who?"

Abby laughed. "I think my grandma formed the group after you'd already left. Hilde and Mabel are the ringleaders—aka troublemakers—of that group. Anyway, apparently you helped Mabel get her groceries out to her car the other day. When she stopped in to see her great-grandson at the Sunshine Corner, she went on and on about it and what a nice young man you are. She also mentioned how she has seven granddaughters from the ages of twenty to thirty-four that she could set you up with. You know, if you're interested..."

She was only teasing, but even just saying the words felt like razor blades on her tongue. Which was ridiculous. She had no claim over him. They'd been a couple once, a lifetime ago. But they were no longer together. Hell, they were barely friends. But if this conversation and these past couple of weeks reminded her of anything, it was how much she missed him in her life.

"Tempting," Carter said dryly.

Abby tried not to let the relief show on her face, but she wasn't sure she succeeded. Carter's lips ticked up the slightest bit, and then he reached out and swept his thumb along the bare skin just above the open neckline of her sweater, and her breathing stuttered.

"Rogue water droplet," his said, his voice low and rough as he lifted his gaze to hers, allowing his hand to drop to his side. "I've missed this, you know."

"What's that, doing dishes?" She tried to control the quality of her voice, but it still came out breathless. She cleared her throat and tried again. "You have one of those fancy machines in your place that does them for you?"

Carter laughed. "No, I mean this. Me and you, talking. It was always so easy between us, wasn't it?"

"Yeah, it was."

Honestly, it'd been everything she'd spent the past eleven years looking for—a relationship with her best friend who also happened to set her body on fire and made her ache with need.

The attraction part was still very much alive and well between them, as her body now humming with life could attest to. And though she didn't know him as well as she once had, easy conversation still flowed between them, as well as comfortable silences.

For the briefest moment, she got lost in a fantasy of

them doing this every night. Cooking dinner together and then cleaning up...long talks about nothing and everything at once. Discussing their days and then getting lost in each other's bodies before collapsing in a heap, tangled in the bedsheets and each other's arms.

If only he lived in Heart's Hope Bay, this could actually be their life. If only he would stick around. But she knew he'd never stay. He'd said it without words in how he'd bailed as soon as possible and stayed away. And now, after learning about the history with his father, she understood exactly why he didn't want to be tied to this town. Why he didn't want to be anchored here.

Just the same as she knew she would never leave.

It was just her and her grandma here, but that family, small as it may be, meant the world to her. The same as the family she'd adopted for herself—her best friends, her coworkers, and all the kids at the Sunshine Corner. Abby's roots were too deep in Heart's Hope Bay to ever leave.

But that didn't stop her from wishing things could be different, because she couldn't remember ever wanting anyone as much as she wanted Carter.

"Abby," he whispered.

She jerked her gaze up. Maybe he'd been thinking the same things, remembering the same shared history, feeling the same irresistible connection. His eyes locked on her lips, and heat stole through her body, lighting her up from the inside out. Determination was written in his eyes, and she froze, her own gaze dropping to his mouth as she wet her lips.

She wasn't sure who leaned in first. All she knew was suddenly Carter's hands were gripping her face, his mouth pressed to hers as he brushed his thumbs across her cheeks, and it felt like coming home.

Carter licked a path across her lower lip and then groaned when she opened to him. He tasted like wine and felt like heaven, and she had to clutch his forearms for dear life, hoping the grip would keep her upright as fireworks rocked her body.

So much between them had stayed the same as it'd once been, but this... Oh, *this* had only gotten better with time. Carter was no longer the fumbling, hurried boy he'd once been. In his place was a determined man who was patient enough to draw things out in order to increase the pleasure. And Abby's pleasure? Good Lord, it was through the roof. Every nerve ending in her body was firing, her skin tingly and warm, a hum settling in her belly... and lower. She ached for more—was desperate to feel Carter's hands along every inch of her.

Just as she pressed her palms to his chest, really letting herself feel the rock-hard solidity of it beneath her fingers, Becca's crutches sounded on the wood floor in the living room.

With a gasp, she tore her mouth away from Carter's and turned in time to watch Becca stroll in, her eyes flitting between Abby and Carter. "Did I interrupt anything?"

"What? No, not at all," Abby said, not daring to even steal a glance at Carter, let alone reach up to make sure she didn't have lipstick smeared across her face.

Apparently content with that answer, Becca stashed her crutches against the wall before dropping into a dining chair. "I forgot to ask you how the renovation is going."

Abby blew out a long breath, grateful that Becca hadn't interrogated them more on what had just happened—mainly because Abby didn't have a damn clue herself. And she could admit she was relieved to have something to focus her attention on other than the man who'd stolen every one of her brain cells.

She tucked her hair behind her ear and nodded. "Good. Well, maybe not *good*. It's going slow. I'm trying to save as much money as I can, so I'm doing a lot of work myself, even if I don't know what I'm doing most of the time."

"Well, that's just perfect!" Becca said, her smile bright. "Carter is great at renovations. I'm sure he'd love to help."

Abby finally slid a glance to Carter only to find his gaze already locked on her, his eyes hot and hungry and not attempting at all to hide it. Her body reacted to the attention, perking up and revving for a hell of a lot more than what she'd gotten. Having Carter in her home for a project of that size would only make things worse. She had no idea how she was supposed to resist him now that she'd been reminded of how good he tasted and exactly how talented that mouth of his was, not to mention how alive her body came under his touch.

She gulped and tore her eyes away from him. "Oh, no, that's okay. I'm sure he doesn't want to spend his time back home doing renovation work."

Becca shot her brother a smirk. "Oh, he definitely does. And he won't take no for an answer."

Chapter Seven

✳

Only a couple days had passed since the kiss that had rocked Carter's world. It wasn't a secret that he and Abby had chemistry, but he'd thought maybe it had languished in the years they'd been apart. *Ha*. That was completely laughable. If anything, the heat between them had only ratcheted up, now practically an inferno. And their connection? It was obvious that hadn't evaporated, either.

He'd had his head up his ass back in high school, hiding so much of himself away from the person he felt the closest to. Stupid pride had kept him from opening up to her about his father then, but it seemed less important to pretend his life was perfect for her now.

Plus there was the matter of Becca airing all their dirty laundry in front of the world.

In the end, it didn't matter. Instead of turning away

from him—the way a part of him had feared she would—Abby empathized with every difficult piece of his past he revealed. The softness in her gaze didn't make him feel like less of a man. It made them feel closer.

And that *kiss*.

It had felt so good to hold her...to feel her under his hands again. It had felt *right*. Enough so that it should have sent him running for the hills.

Now, instead of keeping his head down and his lips to himself like he should have been doing while he was in town, he'd been roped into helping Abby with her renovation. Which was why he had no choice but to kill his sister.

After picking Sofia up from the Sunshine Corner a couple hours ago, he'd made sure she and Becca were settled in for the night. Then he headed to Abby's to fulfill the promise Becca had made on his behalf.

Carter parked in the street, grabbed his tools out of the back, and made his way up the winding front walk toward the huge wraparound porch. Abby's grandmother's house hadn't gotten any less grand with time, the bright yellow double front door embodying sunshine—completely apropos of the day-care name. The white porch boards were a little worse for wear and the window trim needed a good painting, but none of that detracted from the stunning, sprawling beauty of the home. He'd been too young and too stupid to appreciate it when he'd been a teenager, but he had no qualms in making up for lost time now.

He pressed his finger to the doorbell and waited only a moment before the front door swung open. It wasn't Abby who stood in the doorway, but rather Hilde, her grandmother. Though they'd seen each other a handful of times since he'd come to town, those had been brief, pleasant interactions. Now she looked him over from head to toe in a way that said she saw far beneath his skin, so much so it had him standing a little taller under her gaze. She'd always had that ability. When he and Abby had been teenagers, he'd been more scared of *her* than of Abby's mom.

Being so young, Rachel Engel had always been more of a friend to Abby than any sort of parental figure. Had, in fact, been the one who'd stocked Abby's drawers with condoms, because she didn't want to see her daughter repeat her mistakes. Just remembering how Abby's voice had quavered the slightest bit when she'd told him that before pasting on a bright smile still made his heart clench.

"Carter," Hilde said, not making a move to welcome him inside. "What can I do for you?"

"Hi, Mrs. Engel. I'm helping Abby with the renovation upstairs."

"Hmm." Skepticism dripped from her tone even on the single non-word. "Isn't that nice." She said the word *nice* like she would have said *tarantula*.

"Grandma?" Abby called from somewhere in the house. "If that's Carter, send him up."

Several seconds ticked by before Hilde finally stepped

back and opened the door wide, allowing Carter into the home. "I guess you can go on up. I suppose I'll just stay down here...where I can hear absolutely everything."

Carter nearly snorted at that but managed to keep his reaction tamped down. From experience, he knew exactly how thin the walls were in this house. He would've liked to say she didn't have anything to worry about, but the other night at his sister's place had proven otherwise. Deciding his best response was none at all, he gave her a brief smile, grabbed his tools, and made his way inside.

The home was stunning, something right out of a magazine. It was a straight shot from the front of the house to the back, with rooms spiderwebbing off in different directions and a rotunda right in the middle where a deep mahogany staircase followed the curve of the room. The staircase had obviously been refinished at some point, along with the rest of the main floor in all its sprawling complexity. But all that stopped at the top of the steps, and he could guess why. Downstairs was home to the Sunshine Corner, the business taking up nearly every inch of what he would guess was nearly three thousand square feet on the main level.

The upper floors, however, were where Abby and her grandmother lived. He wondered if Abby's bedroom was still located on the third floor, and if her favorite place in the house was still the turret on the far side of the space. Though she and her mom had jumped from place to place—three just in the time she and Carter had been together—she'd always had a room in the home to fall back on. Though she'd been there long before, Abby had officially moved in with her grandma the day after she'd turned eighteen, her mom bailing from town faster than either of them could blink. She'd had the entire floor to herself, and the vast space, with all its privacy and seclusion, had been something teenage him had loved.

He found Abby on her hands and knees in the corner of the landing. The sight of her bent over, her sweet curves presented to him like an offering, did absolutely nothing to keep his mind from going to where it'd been on vacation the past two nights ... and every hour in between.

She glanced at him over her shoulder, her face blank for a split second before she pasted on a bright smile. "Hey. Thanks again for helping."

"No problem." He placed his tools on the floor, taking stock of the space. She'd already started to pull up the carpet that covered the entire second floor, but there was enough of it that it'd take both of them a while to complete.

"I know your sister sort of roped you into it, but I appreciate it."

He lifted a single shoulder. "It's really not a big deal. I actually miss doing this kind of stuff."

Which was one hundred percent true. While he enjoyed his job at Mosley & Associates, he missed being elbow-deep in the actual renovations. As the firm had grown, there'd been less time for him to get his hands dirty when what he'd needed to spend his time and focus on was retaining current clients and attracting new ones. After all, it wasn't going to be his wood-working or refinishing skills that got him where he wanted to be. That didn't mean he didn't love it. And that certainly didn't mean he didn't miss it.

"I know the polite thing would have been to tell you that you didn't need to come over and help, but the truth is, I have absolutely no idea what I'm doing. I'm completely shooting in the dark over here. Pulling up the carpet is pretty self-explanatory, but after that, I'm completely lost. A girl can only Google so much."

He laughed, his shoulders relaxing infinitesimally as he realized maybe it could be this easy. So they kissed. It wasn't like they'd never done it before. They were both adults. So there'd been a temporary lapse in judgment. It didn't have to be a big deal.

"First the wallpaper, and now demo…Do you have anybody helping you with this?" he asked.

Abby sighed, her shoulders slumping as she sat back on her heels. "I did, but not so much anymore. I hired Bobby Kramer—you remember him? He was a couple years ahead of us in school. Anyway, he was helping me as a side job because he was cheaper than any of the contractors I found. But his world kind of imploded a few weeks ago when his pregnant wife got put on bed rest. He's been trying to make sure she's doing okay, while at the same time taking care of their twin two-year-olds *and* still working his full-time job."

Carter grimaced. "Yikes. That's a rough hand to be dealt."

She laughed. "For him or for me?"

"Both."

With a shrug, she said, "Yeah, I guess. But it's fine. A few of the parents talked me into hosting a fundraiser for the preschool in a couple weeks. One way or another, I'll figure out how to get the preschool done in time to accept students by the fall."

It didn't surprise him in the least that Abby was rolling with the punches and not letting any setbacks get in the way of her dreams.

"A fundraiser's a great idea."

"I can't take credit for it. It was Becca's brainchild, actually, so I have her to thank."

Carter grinned. "I like how you oh-so-kindly made that out like she hadn't strong-armed you into it."

Abby smiled and ducked her head, a faint blush sweeping over her cheeks, proving Carter's assumption correct. "Well...however it came to be, I'm grateful for it. I can't wait for the preschool to open."

"Speaking of...we should probably get on the same page for what you envision up here. What are your plans for the space?"

Abby's eyes lit up with passion, her excitement so contagious he found himself drawn to her. She stood, gesturing to the large, open landing. "This will be the coatroom. All the preschoolers will have their own cubbies over here where they can hang up their coats, hats, backpacks, that kind of thing. They'll have bins with their names on them where they can put any projects that they've worked on, and then the parents can pick them up at the end of the day. I'm thinking I'll need to take down a couple of these walls separating the smaller rooms to make them practical for classrooms. And then over here..."

As Abby continued, her eyes bright and her voice excited, she mesmerized him. She truly loved what she did. And there was no doubt she was good at it. She was caring and compassionate and sensitive, but also smart and driven. Given what he knew of her, he didn't have an ounce of uncertainty that she'd chosen the right career. The Sunshine Corner and the kids she looked after, day in and day out, was exactly where she was meant to be.

That only reiterated why he needed to stay away and keep his hands to himself for the remainder of the time he had in Heart's Hope Bay. They were on two very different paths. And he had absolutely no business being with her, because Abby was meant for so much more than what Carter had it in him to give.

* * *

It was after ten by the time they decided to pack it in for the night, but they'd gotten further than Abby had anticipated. After listening to her ideas, Carter had sketched out a renovation plan, and then they'd managed to rip up all the carpet on the second floor, save for the rooms currently in use. They'd already made plans for Carter to come back later in the week to help with the next steps.

"Thanks again for coming by," Abby said. "I really appreciate it."

They stood in the entryway, their voices hushed so as not to carry throughout the old house. Probably wouldn't matter anyway—Abby's grandma was a night owl, and she'd place bets on the fact that Hilde was straining to hear every single word from wherever she sat.

Carter shrugged into his coat before grabbing his tools. "It's seriously not a big deal. You can stop thanking me now, Abby," he said, his lips tipped up at the corners.

The move drew her gaze to his mouth, and, without permission, her mind conjured up what it'd felt like to have it pressed against hers again. He'd been just the right amount of confident and commanding—something he hadn't yet grown into back when they'd been a couple. What else about him might have changed in the years they'd been apart?

He cleared his throat, and she jerked her eyes up to his, surprised to find heat in their depths. At the memories they silently shared between them, her body warmed under his gaze, aching to step into him...to remind herself just how firm and solid he'd felt beneath her hands the other night. To feel his heat and the security of being held in his arms.

"I should go." His voice was rough and low, sending shivers racing up and down her spine. Temptation pulled at her to lean into him and see if he would close the gap. Finish what he started the other night.

But that wasn't going to happen. Without either of them saying a word, they'd both acknowledged that the kiss between them shouldn't have happened and wouldn't be happening again. He was only in town for a short while, and she was looking for a forever love, not whatever it was Carter could offer.

"Yeah." She broke eye contact and opened the door for him, leaning against it as he stepped out into the cool night air. "I'll see you tomorrow when you drop off Sofia."

"Bright and early." With one final sweeping gaze over her, he descended the steps and strode to his car. Once he was settled inside, he gave her a quick wave before driving away.

Abby shut the door, sighing as she closed her eyes and sagged against it. She may not have been ready for Carter to be back in her life, but just because she wasn't ready didn't stop it from happening.

Despite how much she craved him—and, oh, how she craved him—she needed to lock that down tight and throw away the key. Because if things were hard for her now, she couldn't imagine how difficult they'd be further along in his stay, especially with the two of them putting in extra hours as he helped with the renovation.

She blew out a deep breath, opened her eyes, and nearly leaped out of her skin at the sight of her grandmother standing two feet in front of her. "Grandma!" she said sharply, her hand flying to her chest. "I swear, you're like a cat sometimes."

Hilde didn't even crack a smile, her eyes narrowing as she looked Abby over. "Perhaps that's because you were lost in Carter daydreams."

Abby rolled her eyes and pushed off the door, making her way down the hallway toward the kitchen at the back of the house. It might have been past ten o'clock, but it was never too late for cookies. She pulled two from the jar that perpetually sat on the counter, replaced the lid, and, on second thought, went back for a third.

"Not even denying it, then?" her grandma asked.

"I'm not denying it because it's ridiculous."

Her grandma heaved a sigh and dropped into the chair opposite her at the table in the breakfast nook. "No, what's ridiculous is that you think it's a good idea to get involved with him after what happened with you two in the past."

"What happened with us in the past wasn't a big deal. We were high school sweethearts, Grandma. We were young, and it traveled its course."

"I'm not sure who you're trying to fool, sweetheart, but you know better than to pull that on me."

"I'm not pulling anything on you. I'm just telling you that you don't have anything to worry about."

"Mmm-hmm ... Don't sit here and try to tell me rain isn't wet. You were more heartbroken after that boy left than you were when your mom did."

Abby rolled her eyes. They didn't talk about her mom often because it didn't matter—her mom had made her choice, and Abby had made her peace with it. "We both know Mom was long gone before she packed her suitcase. And you've said yourself it was the right move for both of us."

"And I still stand by that. Your mom sticking in Heart's Hope Bay was only going to bring you both down. Better she go off to do whatever it was she wanted and you stay with me. But the staying with me part means I witnessed every tear-filled night for months after that boy left. And I don't want to see you get hurt like that again."

Abby's shoulders sagged, her eyes softening as she looked at her grandma, who truly did only want the best for her. Was the solitary person in her life who had ever only wanted the best for her.

She reached out, placed her hand against her grandma's papery soft skin, and squeezed. "I'll be fine. All Carter's doing is helping with the renovation. And the only reason he's doing that is because Becca forced him into it. That's it. That's all. And there's no reason that, while he's back, we can't be friends. What we had together was a long time ago, and we didn't end on bad terms. It would be a bigger deal if we *weren't* friendly while he's home. I'm not a kid anymore, so you don't need to worry about me."

Her grandma stared at her with narrowed, assessing eyes, as if she could see directly into her soul. And based on what Abby knew of her and the miraculous— and sometimes eerie—things that happened around her, Abby actually wouldn't put it past the woman to have another trick up her sleeve.

"I've never been one to tell you what to do with your life, Abby. You know that."

Abby met her grandmother's stare with a wry look of her own. "No? You sure have a funny way of showing that."

Hilde rolled her eyes. "So I look out for my granddaughter. Is that such a crime?"

Abby softened and she squeezed her grandma's hand once again. While her mom called once or twice a year, she spent the majority of those phone calls talking about herself. Abby's grandmother had been the only person she could truly count on for as long as she could remember. She also knew, without a doubt, that Hilde was just trying to look out for her and only had her best interests at heart. Even if those interests were incongruent to her own.

Getting over Carter had been one of the hardest things she'd ever done, and her grandmother had been her rock through all of it. Of course she would question Abby spending so much time with him again.

No matter how right it felt to Abby to let him close, she would do well to remember she was treading dangerous waters.

"I know you do, Grandma. And I'll be fine. I promise."

Maybe if Abby said it enough times, she'd be able to take a page out of her grandma's playbook and actually will it into existence.

Chapter Eight

✺

Carter had slipped seamlessly into life back in
Heart's Hope Bay. He'd been back in town for three
weeks, and he hated to admit how much he actually
enjoyed being here. While he loved his job and the
people he worked with—and he actually enjoyed living
in Vegas—there was no denying how very different
the two places he'd called home were. Las Vegas was
dry martinis at the latest nightclub while talking loud
enough to be heard over the pumping music, and
Heart's Hope Bay was BYOB around a bonfire on the
beach with the crashing ocean waves providing the
evening's soundtrack.

Abby had invited him to a get-together tonight, and
despite his better judgment, he'd agreed. Carter's job
had been more demanding recently, taking up most of
his free time, so he'd only been out to help with the

renovation a couple more times. Though maybe that was for the better.

He'd already proven to himself that he couldn't be in Abby's presence and not want her. He'd also proven that he couldn't keep his hands—or his lips—to himself. They had yet to re-create that one impulsive kiss they'd shared at Becca's house, but it had only been through rigid self-control on his part. Not only was it easy being with her, but his blood thrummed for her whenever they were in near proximity to each other. More than once, he'd barely caught himself before he could grip her hips and haul her in against him the way he'd done countless times before.

"I'm glad you decided to come." Abby glanced at him, smiling as if he hadn't just been fantasizing about having her in his arms again. She wore jeans and a long-sleeved T-shirt, the thin cotton molding to her curves like a second skin.

He cleared his throat and adjusted their canvas chair totes slung over his shoulder, trying to steer his thoughts back to just-friends territory. "Me too. You guys do this a lot?"

She shrugged, keeping pace as they walked down the rocky path toward the shore where laughter and chatter rose above the sound of the ocean. "Not as much as we used to. We still manage to get out a handful of times a year, but it's been hard to maintain. Everyone's busy with their spouses or kids."

Carter studied her in the fading twilight, the setting

sun casting a glow on her skin, her red hair catching fire. There was no disguising the wistfulness in her voice. Yep. She definitely still wanted a family, badly— something he actively shied *away* from.

He averted his gaze from her and looked out at the ocean spread before him, breathing in the salty air. Though the mountains in Vegas were certainly appealing, he couldn't deny that the ocean, beautiful and deadly at once, had always called to him like none other. "So are you trying to tell me that you guys don't have raging parties down here all the time anymore?"

At that reminder of how they'd spent every weekend possible during their senior year of high school, complete with an ill-advised cliff dive or two, Abby threw her head back and laughed, the sound bright and vibrant and piercing straight through his chest. He'd missed hearing it, and now that he'd gotten to spend more time in her presence than he had since high school, he could admit that he'd missed *her*. They may have broken up and not been a couple anymore, but that didn't mean he'd suddenly stopped caring about her. She'd been one of his closest friends, and then, suddenly, they were done.

"We had fun, huh?" Abby turned toward him, her eyes bright as she gripped his forearm. "Oh my God, do you remember the time when we nearly got caught by the sheriff?"

Carter chuckled quietly, his head tipped down as he

nodded. "Yeah, I remember. Nearly shit my pants I was so scared."

While it was legal to have a bonfire on the beach, underage drinking...not so much.

"Well, it all turned out fine. We only had to hide out for an hour or so."

Carter's gaze met hers, and he knew he couldn't hide the way his had heated. She looked up at him, her lip caught between her teeth, and it was clear she remembered exactly how they'd filled that hour *hiding out*. He'd never been more grateful that he kept an emergency condom in his wallet than he had been that night.

"You guys made it!" Savannah jumped up from her perch on a folding chair and ran toward them. As soon as she was close enough, she threw an arm around Abby's shoulders and leaned in. "My overbearing brothers and their jackass friends are driving me *crazy*."

"Friends who you've said more than once are hotter than sin."

"And your point?"

Carter chuckled, lifting his gaze to take in exactly who was here. And, sure enough, three of Savannah's four older brothers sat around the bonfire—somehow none of them had changed a bit in the eleven or more years since he'd last seen them—laughing and joking with a handful of others he vaguely recognized but couldn't name.

Abby bumped her hip into Savannah's. "They just want to keep you safe."

"They just want to keep me from having fun is what they want to do." Savannah rolled her eyes. "And someone needs to tell them I'm twenty-nine not twelve, and they can stop with their overprotective bullshit."

Abby laughed. "Maybe that someone should be you."

Savannah pursed her lips, sliding her brothers a look out of the corner of her eye. "Whenever I tell them anything, they do the exact opposite, just to irritate me. Older brothers' prerogative apparently." She leaned forward, meeting Carter's gaze around Abby. "Would you ever do something like that to Becca?"

He laughed. "Have and do. Quite frequently, actually. Like you said, older brother's prerogative. You guys made our lives a living hell when we were younger, so it's only fair that we return the favor tenfold."

Savannah narrowed her eyes at him. "Well, I see you're of absolutely no help. I hope you at least brought the good beer."

He held up the six-pack he'd grabbed before Abby had swung by to pick him up, and Savannah brightened as she plucked out a bottle.

"For me? Thanks!" She turned and headed back toward her chair, immediately getting pulled into an argument with her brothers and a few others, one guy glowering at her more than the others. She'd always been able to hold her own around them and their friends, though, and that still appeared to be true.

"I see nothing has changed in regards to that," he said, tipping his head toward them.

Abby laughed. "Nope, not even a little. It's actually managed to get worse, if you can believe it. In case you haven't noticed, Savannah doesn't do well with people—namely men—telling her what to do. And that goes double for her brothers and their friends, especially Noah." Abby lifted her chin to the guy Carter had noticed shooting laser beams Savannah's way.

He opened his mouth to ask what that was about when Marco's booming voice interrupted him.

"Hey, man!" Marco waved from where he sat in a canvas chair. His wife, Gia, was perched on his lap, and their dog, Ollie, sat at their feet, tail thumping against the sand. "Glad you could make it. What kind of beer did you bring me?"

"If I'd known this was for everybody else and not just myself, I would have brought more."

"It really has been a long time since you've been back here. Sharing is caring. Isn't that what you teach the kids at the Sunshine Corner?" Marco asked Abby.

Abby grinned up at Carter. "He does have a point—sharing *is* caring." And with that, she placed the six-pack she'd brought among a collection of various alcoholic beverages and grabbed a different bottle of something else entirely. "Anyone else need another?"

Once Abby had delivered the requested refills, she and Carter set up their chairs in the large circle surrounding the bonfire, greeting the dozen or so people he knew by name and being introduced to a few of the others he hadn't been able to place, including

Savannah's brothers' friends. Every single person there tonight, with the exception of him, was a Heart's Hope Bay lifer. People he'd known in one way or another since at least kindergarten.

This place truly did suck you in and hold on tight.

"How've things been going? You get what you needed to your client earlier this week?" Marco asked, taking a pull from his beer.

"Yeah. I had to iron out some kinks working remotely, but I'm getting used to it. How about you? You hire anyone yet?"

"That depends—are you sticking around?"

Carter chuckled quietly and shook his head as he opened a beer for himself. "When are you gonna let that die?"

"Probably when you stop being such a stubborn ass and agree to work with me."

"Stubborn's in my bones—you know that."

Marco laughed. "Well, we need to do something. Carlos and I are both working our ways toward divorces. Isn't that right, babe?" Marco glanced up at Gia, who was completely ignoring him, instead talking with Abby and Savannah over his head.

Carter turned toward the girls, his eyes landing on Abby as she laughed with her friends. The firelight danced in her eyes, her face cast in flickering shadows. His head was already stuck in the past after their reminiscing earlier, and the mingling scents of the fire and the ocean just placed him further back. She looked so beautiful against the night sky, it was all he could do not to haul her up against him and finish what they'd started the other night.

"And then I took that briefcase of money and set the whole damn thing on fire," Marco said.

Carter made a hum of acknowledgment, his eyes still locked on Abby, before he snapped his head toward Marco. "*What*?"

With a low laugh, Marco said, "Damn, man, I've been feeding you complete bullshit for a solid three minutes now, and Ollie has licked your hand at least twice. Something else got your attention?" Which might as well have been a rhetorical question for the knowing lilt in Marco's voice as he smirked at Carter.

"I don't know what you mean." Carter avoided his friend's gaze and reached out a hand to Ollie, rewarding the dog with some ear scratches when he nuzzled into Carter's touch.

Marco leaned over, wrapping a hand around Gia's hip as she continued chatting with the girls. "Don't play me like an idiot. A blind person could see how much you've been staring at Abby since you guys got here."

"That's the beer I'm looking at. She's right in front of it."

Marco let out a loud boom of laughter. "If you were looking at beer like that, you'd have bigger problems than just wanting to sleep with your ex-girlfriend."

Sleep with? Yeah. That and a whole lot more.

Carter flicked his gaze up to Gia, who was still engrossed in her animated discussion with Abby and Savannah on the versatility of tacos, then met his friend's knowing stare. "Just because I want to doesn't mean I'm going to. I do have some self-control."

Marco whistled low and leaned back in his chair. "Goddamn, I thought it'd take a lot longer to get a confession out of you."

Carter rolled his eyes and took a sip of his beer, not wanting to even justify that with a response.

"Okay, all right...I'll stop giving you shit."

"No, you won't."

Marco laughed. "You're right. But you're still here for, what, a couple weeks?"

Three. He still had three weeks, give or take, left in town, depending on Becca's doctor's orders. Carter had kept a mental tally of his remaining time, and the funny thing was, he wasn't sure if it was because he was savoring what little he had left or because he was anxious to get back to his real life.

"Something like that," Carter murmured.

"So why not have a little fun while you're home?"

Carter's brows lifted. "You think Abby and I could just have a little fun, with our history?"

Marco lifted a shoulder. "Why not? As long as you both know what it is—and what it *isn't*—going into it..."

He couldn't deny the appeal of filling his remaining

time in Heart's Hope Bay while warming Abby's bed. Just the brief thought had him shifting in his seat.

A tap on his left shoulder had him twisting away from Marco and to the person who'd so completely taken over his thoughts in the short time he'd been back. "Do you want it?" Abby asked, the roaring fire light making her eyes dance.

Did he want it? Hell yes, he wanted it, with every fiber of his being. Whatever *it* was, if it was coming from her, the answer was a resounding yes.

"Yeah," he managed.

Her lips curved, her smile sweeping over her mouth slow like molasses, and he realized he may need to drive them home tonight because she was just this side of tipsy. She pushed something into his chest, and he grabbed it instinctually, glancing down to see what it was. Another beer.

Abby hadn't been asking him if he wanted *her*, but rather another drink. And if that wasn't a bucket of ice water on his fantasy about following Marco's advice, he didn't know what was.

"How about you, Gia?" she asked, waving a bottle toward her friend. "I haven't seen you have even one, and I brought your favorite!"

"No, I'm good."

Savannah snorted. "You're *good*? Since when do you not want one of these? We've been friends for five years, and I've never once known you to turn down anything from Burnside Brewing."

"Well, actually, it's not that I don't want it. It's that I can't have it." She paused, taking a deep breath as she brought a hand to her stomach. "I'm pregnant."

There was a heavy beat of stunned silence before chaos erupted. Savannah and Abby jumped up, pulling Gia out of Marco's lap as they hugged and squealed and—yep—he watched as Abby swiped away a happy tear or two.

Carter turned toward Marco, offering him his hand and slapping him on the back. "Congratulations, man. You're gonna be a daddy. What the hell!"

Marco chuckled, nodding as his attention was snagged on his wife while she celebrated with her closest friends, Ollie leaping along beside them, desperate to get in on the fun. "I know, right? I can't believe it."

"I didn't even know you guys were trying."

"We definitely weren't. You know how crazy things are at work, and now this. Gia's been freaking out because it wasn't in the plans yet, so we're completely unprepared."

"Good thing you've got nine months to get your shit together."

Marco grimaced. "Seven, actually. She's already eight weeks along."

Carter whistled lowly. "Still, you'll get it done. You planning to take time off after the baby comes?"

"I'd like to, but I'm not sure it'll be possible with how things are going now."

"Better get a help wanted sign up in your window real quick."

Marco pinned Carter with a look, his eyebrow raised. "Any chance this will make you take pity on me and finally come work with me?"

Carter laughed outright. "Not a chance."

Chapter Nine

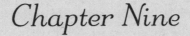

A few days later, after Gia's weekly art class had finished up, she hung around the Sunshine Corner with Ollie by her side and just...watched. Absorbed everything she possibly could. Abby had never seen her friend quite so excited and scared at the same time. She knew Gia and Marco hadn't planned this, but that didn't stop her friend from being over the moon at the idea of a new baby.

"So, I figured the best thing for me to do is make lists," Gia said, brandishing a leather-bound notebook and an assortment of different colored pens—Staedtler Triplus Fineliners, Abby's favorite.

Savannah, Jenn, and Abby all laughed as Hilde simply shook her head. Gia's list-making abilities rivaled even Abby's, which rivaled Ryder Carroll, the inventor of the bullet journal himself.

Gia opened the notebook and skimmed over the contents. "I've got one started for what to pack in my hospital bag, what I want on my playlist, what to do before the baby arrives, items that we want on the registry, things I need to research, and what I want on my birthing plan...Am I missing anything?"

"Maybe to take a breath," Savannah said dryly.

Gia shot her a grin. "You know this is how I deal with stress. Lists are soothing for me. So, if I make enough lists, maybe I'll feel like I know what I'm doing and that my life isn't completely spiraling out of control."

"Hey," Abby said soothingly at the tinge of panic in Gia's voice, rubbing a hand down her back. "Everything's fine. Your life is not out of control. This is just a little speed bump in your five-year plan that decided to come along in two. You guys wanted kids, right?"

"Well, yeah, but—"

"But nothing. So it happened after you've only been married for a couple years instead of the five that you originally planned. You just don't have quite as much time to prepare as you would have liked."

Gia laughed before promptly bursting into tears as Ollie nuzzled his snout into her hand, attempting to comfort her. She accepted the tissue Savannah offered and shook her head. "Oh my God! What's wrong with me? I'm like this all the time. My emotions are absolutely off the rails. Marco doesn't have any idea what to do with me. I'm laughing one minute, yelling at him the next, and then breaking down in tears. I'm giving him whiplash. Even Ollie doesn't know what to do with me. Is this normal?"

Savannah raised her hands and split a look between Jenn and Hilde. "That's all you guys."

The two women shared a knowing smile before Jenn said, "Not only normal, but completely expected. I was a disaster the first trimester. And the second. Aaaaand...the third. I think Lori was at her wit's end by the time Brayden came."

Everyone chuckled and even Gia managed a laugh through her tears.

"Honey, you're doing just fine. You are more prepared than any person I've known. Except maybe Abby." Hilde shot Abby a wink before focusing again on Gia. "You just need a little confidence is all."

"But that's the problem—I don't know what I don't know. Teaching art here is the most I've ever interacted with kids, and I don't think this baby is going to come out able to walk and talk and wipe its own butt."

"Oh, sweetie..." Savannah said. "It's cute that you think four-year-olds can wipe their own butts."

"Oh my God, *see*? I have no idea what I'm doing, and that's what terrifies me the most. Like, how am I supposed to know if we should let the baby cry it out or not?"

"Well, that's an easy one," Savannah said. "You don't have to do either—just invite the Baby Whisperer over to put that baby to sleep in the first place, and they won't make a peep until the morning."

"I volunteer my services anytime," Hilde said with a sage nod.

Gia shot her a grateful smile. "Okay, that's one less thing to worry about, but what about everything else? Cloth or disposable diapers? Store-bought baby food or make our own? I don't dare ask in any of the forums I'm part of because the moms on there are freaking terrifying."

"You do whatever is right for you and Marco," Jenn said with a shrug.

Gia tapped her pen on her notebook, her mouth dropping open. "It can't seriously be that easy."

"Oh, it's not." Hilde laughed. "You're going to second-guess yourself every step of the way."

"And then you're going to have to deal with the unwanted and unasked-for opinions from everyone in the world who thinks they're an expert on *your* kid," Jenn said. "Not only that, but all their messages will be mixed, too. Take breastfeeding, for instance. People will make you feel awful if you can't—or choose not to—while at the same time shaming you for doing so in public. Um, babies don't just eat at home, you know?"

Savannah made a frustrated sound in her throat. "And a lot of the times, the ones who are doing it are fellow women! Completely uncool."

"Yep," Jenn said. "That's why those forums can be toxic cesspools. They have opinions on everything from the brand of laundry detergent you should use to when you should start solid foods for the first time. If you have a question, come to us. Hilde and I can answer your pregnancy questions, and all of us can help with the new baby questions."

Abby wrapped an arm around her friend. "We're all here for you. I'm not a mom yet, but I play one in my day job. I'll help however I can."

Gia's shoulders slumped as she leaned into Abby's side. "I just don't want to screw up."

Hilde walked over and took one of Gia's hands between both of hers. "As long as your baby is happy and healthy, everything else is just the details. You remember that."

"But the details are my favorite part."

They all shared a laugh just as a baby wailed from the quiet room reserved for nap time.

Jenn stood, shooting Gia a look. "Your new favorite part is going to be sleep."

Abby squeezed Gia into her side. "You'll be fine. And Marco will help, right?"

"Definitely. He's so calm and collected. He's been my rock this whole time."

Abby tamped down the envy that bubbled in her gut as Gia continued on about Marco's late-night runs to the grocery store to contend with her every craving and how he massaged her feet every night, even when she told him they weren't sore. This unwanted jealousy had no place in Abby's life and certainly not in her friendships—she only wanted the best for Gia. But she couldn't deny how much she ached for the very thing her friend was facing.

Gia had had a five-year plan, but so had Abby. The problem was, she was four years into that five-year plan of starting a family of her own, and she was no closer to managing Step 1—finding a boyfriend—than she'd been when she'd gone out with the guy who knew about his mom's reoccurring UTIs...or the twelve duds before him. And now that all her spare time was spent on the renovation to ensure the preschool would be ready by the fall, she wasn't sure when that would actually happen.

Especially when the person she was spending all that time with was the one person who was completely off-limits.

* * *

Shuffling the plans in his hands, Carter opened the front door to Alvarez Architecture. He'd called earlier in the day to see if he could borrow their scanner again, and Marco had told him to just go straight back if Dotty wasn't out front. A quick glance around showed he was alone, so he stepped through the archway and headed toward the offices.

As soon as he stepped foot in his friend's office, he froze. Books were spread across every available surface, and not books on renovations or architecture or anything of the like. Nope, it looked like the parenting section of the library had thrown up in there. It was a far cry from the neat and tidy space Carter had seen the last time he'd stopped by.

"Holy shit," Carter said, his eyes darting to the half-dozen open books strewn across the room. "What the hell happened in here?"

Marco collapsed back in his chair, his hands fisted in his hair. "I don't know what I'm doing, and Gia's freaking out. *She's* normally the levelheaded one between us. She always has all the lists and knows exactly what needs to happen and when it needs to happen, but she is *freaking out*."

"Okay...," Carter said, a little warily.

"No, not okay! If she's freaking out, that means I need to calm her. I need to be the one who knows all this stuff, so when she turns to me, laughing one minute and then tears in her eyes the next, asking about some random baby crap, I can tell her, 'Don't worry, babe. I've got this handled.'"

"That seems...reasonable?" Carter could hear the question in his voice, even though he'd intended it to come out as a statement.

"You'd think! Except apparently there's a lot to learn about being a parent." Marco gestured to the open books littered across his desk. "*Obviously*."

Carter sat in the chair across the desk from Marco and blew out a sigh. "I had no idea you were freaking out so bad. At the bonfire, you seemed excited."

"Don't get me wrong, I am. I mean, we've always

wanted kids. We just didn't think they'd come quite so soon. But nothing can stop my swimmers, I guess." He flashed a grin. "I've got superhero sperm."

Carter grimaced. He could've gone his whole life without hearing his friend utter those two words.

"But because it's happening so soon, we don't know what the hell we're doing. Gia's an only child. My brother's only two years younger than me, so I never really helped with him. We're both completely out of our element."

Carter couldn't help him there. Becca was also only two years younger than him. And though he knew enough now that he could take care of Sofia, she was three but getting more and more self-sufficient. Things had to be completely different for a brand-new baby who was one hundred percent reliant on your every last move. Who wanted that kind of pressure and responsibility?

"Doesn't Gia work at the Sunshine Corner with Abby? Wouldn't she have picked up some tips there?"

Marco blew out a heavy sigh and propped his forearms on his desk. "Nope. She's the art teacher. She works with the toddlers and that's it, so she's never spent time with the babies. She knows as much about them as I do. And I know jack shit."

Marco's phone rang, the sound echoing down the hall from the reception area. Dotty must've been at lunch again. Instead of answering it like he'd done the last time Carter had stopped by, Marco pressed a button on his phone to send the call straight to voice mail.

Carter's brows lifted. "Don't you need to get that?"

"Nah, man. Haven't you been listening? *This* first. Dotty can listen to the voice mails when she gets back, but if I don't figure out what the experts say about banking the baby's cord blood before I get home tonight, I'm going to have a crying pregnant woman on my hands. Again."

Carter had absolutely no idea what that meant, and he could only blink in astonishment at his friend. He barely recognized him. The Marco from today versus the Marco from when Carter had first arrived in town were like night and day. Marco had always been like him—career focused, determined, and unwilling to let anything stand in his way. He'd always put his work first. But seeing him now, so distracted and willing to put everything else aside to look up some stuff in baby books left Carter unsettled.

"You know they have this thing called the internet now, right?" Carter said on a laugh. "I don't think you need to read a library's worth of nonfiction to get the answers that you want. I'm sure you can find everything you could possibly be wondering about with a simple Google search."

Marco shook his head. "You'd think so, wouldn't you? But then you don't get just facts. You get everybody's opinions on whatever it is you're searching for. You got Mommy A telling Mommy B why her way is horse shit, and then Daddy C comes strolling in and tells them they're both wrong."

"And no one likes a mansplainer."

That didn't even pull a smile from Marco, so Carter blew out a breath and leaned forward, resting his arms on the desk. "Look, I'm no expert, but isn't like ninety-nine percent of parenting just opinion? And don't you guys have a while to figure all this out? I'm sure everything will be fine."

Except when the phone rang again and Marco silenced it once more, Carter wasn't so sure that everything would be fine after all. He'd never seen his friend so panicked and distracted, and Carter had no idea how that would affect his business or his clients.

What he *did* know was that he was just relieved and damn glad it wasn't him in Marco's shoes.

Chapter Ten

※

The first few times Carter had been by after hours to help Abby with the renovation, Hilde had answered the door, giving him the stink eye and the third degree. Letting him know in no uncertain terms that she had her eye on him. He wasn't sure which she was more worried about—Abby's heart or her virtue, the latter of which was laughable since he'd already divested her of that more than a decade ago.

She had a good right to be concerned, though, considering how close he'd come to slipping up at the bonfire. Abby had been so loose and relaxed and beautiful, the memories of their past—not to mention that kiss—fresh in his mind.

Hilde must have been busy tonight, though, because Abby answered the door in her place. She wore ripped, faded jeans and a battered T-shirt that had seen better days, a hole along the hem showcasing the creamy smooth skin of her stomach. Her long hair was on top of her head in a messy bun, held in place with a pencil, and it didn't matter that she was a little bit unkempt. In fact, the sight of her in clothes that proved she was ready and willing to get dirty did nothing to tamp down the desire he felt toward her.

He swallowed, attempting to impart some moisture into his too-dry mouth, but it was no use. His throat was still full of gravel as he said, "Hey."

She smiled at him, leaning against the opened door. "Hey, yourself. Come on in. Everything's already set up." She shut the door behind him, then led them into the house and up the stairs. "Thank God we don't need to paint the cubbies yet. I think I'll probably spend at least a week picking out the color."

"Sounds like the senior float all over again."

She'd been so determined for their group of friends to win the contest, she'd micromanaged every detail of their float—including the paint color. From anyone else, it would have been aggravating, but with Abby, it was just...her.

With a laugh, she glanced at him over her shoulder. "Hey, there's a reason we won, you know."

"I know, I know."

And the joy on her face when they'd announced it had made all the work worthwhile.

"I'll try to keep things under control," she promised. "The last thing I need to do is spend a week buried under paint samples, but I just want everything to be perfect."

He hummed in acknowledgment. No matter what Abby did, she put her whole heart into it.

All the more reason he needed to stay grounded in the present.

Despite Marco's suggestion to go wild and try for a quick fling with Abby while he was here, she wasn't the kind of person who could stay casual about anything. And Carter wasn't the kind of man who could be causal about her.

They'd had an amazing time together in high school, but they were adults now. Adults who wanted completely different things from life. He couldn't afford to lose sight of that, for both his sake and hers.

Once upstairs, she walked to where she had a tarp laid down on top of the paper they'd covered the original hardwood floors with in order to protect them before refinishing. She turned to him, hands settled on her hips. "So, where do we start?"

Christ, she was cute, all determined and focused, pride shining in her eyes as she stood in the space that would soon be the Sunshine Corner's preschool. That was one thing that had always attracted him to her—her tenacity and grit. You wouldn't know it by looking at her, all smiles and sunshine, but she was built of tough stuff.

Grinning, he set down his tools, pulled out a tape measure, and held it up. "Measure twice, cut once.

Once we know the measurements, we can head to the garage and start cutting."

"Ooh," she said, a teasing flirtiness to her tone. "Talk to me more about your plans to be careful and precise."

He rolled his eyes, but he couldn't stop the warmth inside his chest. Of course Ms. Bullet Journal Life Plan Girl would be on board with his approach.

Pulling out the end of the tape measure and then letting it snap back, he lowered his voice to the same mock-sultry timbre. "I can do better than that. I can show you."

She pursed her lips and beckoned him forward. "Right this way."

As they kept up their banter, it struck him that he'd almost forgotten how much fun they used to have together. It didn't matter if they were studying at her grandmother's kitchen table or hanging out after a football game or—yes—even doing some sort of DIY build together. Abby's presence made everything better.

He followed her to the future location of the cubbies, sure to maintain a careful distance between them as he did. Right up until she stopped short a few feet from the wall and he almost walked into her. He reached out to steady himself, his hands landing on her lush hips, heat emanating from the sliver of skin above her waistband as a barrage of other memories slammed into him.

He jerked his hands away, but it was too late. Their eyes met as electricity crackled between them. "Sorry," he said, his voice too rough and low for what the situation called for.

She rolled her lips between her teeth and blinked away the haziness in her eyes before nodding. They got back to work, but there was no way not to be in each other's spaces, especially when she insisted on him teaching her how to do all the steps herself.

He couldn't even take a breath without inhaling her sweet scent, without a piece of her hair being caught up in his scruff. Couldn't walk more than a foot without brushing up against her. And that was all child's play compared to when he had to show her how to work the table saw Marco had dropped off earlier in the day for them to borrow. Standing right behind her, their hips practically aligned, mere inches between them, had his blood heating and his skin feeling too tight.

"Like this?" she asked over her shoulder, her hands exactly where he'd told her to place them.

He swallowed hard and nodded, willing away the images his brain was all too happy to supply of her in that same position, saying those very words.

She grinned at him, doing an excited little wiggle of her hips, and he barely stifled his groan. This whole night was one big willpower challenge, and it was dead set on seeing to it that he failed.

* * *

Once they'd gotten all the wood cut to the proper dimensions, they hauled the pieces upstairs. Because of the size of the unit, their best bet would be to assemble it inside the space. While Carter had assumed he'd be doing most of the work on this, Abby had proven him wrong, stepping in, asking questions, and completing each step herself—that tenacity on full display. Much like him, she hadn't had anything handed to her, and that only made him admire her all the more for what she'd managed to accomplish already. He couldn't deny how hot it was to see her like this, determination written on her face as she wielded a nail gun, her brows pinched in concentration.

She blew a strand of loose hair out of her eyes and, with a smile, met his gaze. "I'm not half bad. Maybe I should start a side job."

He laughed as he held two boards together for her. "With all your spare time, huh?"

Pressing the nail gun against the wood, she smiled but didn't lift her eyes from her task. "Well, you've got me there."

They'd already spent countless hours working on the renovation—not to mention all she'd done before he'd come along to help—and he knew she still had a laundry list of items she wanted to complete.

"This is an awful lot of work you're doing for this preschool. You sure you want to do all this?"

"Absolutely. It'll all be worth it." She said the words with such conviction, he couldn't help but hear the truth in them.

"You told me how you're designing the place, but you haven't told me what's going to make the Sunshine Corner preschool special. So...?"

A smile swept across her mouth, and her eyes lit up. "Well, in the beginning, we'll just have two classrooms—one each for the three- and four-year-olds. We'll be teaching the typical reading, writing, counting, that kind of thing. But we're also going to have some unique offerings, like cooking classes with my grandma. We'll have science labs once a week. And we'll continue the art classes with Gia, of course. I'm also considering hiring a second language teacher, because children pick up foreign language faster than adults do, so it's the perfect time for them to start. I just need to figure out if it's in the budget."

"How long do you think it'll take before you've got a full roster?"

"Oh, I've already got a full roster. Parents started putting their kids' names in as soon as I mentioned I was planning to expand our offerings." She blew out a deep breath. "Which is why I need to make sure this gets done on time—I've got so many families counting on this."

After hearing how much Sofia loved coming here—and the horror stories Becca had told him of her friends who weren't so lucky to get their kids into the Sunshine

Corner—he had no doubt they were. And he had no doubt Abby would do everything in her power to make sure to deliver.

"It sounds like an awesome place, Abby. You should be really proud of what you're doing."

"Thanks." She glanced down and nodded. "I am."

"Did you end up getting your degree in early childhood education?" he asked, remembering what her plans had been when they'd gone off to college.

"Yeah, I did."

"What made you decide to open the Sunshine Corner instead of becoming an elementary teacher?"

She shrugged. "It wasn't just one thing, you know? Once the preschool is complete, I'll still be able to teach. But I wanted something more. I wanted something that was *mine*. Plus, not every kid has a loving parent to go home to or a place to build childhood memories. I want the Sunshine Corner to be that for those who need it."

The way she said it so reverently made his chest ache. It was clear how much Abby loved not just the business, but each and every child who attended the Sunshine Corner. And Carter knew enough— hell, he and Abby both knew more than most—just how important that comfort was in a child's life. They knew, too, just how damaging the lack thereof could be.

"Doesn't surprise me that you're giving so much to all these kids, even if that cuts into your off time."

"It's all I've ever wanted to do," she said with a helpless shrug.

"I remember," Carter murmured, his eyes locked with hers.

They stood barely a foot apart, so close the scent of her filled his nose—lemons and sawdust...familiar and yet at the same time, completely new. A lethal combination if the state of his body was any indication. It heated, thrumming to life under her gaze. It'd be so easy to lean down, brush his lips against hers. Feel her tongue sweep into his mouth again. This time, he wouldn't be as hesitant as he'd been at his sister's. There'd be no one to walk in on them now.

He could take his time, relearning the taste of her and all the things that made her moan. Finding out if she still liked it when he scraped his teeth against her soft bottom lip. Or when he hauled her up against him, his hands greedy and his mouth—

Abby cleared her throat and shook her head, breaking their gazes. When she spoke, her voice came out husky. "What about you? Tell me about your job. Do you love it?"

Grateful for a distraction, Carter nodded. "I do. I haven't been able to do much of this kind of thing lately." He gestured toward their current project, as well as the space around them. "But otherwise I'm happy, and I'm on track with my goals."

"And what goals would those be?"

"I have one last promotion to nail." His current

projects should seal the deal by quarter's end, even with him working remotely. "Then I'll have all the experience I need to open my own firm within a year."

"Wow, really? Becca didn't mention that."

"That's probably because I think she's blocked it out entirely." He chuckled softly. "She's been trying to get me to move back since I graduated college."

"I don't blame her. I know how much she loves having you in Sofia's life. And that little girl adores you."

"She adores me because she's got me wrapped around her finger and she knows it. If she wants something, I'm the one who's going to give it to her."

Abby laughed. "Are you sure they aren't going to sweet talk you into staying?"

"Nope. I've worked too hard to get where I am. I've been strengthening my connections in the Vegas area and socking away every extra penny so I'll have the capital I need to open up down there."

"It's not all it's cracked up to be, you know. Owning your own business is a pain in the ass most days. You have to be *really* sure you want it."

"I do," he promised, determination filling him.

That hadn't changed, no matter how much he'd been enjoying his extended stay in Heart's Hope Bay. Spending real quality time with Becca and Sofia, getting reacquainted with old friends.

Reconnecting with Abby.

That, more than anything, gave him pause. He connected with her in a way he'd never done with anyone else. Everything about her drew him in, from her drive to her kindness ... Hell, even her obsessive planning. She was beautiful and capable, intelligent and sexy, and his body thrummed with want whenever he was within arm's reach of her. He'd bet anything she felt the same deep connection.

But if this conversation had reiterated anything for him, it was that he had a goal he intended to meet. A goal that was in Las Vegas ... not Heart's Hope Bay, Oregon. There wasn't room in this tiny little town for more than one architecture firm, and Marco's family had owned that sole business for more than thirty years. Besides that, in a town this size, Carter wouldn't dream of hanging a shingle out in direct competition to one of his closest friends. Yes, he'd be doing that very thing to Jake in Las Vegas, but it was different there. Competition was expected in a market that large. Plus, he'd never kept his plans a secret from his boss.

"I'm glad you're happy, Carter," Abby said quietly, her voice pulling him out of his thoughts. "It sounds like you've got everything you could possibly want there."

As Carter looked at her, into the bottomless blue eyes of the girl he'd once loved—the girl he was currently starving for—he knew, without a doubt, Vegas didn't hold *everything* he wanted.

Chapter Eleven

Abby had always loved her hometown. True, she'd never gone farther than Ashland, Oregon, for college, but she didn't have to travel around the world to know that the *heart* in Heart's Hope Bay was justified. They may not have had every chain restaurant or business, but what they lacked in those things, they more than made up for in their residents. When one of them needed help, they rallied around each other, no questions asked. And they did so, not out of misplaced duty, but rather a genuine desire to help one of their own.

It was for that reason that Last Call, the local bar and tavern that sat on the ocean's edge just a few blocks west of downtown, was crammed full tonight for the fundraiser Becca had talked Abby into hosting.

Not only was the location packed, but she'd also had more than two dozen businesses offer up goods and services, ranging from gift baskets full of nontoxic and organic skincare to surf lessons to a night for two at the Seascape Bed-and-Breakfast.

Abby had never been so humbled in her life, and she was full to bursting with gratitude. She hadn't ever known what it felt like to grow up in a large family, but she wondered if maybe it felt a tiny bit like this.

"What put that look on your face?"

At the deep male voice in her ear, Abby startled and spun around only to find Carter standing there looking so completely drool-worthy she could hardly stand it. He wore well-loved jeans and a black sweater that clung to his chest in a way that made Abby long to feel it under her fingers.

"Carter, hi. I didn't know you were coming tonight."

He lifted his shoulder. "Becca was feeling pretty run-down after her day, so she sent me in her place. Hope that's okay."

"Of course." Abby was going to completely ignore the way her stomach somersaulted at his mere presence here to support her. "Is she feeling all right?"

He shot Abby a wry look. "My sister, the demonic conniver, will be just fine. Believe me, this was more about getting me here than it was about her being in pain."

Before Abby could ask what he meant by that, he lifted his head and glanced around at the people lined up to bid on the silent auction items. "She was wrong about one thing, though."

"What's that?"

"I don't think you would have missed one less person here. This is quite the turnout. You must be liked around town or something."

Abby smiled at his gentle teasing tone and then stepped to his side, her shoulder brushing his biceps. "I can't believe so many people showed up. I was worried nobody would, and then I'd have to tell these businesses, 'Thanks so much for the donations, but you can keep them.'"

He nudged her with his elbow and turned his head to look down at her. "Come on, Abby. You have to know by now how much you're loved here. Besides, I've only heard people rave about the Sunshine Corner. Of course everyone would come out to help you in whatever way they could."

Abby swallowed through her tight throat, her eyes stinging as she furiously blinked back tears she absolutely did not want to fall. She nodded. "Yeah. It's just unexpected to see it in action."

At her tone, he made a gruff sound in his throat, wrapped his arm around her shoulders, and tucked her into his side, pressing a kiss to her temple. With a sigh, she melted into him, one arm going around his waist as she pressed her other hand to his firm stomach. She tried to ignore the ridges of muscle she could feel even through the material of his sweater, because it was the last thing she needed to be thinking about. This embrace was too good to spoil it with senseless, unwanted attraction.

"Have you been drinking already, Abby?" he asked, his voice teasing.

She breathed out a watery laugh and looked up at him, grateful he'd lightened the moment. "I was so nervous about who would and wouldn't show up that Savannah made me do shots before everyone got here. I was never able to hold hard liquor very well."

"Well that's your problem right there. Savannah was always a troublemaker."

"Hey!" Savannah snapped, suddenly standing in front of them, her eyes narrowed. "I heard that."

Carter simply raised an eyebrow. "And are you denying it?"

Savannah pursed her lips and crossed her arms, her toe tapping out her irritation. "Well…no. It's just a little rude of you to say it aloud, Mister I Haven't Been Home In A Hundred Years. Don't you think?"

"I call 'em like I see 'em."

As quickly as her irritation had come, it vanished, and Savannah shrugged. "Fair enough." She slid her eyes to Abby, and then pointedly to where Carter's arm still rested across her shoulders. "I'm not interrupting anything, am I?"

"What? No," Abby said, stepping away from Carter's side as she tucked her hair behind her ear. "What's up?"

Savannah looked at Carter, but Abby didn't dare, too scared of what she'd find. But whatever Savannah saw made her cock her brow before turning her full attention to Abby. "My parents just got here and they wanted to say hi. I told them I'd see if you were too busy."

"For them? Never."

She turned to Carter and found him with his hands in his jeans pockets, his eyes unerringly on her. "I'm going to run and say hi to them quick. Will you be all right by yourself?"

An amused grin tipped the corner of his mouth and he nodded. "I'm a big boy, Abby. I think I can probably manage."

Just then, Marco came up and clapped a hand on Carter's shoulder, greeting him warmly. The murmur of their voices followed Abby and Savannah as they walked away.

Savannah tugged her arm and hissed, "Stop staring at him! God, have I taught you nothing? At least play a *little* hard to get."

Abby whipped her head around to face the direction they were walking, her cheeks flaming at being caught. "I don't know what you're talking about."

"Uh-huh. And my favorite position is missionary."

Abby turned to her on a gasp, her mouth hanging open. "I cannot believe you just said that at a fundraiser for our preschool."

Savannah shrugged. "What? Do you see any actual preschoolers around here? Don't worry, I promise not to whip out the Kama Sutra for show-and-tell on our first day of school."

"Oh, there you both are!" Pauline, Savannah's mom,

wrapped Abby up in a hug, her arms warm and welcoming. With one last squeeze, she stepped back and
grabbed Abby's hands as she regarded her with nothing
but fondness. "We're just so proud of you, Abby, and
all you've accomplished."

Abby waved a hand in front of her face, brushing
aside the compliment. "Oh, I haven't done—"

"Nonsense," Alan, Savannah's father, boomed as one
large hand settled on Abby's shoulder, squeezing lightly.
"It's quite a feat what you've done. Opening your own
business, and now expanding? All before you're even
thirty. You should be very proud of that."

Dammit. Those traitorous tears were burning behind
her eyes, the tingle in her nose telling her she was about
three seconds away from losing it.

Savannah's parents had played a huge and much-
needed role in Abby's life when her own mom couldn't
be bothered. She didn't know much about her father,
only his name and that he wanted absolutely nothing
to do with her. So she'd always looked upon Savannah's
parents as the next best thing. When she and Savannah
had been younger, Abby had stayed over there countless times, Abby's mom all too willing to relinquish her
responsibility so she could spend the weekends doing
what she'd insisted she should have been able to do
all along.

When they weren't at Savannah's house, they'd
stayed at Abby's grandmother's. And though she loved
Hilde with everything she had, she couldn't deny her

grandma was a bit . . . eccentric. She allowed Abby to do things that most parents would probably be horrified about. Abby never needed much discipline or supervision, though, all too willing to keep herself in line if that meant easing the burden on her mom, and consequently on her grandma when her mom would pawn her off.

But at Savannah's house, there were fights and yelling, groundings and apologies. There was raucous laughter and pancakes on Saturday mornings and family movie night that all five siblings grumbled about but sat through every weekend nonetheless. Abby had soaked up every ounce of it, longing for a bond like the Lowes shared.

Once Abby was able to get her emotions under control, she cleared her throat of any sign of tears. "Thank you both. That means a lot to me. I'm so glad you were able to come."

"Nonsense! We wouldn't have missed it for the world." Pauline wrapped Abby up in another hug, and she breathed in the familiar combination of Chanel No. 5 and cinnamon chewing gum that she'd always associated with Savannah's mom.

Alan tugged his wife away. "Come on, now. Leave the poor girl alone. You're smothering her."

Abby laughed as Pauline stepped back, but she shook her head. "She gives the best hugs, so I don't mind."

As if they'd been called by name, three of Savannah's brothers strode up looking like they'd stepped off a set for *GQ*, and suddenly Abby was surrounded by

Captain America, Thor, and Star-Lord—she wasn't a huge superhero fan, but she damn sure knew the Chrises. She could admit, in a completely impartial way, that they were attractive. For one brief moment in middle school, she had, in fact, crushed on Caleb, the second oldest Lowe boy and the only one not in attendance tonight since he lived in San Francisco. He must've sent his best friend, Noah—the solitary friend Savannah clashed the most with—in his stead, as he stood stoically in the mix, the only dark-haired man in the bunch, though certainly not the only attractive one. But though Abby could admit they were all good-looking, all she felt for them now was sisterly fondness, even if they weren't hers to claim as such.

Tossing an arm around Pauline's shoulders and tucking her into his side, Jackson said, "She does, doesn't she?"

Pauline rolled her eyes but slid an arm around her youngest son's waist. "That's not what you said once upon a time. I used to have to sneak my affection after you'd fallen asleep for the night."

Horrified, Jackson stared down at her. "Jesus, Mom. You actually did that?"

Sounding not even a little bit remorseful, she said, "Every night until you moved out. Used to sneak into your bedroom in the middle of the night and stick my hand under your nose to make sure you were still breathing. And, in fact, I did it every time you were home, all through college. A mother's work is never done."

Spencer, the oldest, crossed his arms over his chest and narrowed his eyes at his mom. "Just him or all of us? Just him, right? On account of the fact that he's so stupid, he might forget how to breathe?"

Without moving his gaze from his mom, Jackson reached out and shoved a laughing Spencer.

Pauline rolled her eyes. "Yeah, just him. I didn't care if any of the rest of you lived through the night."

Aaron, second youngest Lowe boy, held up a hand to his chest as if he were wounded. "That was harsh, Mom. I didn't even say anything."

"What's harsh," Alan piped in, "is you three little shits taking the spotlight off of Abby on her well-deserved night."

"Oh damn." Spencer turned to Abby, true remorse written on his face. "Sorry, Abs. The event is great. I'm glad Ben was able to host it tonight."

Spencer's best friend, Ben, owned Last Call and had been kind enough to let her use the space for the event, free of charge. As if that wasn't enough to forgive him, the use of her nickname certainly would've tipped it over.

Abby waved off his apology. "No sorry needed. Have I thanked you yet for setting this up for me?"

He grinned, rolling his eyes. "I think maybe once or twice."

Okay, so she'd thanked him at least a dozen times, but her gratitude for this big family that had taken her in as if she were their own couldn't be capped.

"Looks like you've got a great turnout," Aaron said, his gaze sliding over the lines by the items up for bid. "I think everything over there's got more than one bid on it."

"I bid on the surfing lessons," Jackson said.

Abby's brows pinched. "You *donated* the surfing lessons."

He lifted one broad shoulder. "And I'm worth every penny."

"How'd you manage to get through the door with your huge head?" Savannah asked dryly.

Without answering, Jackson locked his arm around Savannah's neck and tugged her to him before she shoved him away. "Speaking of, it's a full moon tonight. Anyone up for a little midnight surfing?"

Savannah's brothers all nodded their agreement, and so did Savannah. "Yeah, I'm in," she said.

As if choreographed, Spencer, Aaron, and Jackson widened their stances, crossing their arms over their broad chests as they scowled at their baby sister. "No," they said in unison. Even Noah got in on the action and mirrored the brothers' scowls.

Savannah snorted and rolled her eyes. "It's cute how you guys think you can boss me around. I'm twenty-nine. And *you*," she said, pointing an accusatory finger at Noah. "You don't have a vote here."

The man didn't back down, but neither did he utter a word, too busy scowling at Savannah.

"I don't give a shit if you're twenty-nine or eighty-nine,"

Spencer said. "You're still our baby sister, and you're not getting out there. It's too dangerous."

"Too dangerous for me, but totally fine for each and every one of you. Have I got that right?"

"Well, yeah..." Jackson said with a shrug.

Savannah made a gruff sound of frustration in her throat, her hands fisted at her sides. "Mom, Dad, would you tell them to knock it off?"

Both parents held up their hands in surrender and shook their heads.

"Oh no," Pauline said. "We stopped having to deal with your squabbles the day the last of you moved out of the house, and you're not pulling us back in."

Savannah glared, mirroring her brothers' stances and crossing her own arms. "You're all the worst. I hope you know that. The absolute worst."

Abby could see where Savannah was coming from. It no doubt got old having to deal with the overprotective nature of four older brothers, plus their friends. But still, Abby didn't think they were the worst at all. She thought they were the best, and she'd give just about anything to create something as equally wonderful with someone she could call her own.

Chapter Twelve

❋

A while later, after making the rounds multiple times, Abby had managed to speak to everyone who'd come out to support her at least once. On one of those passes around the bar, she found her grandma at a high-top table surrounded by the Bridge Bunch, the group of them laughing uproariously.

Hilde snagged her arm as she passed. "Abby! Come here a second."

She stepped up to her grandma's side, grinning. "Hi, Grandma. Ladies. Thanks so much for coming out to support me tonight."

Mabel reached out, covered Abby's hand with her own, and squeezed. "Oh, honey, you couldn't have kept us from it! We're all so proud of you."

Abby could feel her cheeks heating over the praise, but she tamped that down and smiled. "Thank you."

"Did you know this place has sand volleyball down on the beach?" her grandma asked. "And these yummy drinks with the little umbrellas." She gestured to her now-empty glass that sat among the collection at the table. "I'm not going to get any of that down at the fuddy-duddy senior center. I want my birthday party next month to be right here."

Abby laughed. "And you think you're going to be down there playing sand volleyball, do you?"

"I don't need to play to enjoy the show," Hilde said with a lascivious smile.

All the ladies in her grandma's little posse hooted their enjoyment, attracting the attention of the other patrons.

"True as that might be," Abby said on a laugh, "I'm not sure how many shirtless men you're going to find on the beach in April."

"I'll take my chances."

"Me too," Mabel said with the other ladies murmuring their agreement.

Abby wrapped an arm around her grandma's shoulders and hugged her tight to her side. "Whatever you want, Grandma. You only turn seventy once, right?"

She talked with her grandma and the rest of the ladies for a little while longer until loud voices reached her from across the room. Glancing up, she found Gia and Marco obviously in an argument, their heads close together, though that didn't do much to keep their voices from carrying.

Excusing herself, she headed their way, her brows drawn together. Carter stood next to the couple, one hand in his pocket, the other holding a bottle of beer. His gaze bounced around the space to anywhere but Gia and Marco, looking like he wished the floor would just swallow him whole.

She touched the back of his arm to get his attention, and he glanced down at her, his relief at her presence evident. "What's going on?" she asked.

Before Carter could respond, Gia threw her hands up. "I'll tell you what's going on. Marco doesn't think I can mother our baby right."

Marco groaned, tossing his head back in clear frustration. "That's not what I said, dammit. All I said was that I wanted to help. We just listened to all these parents talk about how hard it is to do midnight feedings by yourself. If you strictly breastfeed, I can't help with that. I'm not saying you *can't*. I'm just saying maybe we look at ways to supplement so I can help."

Crossing her arms, Gia said, "You think I can't do it on my own."

"Jesus, Gia. That isn't what I said." Marco slid a frustrated hand down his face and took a deep, calming breath. Reaching out, he gently gripped her arms. "You're getting worked up over nothing, babe. You're turning this into a fight when it doesn't need to be."

Narrowing her eyes, Gia stepped back from his touch and, without a word, strode past them before disappearing inside the bathroom.

Marco ran his hands through his hair before dropping his arms to his sides, groaning out his frustration. "What the hell just happened here?"

Carter only managed a shrug and a bewildered expression. "No idea, man."

"I'm going to go check on her," Abby said.

Marco didn't put up an argument, so Abby turned and headed toward the bathroom. Inside, she found Gia at the sink, attempting to save her mascara with a tissue, before she whirled around to see who'd come in.

Abby held up her hands and walked toward Gia. "Just me." She ran a hand down her friend's arm. "What was that all about?"

Gia shook her head and lifted her gaze toward the ceiling, blinking at the sudden sheen in her eyes. "It normally wouldn't even be a big deal, but everything just piled on tonight. We had all these well-meaning people coming over to congratulate us, and then every single one of them gave us advice on how we should do this and that. Co-sleeping, epidural or not...and do we really want someone else raising our kids? *Hello*. I teach classes at a day care!" Gia threw her hands up in clear exasperation.

"Yeah, they needed to read the room on that one..."

Gia breathed out a watery laugh before shaking her head. "And then there was talk of discipline, and whether or not it's cruel to let the baby cry it out. And breastfeeding versus bottle feeding, and how if you don't breastfeed, you don't want the best for your child.

But how if you *do* breastfeed, you aren't interested in allowing your partner bonding time with the baby. How am I supposed to know what's right, Abby? I *don't* know! I don't know how to do any of this."

As Gia started crying again, Abby wrapped her arms around her friend and held her tight. "I don't know either. But you and Marco have always been a great team. You listen to each other and support each other, and that's going to trickle down to your baby. You just have to talk to each other with an open mind."

"If he doesn't tell me I'm getting worked up over nothing…"

"Yeah, he didn't need to be so dismissive of your concerns." She grabbed her friend's hands and stepped back, holding her at arm's length. "Can I be honest with you about something, even if it makes you upset?"

Gia laughed through her tears and rolled her eyes, gesturing toward herself. "I think that ship's already sailed."

Abby smiled softly and squeezed Gia's hands. "I didn't hear the whole thing, but what I did hear was a husband worried about his wife. Marco would do anything for you, and I'm sure he just wants to make sure he helps out in any way he can. That he pulls his weight so it doesn't all fall to you."

At that, Gia's tears ran faster, and Abby made a gruff noise in her throat. "Oh, honey, I didn't make mean to make you cry more."

Gia waved a hand in front of her face, blotting at

her tears with a tissue. "I cry all the time. *All* the time. *I* might as well be a newborn baby." She blew out a deep breath, her shoulders slumping. "And I'm not upset. I'm crying because you're right. It's just… It's hard, Abby. We've never had to deal with something like this before."

"That's not true. You did it when you adopted Ollie and went through the adjustment phase of bringing him into your life."

"A dog and a baby are hardly the same thing."

"Well, obviously they're very different, but you still had to discuss what you were going to allow and not, discipline, who would get up in the middle of the night for potty breaks…"

"I guess."

"See? And you got through that just fine. You'll get through this, too."

At Gia's nod, Abby wrapped her friend in her arms and held her until her tears finally abated before they ventured back into the bar.

* * *

Later that night, after Abby had seen Gia off with Marco, she collected the sign-up sheets from each of the silent auction items. Aaron had been right—each and every item had more than one bid… some *plenty* more—and her eyes nearly bugged out as she mentally tallied up how much the event had raised. This night alone was enough to cover the long list of equipment she needed for the preschool. Once again, she was overcome with gratitude to the people of Heart's Hope Bay who came out to support her and her dream.

"Looks like it was a success."

Abby turned at the sound of Carter's voice, smiling at him and hoping he didn't catch the sheen of tears in her eyes. Swallowing, she nodded. "It was. I wasn't anticipating quite this big of a turnout."

He stepped up next to her, so close his arm brushed her shoulder, and she barely suppressed a shiver. "I could've told you otherwise."

"Oh yeah? Since you're so familiar with the people in town?" she teased.

"I don't have to be familiar with them to see how much they love you. Next time don't sell yourself so short."

Instead of responding to that, she asked, "What are you still doing here?"

Carter glanced around the nearly empty bar and lifted a shoulder. "Thought I'd stick around and see if you needed help with anything. All I have waiting for me at home is a passed out three-year-old and a sister who's going to grill me on every single detail even though she could've just come herself."

With a grin, Abby said, "Well, thanks. I think I've got everything. I just need to get these baskets out to my car, and that's it. I was going to wrangle Savannah's brothers into helping, but it's a full moon tonight and apparently that's a good time to risk your life with midnight surfing."

Carter laughed. "Shit, they're still doing that? I figured they'd have outgrown that by now."

"They haven't outgrown a single thing in their entire lives."

He made a noise of acknowledgment and said, "Well, I can help you get the baskets to your car. But how about a drink and a game of pool first?"

Abby's feet ached and she couldn't wait to get into her pajamas, but she'd done something great tonight. She deserved to celebrate, and she couldn't think of anyone she'd rather celebrate it with than Carter.

"That sounds great."

He smiled down at her before guiding her toward the bartender, and she valiantly ignored the way her insides warmed over the affection showcased in his gaze.

Fortunately, since they were some of the last people left in the bar, they didn't have to wait for either their drinks or a pool table. Before long they were set up with both.

Abby stood off to the side with a pool cue in one hand and a bottle of beer in the other. She watched Carter rack the balls, the muscles of his biceps bunching against the fitted sleeve of his T-shirt. He must've taken off his sweater earlier in the night when the crowded bar had gotten a bit heated, but Abby couldn't say she minded the view.

"So . . ." Carter started with a deceptive casualness to

his tone. "Which of Savannah's brothers was going to help you get everything loaded in your car tonight?"

"Jackson, probably. I can usually talk him into just about anything."

"Is that so? Anything, huh?"

"Well, I haven't tested the theory, but I don't think Jackson's said no to anything a day in his life."

"Even you?"

Abby's brows hit her hairline, and she froze with her bottle poised in front of her mouth. She stared at Carter, seeing the lines of tension across his shoulders, and nearly laughed internally. "Is that your way of asking if I've dated Jackson?"

Carter shrugged before leaning over to break. "It makes sense. You guys always got along."

Abby snorted at the sheer ridiculousness of the thought of her with any one of Savannah's brothers. "Got along like siblings...I haven't had a crush on one of Savannah's brothers since I was thirteen."

Carter narrowed his eyes. "You never told me that."

She tossed her head back and laughed at how put out he sounded. "Did you want me to tell you about my teen crush on Chad Michael Murray, too?"

Carter didn't seem to be quite as amused with the entire thing as she was. He stood, stone faced, as she grinned. Finally, he said, "So you never explored anything with one of them?"

"With them? No. But I have been in other relationships, Carter. If I give you their names, do you plan on stopping by and beating up each and every one of them?"

Seeming to realize how he'd been holding himself, Carter relaxed, letting his shoulders drop as he shook his head on a low laugh. "It's none of my business."

Abby wasn't so sure about that. Since Carter had been home, it had been easy for them to fall back into the bond they'd once shared. And though it was different, that wasn't necessarily a bad thing. Besides, she wasn't so sure that she didn't *want* it to be Carter's business. She'd spent the entirety of his time back here fighting this undercurrent of chemistry that always arced between them. She wasn't sure how much longer she could hold on.

"What about you?" she asked. "Any relationships I should know about?"

"If it didn't stick with you, Abby, it's not gonna stick with anyone. You should know that by now."

His words floated over her, settling deep in her chest, making her feel buoyant. As their eyes met across the pool table, heat sparked between them, and she was snared in his gaze, unable to look away.

Carter shook his head and broke their connection, taking a pull from his beer. "Would you rather have whatever you're thinking appear as thought bubbles above your head, or have your life be live-streamed?"

Abby laughed at the old game they used to play, forgetting until just then how they'd talk until the early hours of the morning, debating different made-up scenarios.

"You're taking me back to high school with that question."

"That was the plan. I want to see if your answers have changed that much."

"How can you even remember what questions we asked? That was a million years ago."

Carter's eyes, when they met hers, were hot and hungry, a lethal combination, especially when she was starving. The chemistry they shared crackled between them, and heat flickered low in her belly.

"I remember it all, Abby."

At just five simple words from him, she bit her lip and had to work to hold herself up. They weren't touching—hell, they weren't even *close* to touching—but it didn't matter. They could have been across the room from each other, and Abby still would've felt this unrelenting tug. This current pulling her closer and closer to him, not caring in the least how much she fought it.

She wanted him. She'd wanted him since the day he'd stepped foot in the Sunshine Corner, even though she'd made a valiant effort to ignore it. She was so tired of ignoring it, though.

"I'd give just about anything to see those thought bubbles now," Carter murmured, bracing his hands on the pool table as he leaned toward her. His eyes flicked down to her mouth before he licked his own lips. "Let me take you home, Abby."

Chapter Thirteen

❋

Having had several drinks that night, neither Abby nor Carter felt it was safe to drive home. Thankfully, Ben, the owner of Last Call, had agreed to store the gift baskets there until the following day when Abby would swing by to pick them up.

She and Carter left both their cars in the lot, unconcerned about being towed, and walked the short distance to Abby's house, the full moon and the streetlamps lighting their way.

Since Heart's Hope Bay was the size of a postage stamp, they arrived far too quickly. The idea of saying goodbye already filled her with dread. The space around Carter practically glowed, the easy intimacy they'd found together tonight almost addictive. She wasn't ready to let it go quite yet.

Fiddling with her keys, she swallowed her nerves and asked, "Do you want to come inside?"

"You asking me in for a cup of coffee, Abby?"

She grinned. "Actually, I was thinking cookies, but if you want coffee, I can put on a pot."

Carter stepped into her and reached to tuck a strand of hair behind her ear. The featherlight touch of his fingers combined with the heat that poured off his body had her breath catching and her nipples tightening into stiff peaks.

"I'll come in for anything you want," he murmured, his voice low and rough and delicious enough to make her knees weak.

Unable to respond, her mouth too dry to muster up an answer, Abby spun around and unlocked the door before stepping inside, willing herself to get it together.

Carter followed, shutting the door behind them. The space was quiet, the only noises the creaky groans of the old house settling.

"Your grandma's not going to pop out of one of these rooms, is she?" he asked.

Abby chuckled softly and shook her head. "After her wild night of too-many umbrella drinks, she must've turned in early. She made me promise to throw her birthday party there next month so she can be a voyeur to beach volleyball."

Carter's eyebrows hit his hairline. "She knows it'll only be April, right?"

"That's what I said."

He chuckled as they both shrugged out of their jackets and hung them on the coatrack near the front door before they made their way back to the kitchen. The hair on the back of her neck stood on end, her entire body humming with awareness at Carter's proximity.

Needing some breathing room, Abby went straight for the cookie jar and plucked out a couple cookies for them to share. "You still like chocolate chip, right?"

He murmured his agreement, and she glanced up to find that he hadn't yet made it to the table in the breakfast nook. Instead, his attention had been snagged by her grandma's old record player—a relic from their high school days—that sat in the sunroom just off the kitchen.

Back then, Carter had pretended to be enthralled with music, and they would spend hours listening to record after record. But she'd learned pretty early on that it hadn't been the music that kept Carter interested— it'd been the fact that so many of her grandmother's records were ballads, perfect to dance to, and Carter would use any excuse to have their bodies pressed up against each other.

It seemed not much had changed in that aspect as he raised a brow in her direction and tipped his head toward the machine. "You mind?"

"If you wanted to dance with me, all you had to do was say so," she teased.

He held her gaze for a beat before breaking it

only long enough to put the needle on the record, the crackling giving way to the slow, crooning voices of the Righteous Brothers. "Well, then, consider this me saying so."

Holding out a hand to her, he beckoned her closer. Without stopping to think too much about it, she stepped toward him and placed her hand in his, allowing him to pull her in. Her breath hitched when he didn't stop until their bodies were flush against each other from chest to thigh and every hard, solid inch in between.

Carter made a masculine hum of satisfaction deep in his throat as he held her hand in one of his and settled his other low on her back, the tips of his fingers just grazing the swell of her bottom. Then they just swayed, barely moving side to side, and she couldn't deny how good...how *right*...it felt to be in his arms again.

She'd missed this more than she'd allowed herself to remember. But that wasn't exactly right either... While being with Carter in high school had been amazing, there was something different about it now. They'd both experienced life—the good and the bad—in the time they'd been apart, and it made her realize just how special the connection they shared truly was.

Before long, Carter dropped his head and murmured her name against the shell of her ear, sending a shudder racing through her. He exhaled and tightened his hold on her back as he pressed his lips to that space behind her ear that made her go half out of her mind. He'd always exploited it, making her stupid in the process, and it was no different now. She melted against him as he kissed a path down her neck, tipping her head to the side to give him more access as his tongue flicked out to lick where her pulse thrummed against her skin.

At her soft moan, Carter pulled back only far enough so she could read the intent in his eyes as he slowly lowered his head toward her.

He paused a hair's breadth away from her lips, giving her time to say no. "Tell me to stop, Abby."

She wasn't sure if he was begging for his sake or hers, but if he was looking for someone to put an end to this, he'd have to look somewhere other than her. She'd decided earlier in the evening that she was tired of fighting this. She was all in for however long he was home, in whatever way worked.

So instead, she tipped her face up toward his and closed the last bit of distance between them. Abby gripped the back of his neck as their mouths touched, electricity sparking between them. He groaned as she parted her lips, allowing his tongue to sweep inside.

And then everything but Carter ceased to exist for her. She lost herself in the feel of him, so solid and sure under her questing hands, and in his taste and his scent and the low groans he released into the barely there space between them.

When they finally broke apart, Abby had to work to catch her breath, though she wasn't sure she wanted to. She wanted to be breathless with him. To feel every inch of his excitement for her as he rocked into her. Wanted to moan his name as they found their releases together.

"This doesn't have to be anything serious," she said.

"What doesn't?" he asked, lifting a brow.

"This. Us. We can do casual." Tucking her hands into the waistband of his jeans, her fingertips narrowly missing the impressive bulge trapped in its denim prison, she silenced the whisper inside her that wondered if this was a good idea and voiced the most important word she'd said all night. "Stay..."

* * *

With that single word, Abby obliterated Carter's self-control, and he was a goner. He was tired of fighting this, tired of reminding himself every day of all the reasons they shouldn't be together. All the reasons he shouldn't sleep with her while he was home. He was so damn tired.

If Abby was willing to venture into this, then so was he.

Even though they were both adults, they snuck upstairs like they were teenagers. And the grin Abby shot him over her shoulder had him feeling seventeen all over again. Like second nature, he sidestepped the creaky stairs along the way, holding his breath as they tiptoed past Hilde's room on the second floor to get to the staircase that led to Abby's room.

"I'm allowed to have boys in my room, you know," Abby teased in a whisper.

"I think your grandma might rethink that stance if she knew all the wicked things I plan to do to you tonight."

"Promises, promises," she murmured as her eyes turned molten.

At that look from his sweet Abby, he actually managed to get harder, though only thirty seconds prior, he'd have sworn it was impossible. He was as stiff as granite, desperate to find out if sinking inside her was as good as he remembered.

If only he'd known what was to come, because as soon as they stepped foot into her room, Abby shut the door behind them and yanked off her shirt without an ounce of self-consciousness, and he wondered if his sweet Abby wasn't actually applicable anymore. She was still pliant but greedy, still the tiniest bit submissive when it came to intimacy, but she no longer held herself with an air of self-consciousness, and he'd had no idea just how hot it would be to see her like this.

As soon as Abby's shirt hit the floor, he reached back and tugged on the neck of his own, tossing it to the side to join hers in a heap. And then he pulled her to him, desperate to feel her skin against his for the first time in far too long.

"Jesus, look at you," he whispered against her skin as he kissed a path across her collarbones, dropping to his knees right there in front of her.

She wore a pale pink bra, and he reached up to trace where the material met her soft skin. The shadowy outlines of her pebbled nipples taunted him enough that he couldn't stop from leaning in and sucking them straight into his mouth, lace and all.

She gasped, her hands flying to the back of his head as she held him to her and moaned his name. At the sound, it was all he could do to keep from exploding in his pants—not unlike the first time they'd done this way back when. Fortunately—for both of them—he had more self-control and stamina now.

When he'd gotten her good and panting and had licked his fill, he divested them both of the rest of their clothes before hauling her up against him and marching them straight to her bed. Laying her out on the plush covers, pillows strewn about, he followed her down, settling himself between her legs. Looking at her, ready and waiting for him, her hair fanned out on the pillow, her lips parted and kiss-swollen, her breasts calling to him nearly as much as the glistening skin between her thighs, was almost more than he could take. Maybe he hadn't licked his fill after all.

He kissed a path down between her breasts, over the soft curve of her stomach, against each damp inner thigh. And then he put his mouth exactly where it was watering to be.

"Carter!" She arched against him, delving her fingers into his hair as he feasted on her until she writhed beneath him as she hit her peak.

"Christ, I love how you taste," he murmured as he tore himself away. He could spend all night pleasuring her with nothing but his mouth, but she was tugging him up, her words trapped in her throat as she tried to catch her breath.

Obliging her, he watched as she sucked in lungfuls of air, her breasts heaving with the effort. With a groan low in his throat, he pulled a condom from his wallet—old habits died hard—and rolled it down his hard length, desperate to sink inside her. He knelt on the bed, kissing a path up her body, once again getting distracted along the way.

At least until she wrapped her hands around his biceps and tugged him up. "Now, Carter. I want you inside me."

He wanted to ask her again if she was sure, because they couldn't take this back once they took this step. But she'd just invited him inside her, still held her arms open for him, and he respected her enough not to second-guess her decision. She knew her mind better than he could ever hope to, and she'd already made it up. Fortunately for him, that decision involved him sliding inside heaven on earth.

Settling between her thighs, he rested his forehead against hers, lined himself up, and pushed inside, swallowing her moan with a kiss. He got lost in the feel of her, in the gripping heat that made him nearly lose his mind. *Jesus*, he couldn't remember it being like this, which was probably for the better. Because if he had, he wasn't so sure he'd have been able to stay away all these years. Not when Abby, with her joyous, giving spirit, and her soulful eyes, and her warm, welcoming body was waiting for him.

Knowing just how creaky her old bed frame was, he rocked into her with slow, deep thrusts, bringing a thumb down to where they were joined and stroking her until he felt the fluttering pulse of her around him. Dropping his head into the crook of her shoulder, he silenced his moan in her neck as she clutched him to her, her panting breaths washing over his skin.

This time, when she came, her walls gripping him tight enough to pull a groan straight from his soul, he went with her, her name on his lips as he settled as deep inside her as he could. Losing himself in her and, for once, not at all certain he wanted to be found.

As they lay there, Abby's fingers lightly trailing over his back while they both tried to catch their breath, he realized she was wrong about one thing tonight. What had just happened between them didn't feel casual at all.

Chapter Fourteen

Carter couldn't remember the last time he'd slept so well, especially when he'd spent the night doing very little sleeping.

He and Abby had reached for each other twice more in the wee hours of the morning. Once as she'd been arching into him, his name a whispered sigh on her lips, and he'd been all too happy to oblige. And the next as the morning sun was just kissing the horizon, bathing Abby's room with pale golden light. She'd sat astride him, a slow, sensual roll to her hips as she'd driven them both out of their minds.

He'd slept with her more times than he could count, but it'd been different when they were younger. It'd been fumbling and awkward, messy and graceless. But now, it'd only taken three times of them being together before they were already in sync.

And he knew that the sight of her riding him, her head tossed back, lips parted, and hair trailing down to whisper across his thighs, was something that would keep him company for weeks, or even months, to come.

It was Saturday, so Carter didn't have to get out of bed to be anywhere, but he was already going to have to meet the firing squad when he got back to his sister's. She'd no doubt noticed that he hadn't come home last night. In fact, he'd bet he had half a dozen calls and texts from her already. But really, this was all her fault. If she hadn't sent him in her stead, none of this would have happened.

That was a lie.

Carter would have gone to support Abby, because if it was important to her, it was important to him. He didn't know when that had changed—or maybe it had never changed and that was the problem. All he knew was that Abby had carved out a special place in his heart. One that was permanently tattooed with her name, which didn't bode well for him. Because the ending to their story was already written. She was destined to be a Heart's Hope Bay lifer, just like all those people down at the bonfire. And he would do anything just to escape this town and everything that came with it.

After gathering his clothes and dressing, studiously avoiding the creaky floorboards, he pressed his hands on either side of Abby and bent to press a kiss to her temple.

Her eyes fluttered open as she stretched. "Are you leaving?" she asked, her voice soft and sleep roughened.

The sight of her lying there, her hair tousled from their night, her eyes sleepy, lips kiss-swollen, made him ache to be back in bed with her. But it was already late, and if he had any hope of sneaking out of here without alerting Hilde, he needed to get his ass in gear.

"Yeah, I'm going to head out before your grandma wakes up. I need to get home anyway. Sofia will wonder where I am."

He lowered his mouth to hers, trapping a groan in his throat as she swiped her tongue against his lower lip. It would be so easy to slip under the sheets, settle between her thighs, and sink inside her. Lose himself for another handful of hours with only the cadence of her moans to guide how much time had passed.

Which was exactly why he pressed one final kiss to her mouth and pulled back. "I'll see you later."

Abby smiled and burrowed farther into her pillow, her eyes already drifting shut. "See you."

By the time Carter had gathered his things and stood at her bedroom door, Abby was already fast asleep again. With one final glance at her, he opened the door and crept out of her room, the move so reminiscent of their high school days, he had an overwhelming sense of déjà vu.

He couldn't count how many times he'd snuck into and out of her room, desperate to escape his home life and be with someone who truly loved him. How many nights he'd slept over, just as he had last night, sneaking out before the sun had even risen. God knew his dad hadn't given a shit about what he'd done or where he'd been. Hell, he'd probably preferred it when Carter just hadn't shown up at all. But Hilde cared where her granddaughter was and how she was spending her time, and given that Abby had spent most of her nights there instead of with her mom—wherever that may have been—he'd been taking his life in his own hands every night he'd stayed.

As Carter descended the steps from the third floor, he weighed his options on taking the front staircase down and slipping out the main door, or taking his chances on the back staircase and hoping Hilde hadn't made her way down to the kitchen yet. Obviously, he and Abby were both adults, and they had every right to do whatever they wished in their spare time—including each other. And Hilde had never been the kind of person who'd tried to destroy that, even when they'd been teenagers. But she *was* the kind of person who looked out for her granddaughter's best interests, and there was little doubt in Carter's mind that she knew he absolutely did not fit that mold.

A quick glance down the hall showed that Hilde's door was shut, a hopeful sign she was still snoozing away. With that reassurance, he crept down the hallway, once again careful to avoid the creaky floorboards, and paused at the top of the back stairwell, taking a moment to listen for signs of life. He didn't hear any clanging in the kitchen, nor did he smell the tell-tale scent of coffee or bacon—Hilde's go-to Saturday morning meal accompaniment.

He decided to take his chances and descended the stairs. A quick glance around proved he was alone, and he breathed out a sigh of relief as he stepped off the last stair and headed straight for the back door. His hand was in midair, poised and ready to unlock the door and make his escape, when a throat cleared from behind him.

"You're a little old to be sneaking out, aren't you, Carter?"

At Hilde's voice, Carter dropped his head and closed his eyes, breathing out a humorless laugh. It was ridiculous that he was nearly thirty years old and this woman could still reduce him to that scared teenage boy all over again.

Knowing he and Abby hadn't done anything wrong, he turned around and pasted a smile on his face. "Good morning, Mrs. Engels. No coffee?"

She held up her mug, the front of which read *If my mouth doesn't say it, my face definitely will*, and toasted him through the air. "Tea's better for the soul."

"I think there are probably millions of people who would disagree with you on that," he said.

She waved a hand through the air, completely unconcerned at what hordes of people would balk at. "Luckily those people aren't in my kitchen right now. Why don't you have a seat," she said, in a way that wasn't so much a question as a demand.

Knowing he'd already lost the battle, Carter blew out a breath and sat in the chair opposite her, where a mug—this one proclaiming *May you have the confidence of a mediocre white man*—already sat in front of him, the tea perfectly brewed and still steaming. Carter didn't even bother to hide his smirk, and he glanced up to find her laughing eyes already on him.

"I have three things to tell you, Carter," Hilde said. "One, you're not nearly as sneaky as you think you are. Two, I wasn't nearly as intoxicated as Abby assumed I was. And three, my ears may not be brand-new anymore, but I'm also not yet at the stage of needing hearing aids. You two might want to work on your inside bedroom voices."

Oh Jesus. Carter could think of twelve thousand other subjects he would rather discuss with Abby's grandmother, including politics *and* religion, than his sex life with her granddaughter.

Not knowing what else to say, he picked up his mug, took a slow sip, and met her eyes. "Duly noted for next time."

Hilde cocked her head, the playful gleam in her eyes vanishing in a blink. She studied him with intensity and focus, and he had to force himself not to squirm under her penetrating gaze. "*Will* there be a next time?"

This was venturing into dangerous territory. He didn't purport to presume what Abby was thinking, or what this between them would be eventually, nor did he want to speak for her. But he also didn't want Hilde to discuss this with Abby and tell her that he had run away scared. Despite it not feeling casual last night, that was what they'd both agreed upon. And if she could keep up her end of the bargain, so could he.

Without getting too much into the weeds, he figured honesty was his best policy. "I'd like there to be."

The answer seemed to shock Hilde, though she tried very hard to keep her reaction under wraps. She cleared her throat and set her mug on the table, wrapping her hands around it as she met his gaze. "How long is it now?"

He didn't have to be a mind reader or have any of her uncanny abilities to know exactly what she was speaking about. She wanted to know how long he had left in Heart's Hope Bay.

"A couple weeks."

At the beginning, being stuck here had felt like a never-ending sentence. Something he did out of obligation to his sister and niece, a roadblock that stood in the way of what he wanted in life. And now he could admit it didn't feel that way at all anymore. He just wasn't sure what to do about that.

"Not a lot of time," Hilde said.

"Depends on the situation."

Hilde steeled her gaze. "The situation is you getting involved with my granddaughter when you have no intention of seeing it through." She paused and raised a brow. "Unless you've changed your mind about our quaint little town?"

Carter clenched his jaw and gave a sharp shake of his head, not dropping his gaze from hers.

She rolled her lips inward and lifted her mug. "I see. In that case, I hope you know what you're getting into, because you two have been down this path before. And you know exactly how it ends."

* * *

Abby didn't want to be *that* girl—the one who was jealous of her friends—but sometimes that jealousy snuck out, just the tiniest bit. Of course, it would probably help if she removed herself from baby situations instead of seeking them out. But then she wouldn't be a good friend either. Especially when Gia was in near-constant freak-out mode because of her pregnancy.

Which was why Abby was currently surrounded by strollers and bassinets and hordes of the tiniest booties she'd ever seen. She'd thought maybe the registry would be a way to make Gia feel more in control when she was unraveling on a daily basis. She'd been quick to tell Abby that it was too early to start one—that all the advice said to begin around twelve weeks—but after Abby had oh so eloquently told her "Who the hell cares?" she'd finally relented and agreed.

"What do you guys think?" Gia stood in front of an assortment of high chairs, scrutinizing them as if they held all the secrets of life. "Between these two, which one should I pick?"

Abby ignored the niggle inside her that wished it was her in Gia's shoes, shopping for her future family. One that had somehow begun to include the one man who'd never be an option. The same man who'd kissed her so sweetly—after not so sweetly rocking her world the night prior—before he'd left her bedroom only yesterday morning.

She cleared her throat, internally shaking herself and focusing back on the present. On *Gia*. "My vote is for the one that transitions to a booster seat. Then you won't be stuck buying that down the road."

Savannah rested an elbow on a shelf, leaning against it as she pointed a finger in Abby's direction. "What she said."

Gia bit her lip, uncertainty written on her face. "That makes sense," she said, but she didn't make a move to scan the item into her registry, still just worrying her lip and glancing between the two choices as if it were truly a matter of life or death.

"Gia, I love you, girl, but I'm gonna need you to move it along." Savannah snapped her fingers. She'd passed *over it* around hour two and was now well into *screw this* territory.

Abby laughed. "What do you think Marco would want?"

Gia sighed, her shoulders slumping. "I have no idea. We haven't really talked about it. Things have been so strained, it seems like all we do is fight."

Abby and Savannah shared a glance over Gia's bent

head before Abby put an arm around Gia's shoulders and tugged her into her side. "What are you guys fighting about?"

"What *aren't* we fighting about? It doesn't seem like we agree on anything for the baby. If things had gone according to plan, this was all stuff we would've hashed out *before* I was already carrying our kid. But now we've got to figure this out while I'm dealing with morning sickness—and afternoon and evening, by the way. Whoever named it morning sickness is a bastard. And probably never even had it to begin with."

"It was probably a guy," Savannah said.

"No doubt," Gia agreed. "So I've been dealing with that, plus all my hormones have gone completely bonkers. And then there's the normal couple stuff, like how he's been working too many hours because they still haven't hired another architect. And if he's working all those hours, when are we supposed to get the baby's room done? Since we moved in, it's been the catchall room we've thrown everything into that didn't have a place."

Sensing Gia was on the verge of tears, Abby squeezed her. "Hey... everything's going to be fine."

Gia huffed out a humorless laugh. "Easy for you to say... You're not the one who's pregnant."

Abby felt those words like a knife to her chest, sinking deep and piercing her heart as sure as if it'd been an actual blade.

"Gia," Savannah said, disapproval in her tone. A tone Abby knew would've been much sharper if Gia hadn't been dealing with mood swings. Savannah turned into a protective mama bear for her friends—even if it was against one another.

On a gasp, Gia swung to face Abby, her eyes wide and apologetic. "Oh my God, Abby, I'm sorry. I didn't mean—"

Abby waved her off, pasting a bright smile on her face and letting her arm drop to her side. "No worries. I know what you meant."

"I just—"

There was no reason for Abby to take it so personally, especially when Gia didn't have a malicious bone in her body, so she interrupted Gia again. "Have you guys talked at all since the fundraiser?"

Gia studied her for a moment before sighing and looking away. Finally, she lifted the scanner and selected the high chair Abby had suggested. "Not really. I mean, we do . . . It's just never about anything important. It's a lot of, 'What do you want for dinner, babe?' and 'How was work?' and 'If we have sex, do you think it'll hurt the baby?'"

"Okay, I kind of want to know the answer to that last one," Savannah said.

"No," Gia and Abby answered in unison.

Yeah, Abby definitely knew more about pregnancy than she probably should.

"Good to know." Savannah guided them toward the

next aisle, no doubt intent on getting this over with as quickly as possible.

"Well," Abby said to Gia, "I'm certainly not a marriage expert, but maybe talking is a good place to start. Instead of falling asleep watching *Queer Eye*, maybe you guys have a conversation about what's been bothering you."

Gia sighed, her shoulders sagging. "You're right. It's just hard, you know?"

Abby knew all kinds of things, but the minutia of married life wasn't among those topics. Still, she could commiserate with her friend without question. Squeezing Gia's hand, she said, "I know."

"Speaking of the fundraiser," Savannah said, raising an eyebrow at Abby. "Don't think I didn't notice Carter still at Last Call when I left. What happened between you two?"

Abby caught her lip between her teeth and pretended to be very interested in the infant bath towels Gia was scanning, giving herself a minute before she blurted out that they'd had sex and it'd been better than she'd remembered.

"He helped me get the gift baskets out to my car, and then we hung around and played some pool." And then she just... stopped talking. That was completely the truth—they *had* done all those things. If she decided not to mention the mind-blowing sex that had followed, well... her friends didn't need to know anything more.

If she told either of them what was going on with her and Carter, she knew they'd be concerned. They'd try to talk her out of it, but she wasn't interested in rehashing that. She'd done it on her own enough for all three of them, and she'd already made up her mind to continue on this path and see where it led. The last thing she wanted to hear was that it was going to take her on a one-way trip to Heartacheville. Mostly because she was already well aware just how probable that outcome was.

Chapter Fifteen

✳

What color do you want, Uncle Carter?" Sofia asked as she sat on the floor in her living room, a dozen bottles of nail polish spread out around her.

Coming over tonight to watch Sofia with Carter was one of Abby's more ill-advised ideas. Her heart was actually in danger of combusting as she watched this gorgeous, muscled man mollify his niece by offering his hand for an impromptu manicure.

He wore a navy button-up with the sleeves rolled up, the color setting off the vibrant green of his eyes, and the scruff on his jaw was calling to her like a siren. She remembered, in great detail, exactly how it'd felt when that rough texture brushed against her neck, her breasts, and between her thighs. And while the night he'd spent at her house had been world-rocking, she'd be lying if she said watching him here, as he painstakingly sorted through each of the colors of the nail polish Abby had brought along for the evening, wasn't affecting her just as much.

"I think I like this one the best," he said without a hint of sarcasm, settling on the lavender.

Sofia's smile widened, and she nodded vigorously. "That's my favorite!"

Abby laughed from her perch on the couch, her second glass of wine settling in her bones in that way that made her feel perfectly warm and content. At the beginning of the evening, shortly after Abby had arrived to hang out with Carter and Sofia while Becca was at a charity work function, they'd started watching *Frozen* as they'd feasted on pepperoni pizza. But the little girl had quickly become interested in the bag of goodies Abby had brought along containing the afore-mentioned favorite lavender nail polish. Apparently manicures outdid Elsa and Anna.

For most people, Abby figured a three-year-old prob-ably served as a gigantic cock block—a wrench thrown in an otherwise intimate evening that would ultimately only function as birth control. The trouble was, for Abby, it was just the opposite. A night in with Carter and his niece, group cuddles on the couch followed by watching him be loving and caring and attentive, was her ultimate kryptonite.

Since she was still on a mission to keep whatever was happening between her and Carter from her friends, she hadn't even been able to talk to them about this. To ask if she was making the right decision by pursuing this casual thing she and Carter had going. She'd doubted herself enough for a lifetime, and she could use some reassurance that she wasn't making a huge mistake. But then again, that was why she hadn't told her friends in the first place. She knew they wouldn't give her empty platitudes, and they'd never lie to her. Which was exactly why she'd never hear them say those words.

As she watched Carter hold out his hand for his niece to absolutely murder his fingertips with the pale purple polish, she couldn't help but play this exact scenario out as if it were years in the future, and this was actually her life. Her family. She knew it was stupid. She knew she shouldn't do it. And she knew doing so was asking for nothing but heartache. But even knowing those things didn't mean she could stop her brain from conjuring up the most optimistic what-if scenarios where Carter was involved.

And that particular scenario was, what if this was *their* life?

"Wow, peanut. You're really good at this," Carter said with a straight face, even as Sofia painted the entire tip of his finger, skin included.

Sofia beamed at him. "I practice on Mommy sometimes."

"I can tell."

"One time, she got mad at me," Sofia whispered, her head bent low over Carter's fingers as she dipped the brush and reapplied.

"How come?" Abby asked.

"I sneaked a bottle even though I wasn't a 'posed to and messed up her bed."

Abby cringed. "Yeah, it's probably not a good idea to do this without your mommy or Uncle Carter knowing about it, huh?"

"Or you, Miss Abby, right?" Sofia asked, her eyes bright and innocent and unassuming as she regarded Abby.

Unexpectedly, a lump rose in Abby's throat, the ache she felt over desiring this very thing sitting like a genuine presence on her chest, nearly suffocating her. Her life was pretty amazing. She had loyal, caring friends, a booming business, and a grandmother who would do anything for her. If her life were a puzzle, it'd be a mosaic of beautiful colors and patterns, fitted together near perfectly... except for a few missing pieces. And those pieces were what she wanted most—the beautiful house and attentive spouse and amazing kids.

And she wasn't sure when—or even *if*—it would be a possibility.

* * *

Hours later, after they'd made it partially through *Frozen* and *Frozen II*—Sofia's interest waning halfway through both—and playing dress-up, complete with a superhero crusade, Carter had just tucked Sofia in.

They'd managed to wear her out tonight, and she'd trotted off to bed late but without much argument.

With a smile, Carter brought out the half-full bottle of wine and held it up, his brows arched in question.

With a smile, she nodded and lifted her glass toward him. Once he'd poured the remaining wine in each of their glasses, he sat down next to her on the couch, closer now than they'd been able to get the entire evening with Sofia running interference between them.

He rested his hand against the back of the couch, stretching out his arm behind her. "Thanks for coming over tonight. I'm sure this isn't your idea of fun."

She waved him off, ignoring the way shivers rushed down her spine at the whisper of his fingertips against the nape of her neck. "I had fun. I never knew you could sing so well or that you looked so good in purple."

His lips quirked up at the corners, and he shook his head. "The things I do for that little girl…"

"It's sweet."

He lifted his eyes to meet hers. "You think so?"

"Definitely."

"Sweet enough to score me enough points for a kiss?" The grin he shot her was all mischief and trouble, but she was helpless to deny him.

She tipped her head toward him, and that was all the answer he needed. He plucked the glass from her hand and set both of theirs on the coffee table before cupping her face, his thumbs brushing gently against her cheeks. With aching slowness, he inched his face toward hers, Abby's eyelids fluttering shut when he became unfocused. And then his lips were on hers, his tongue sweeping into her mouth, and she breathed out a sigh of pleasure. He tasted like wine, the chocolate truffles Abby had brought for dessert, and the best bad decision she'd made in a long time.

She gripped his forearms, anchoring herself—though if to keep from floating away or from pouncing on him, she wasn't sure. They used to spend hours making out on the couch, exactly like they were tonight, but there was something different now. Something hotter and hungrier just below the surface. Maybe because she knew exactly what was waiting for her if they moved beyond frantic mouths and over the clothes petting.

When she was wholly and completely worked up and *this close* to stripping down in Becca's living room, Carter placed one last chaste kiss on her lips before pulling back with a groan. He swept a hand through his hair, his breaths coming in pants, much like her own.

"Christ, I could spend a whole day just kissing you," he said, his voice a gruff whisper as he locked his attention on her lips. When he lifted his gaze, the heat in his eyes was unmistakable, as was the promise behind them—if they weren't on the clock as babysitters, he'd have already divested her of her clothes and he'd be working them both toward ecstasy.

The sound of keys in the lock jolted Abby, and she jumped away from Carter as if she were a teenager again, in danger of being caught by an adult.

"Hey," Becca said, not sparing them a glance as she strode in on her crutches, wielding them like a pro. "Ugh, I could not get out of there! Sorry I'm so late."

Abby glanced down at her watch, shocked to find just how close to midnight it was. Even though they'd put Sofia down past her bedtime, there was a whole lot of time unaccounted for. Well, except that the inferno raging inside her and the rough shape her panties were in said it wasn't altogether unaccounted for.

"How was it?" Carter shifted on the couch, no doubt trying to hide his not-so-easy-to-conceal reaction from his sister.

"Boring, but the event raised a lot of money, so I'll give it a pass." She tossed her purse on the side table. "I'm exhausted, though. I think I'm gonna turn in. Abby, you should just stay over since it's so late."

"Oh, that's okay. I'll head home." Abby didn't dare meet Carter's eyes, but she couldn't help but wonder what he thought of his sister's invitation and would give just about anything to know.

"That's silly. There's one hell of a storm out there. It took me ten minutes to get home, and I could normally walk that route faster, even with these," she said, lifting up one of her crutches. Even as she did so, lightning flashed outside, and a crack of thunder shook the house.

God, how lost had Abby been in Carter's kisses that she hadn't even noticed a severe thunderstorm rolling through?

"She's right," Carter said. "I don't want you driving home in that. You can stay in my room, and I'll sleep down here."

Abby could've sworn she heard Becca snort, but when Abby lifted her gaze to meet the other woman's, it was wiped free from everything but a serene smile.

Carter stood and reached for Abby's hand to tug her up. "C'mon, I'll show you to my room and grab you something to sleep in."

"Thanks again for coming over, Abby," Becca called as she strode down the hallway toward her bedroom. "Hope you get a good night's sleep..."

Okay, Abby definitely heard the teasing lilt in Becca's tone that time.

She tugged on Carter's hand as he led them both up the stairs and to the single bedroom that took up the majority of the peaked second floor. "Did you hear that? Your sister totally thinks you're dragging me up here to have your way with me."

Once they were both at the top of the stairs, Carter stepped into her, not stopping until she was sandwiched between his body and the wall, his hard, solid erection pressing against her belly and making her ache with need.

He dipped his head, brushing his lips against the slope of her neck. "I *am* dragging you up here to have my wicked way with you..."

Then he dropped to his knees, flicking his eyes up to hers as he lifted her skirt. He tucked her panties to the side and fitted his mouth to her, testing every ounce of her self-restraint... not to mention her ability to be quiet.

And she didn't mind a bit.

* * *

The following morning, Abby woke up well before the sun, and that, compiled with the activities she and Carter had gotten up to the night before, meant she'd gotten *maybe* four hours of sleep. Even still, she couldn't keep the smile off her face as she greeted each and every family who walked through the bright yellow doors of the Sunshine Corner, much to the suspicion of basically everyone.

When her grandma had walked downstairs that morning, she'd given Abby a knowing look, complete with thinly veiled concern, but Abby couldn't even bring herself to care. Nothing could take the spring out of her step today.

"Seriously, what is your deal this morning?" Savannah asked for the third time.

Abby shrugged. "Can't I just have a good day?"

Savannah and Jenn didn't even try to hide the looks they shot each other, but Abby ignored them. Whereas last night, she'd wanted to be able to confide in her friends even though she knew it was a bad idea, today she had no such desires.

At this time of the morning, with near-constant

drop-offs, it wasn't unusual for parents to hold the front door open for others who attended the Sunshine Corner. Because of that, she should have been prepared to see Carter suddenly there, looming large in her space, but she still would've liked some forewarning. Then maybe she could have stopped the stupid smile from sweeping across her mouth or at least tamped it down so she didn't look like an idiot. Fortunately, she wasn't alone in that respect, as a matching grin appeared on Carter's face when he spotted her.

"Hi," she breathed.

He ran a hand through his hair, the move reminding Abby of when she'd had her fingers locked in the strands the night before as he'd driven her half out of her mind with his mouth alone. Without her approval, heat flooded her cheeks as she bit her lip and met Carter's gaze.

"Hey," he said, the low timbre of his voice reenergizing parts of her body that were still humming from last night.

"Miss Abby, Miss Abby! Thank you for bringing your nail polish last night!" Sofia grinned up at her.

Abby squatted down to her level and reached to hold the little girl's hand, lifting it up to inspect her nails that Carter had painted. "You're very welcome. They look so pretty."

"How come you slept at my house?"

After working with kids for so long, Abby should've been prepared for their random subject changes and blunt questions, but she wasn't sure anything could've prepared her for this. Her wide eyes flew to Carter's just as Savannah's gasp met her ears.

Letting her eyes flutter closed, she exhaled a deep breath before turning her attention back to Sofia. One issue at a time, which meant the grown-ups would have to wait. "What do you mean?"

She and Carter had specifically set an alarm for pre-human hours to avoid this very situation. She'd thought she'd gotten out unnoticed, but then again, she'd lost who knew how long to Carter's kisses against the front door. Apparently, they hadn't been stealthy after all.

Sofia's eyes darted to the side, and she didn't respond.

Carter rested a hand on her head. "What do you mean, peanut?"

Sofia looked up at him, her eyes worried. "I got up before I was a 'posed to, and I saw Miss Abby's bag was downstairs. Don't tell Mommy, 'kay?"

Abby stood to her full height and met Carter's questioning gaze. His cocked eyebrow told her however they played this was up to her, and he'd follow her lead. Normally, she didn't condone lying. In fact, she hated it. But in an instance like this, it seemed a white lie was the best solution.

"I left that for you in case you wanted to paint your mommy's nails."

Sofia's eyes brightened as she grinned up at Abby. "Thank you, Miss Abby!"

With that, she hugged Carter's leg before yelling

a goodbye over her shoulder as she fled toward her best friend.

He stepped closer to Abby, his voice low so as not to be overheard by any of the other nosy people milling about. Sadly, it wouldn't matter. Abby would most definitely be grilled as soon as he left. "Quick thinking," he said.

Abby lifted a shoulder. "Seemed like the easiest solution."

"Maybe tonight I can leave a bag behind at your place."

Abby knew her friends and grandma were watching them, so she tried to keep her emotions in check. She rolled her lips between her teeth in an attempt to tamp down her smile, but it was no use. "That sounds good."

"Great. I'll see you later." Carter dipped his head the tiniest bit, as if he was intent on giving her a kiss, but he seemed to think better of it at the last minute and froze. Even though his lips never touched hers, the scorching look he sent her managed to set her body ablaze all on its own.

Tonight couldn't come fast enough.

"What the crap was that?" Savannah hissed.

Abby snapped her gaze away from Carter's retreating form to find Savannah, Jenn, and her grandma all staring at her, varying looks of concern on their faces. "What was what?"

Jenn laughed and rolled her eyes. "Honey, do you really think we're that stupid?"

"I don't think you're stupid at all. I just don't know what you mean."

"Um...you and Captain McHot Pants over there," Savannah said.

Abby snorted and shook her head. "Nothing."

"Uh-huh." Savannah crossed her arms and attempted to coerce Abby into spilling with her glare alone.

"I still don't think this is a good idea, Abby," her grandmother said, her voice quiet but firm.

Savannah scoffed. "Not a good idea? That's like saying the Grand Canyon is a pothole. This is an *epically horrible* idea. And if there weren't little ears around, I'd throw in some colorful words to go along with my description just to really drive home the point."

Abby rolled her eyes and shook her head, busying herself as she readied the science experiment they were doing that morning. "You guys are making a bigger deal out of this than you need to."

"And I don't think you're making a big enough deal out of it," Savannah said. "You do know who this is you're getting involved with, right? You remember him—the guy who already broke your heart once? And, last I checked, is on schedule to do it again in, oh, a week or two?"

"And you realize that I'm a fully grown woman perfectly capable of making her own decisions, and said decision has already been made regarding this?" Abby sighed, tamping down her frustration. "Look, I appreciate the concern, but I'm not a starry-eyed teenager anymore. I walked into this with my eyes wide open, and I knew exactly what I was getting into. I can handle it. Whatever may come."

Jenn just shook her head while Savannah pursed her lips, crossing her arms over her chest. "I sure hope you're right."

It appeared Abby hadn't had as much luck tricking her friends into believing it as she'd had tricking herself.

Chapter Sixteen

✺

Carter was playing a stupid game, and the worst part was he knew it, but he couldn't stop. Even though this thing between him and Abby was supposed to be casual, it hadn't felt that way from the beginning. And it sure as hell didn't feel that way now as they spent every night in one of their beds. Ill-advised or not, he couldn't say he regretted it. He hadn't enjoyed a woman's company this much since...well, since her. And if that said a little bit too much about exactly how dangerous their involvement was, well, it wouldn't be the first time he'd ignored his instincts.

The back door opened, and Carter looked up from his makeshift desk at the dining table. Great. Becca was home, which meant it was already noon, which also meant he'd managed to piss away the entire morning fantasizing about Abby. Yeah, getting lost in daydreams was definitely going to get him his own firm.

His sister strode in on her crutches before propping them up against the counter. She leaned back alongside them and immediately pulled out her phone.

"Um...hi?" he said.

"Hi," she answered distractedly, her attention completely focused on her device.

He glanced at his watch only to realize he hadn't pissed away nearly as much time as he'd worried, but rather, Becca was actually home earlier than usual for lunch. "You have brunch plans today instead of lunch?"

"What?" Becca asked before slowly lifting her head from her phone and meeting Carter's gaze. "Oh, no...I just, um, wanted to come home real quick and make some calls. I'm going to head to my room for that."

With a furrowed brow, Carter watched her leave, her crutches thumping against the wood floor as she glided toward her bedroom. Weird. His sister hadn't ever much cared about privacy. Didn't much care about providing *him* with privacy either, but that was a whole other issue. He leaned back, balancing the chair on two legs as he glanced down the hallway toward her room. The door snicked shut behind her, which only piqued Carter's curiosity more. Who the hell was she talking to that she didn't want him to hear?

"Whatever," he mumbled, focusing his attention once again on the lengthy to-do list he had looming for him today. He'd already wasted enough time, thanks to a certain redhead who'd snagged all of his attention. He couldn't get sucked in to whatever was going on with his sister, too.

Five minutes later, Becca reappeared in the kitchen, her mouth pursed, a V between her brows showing her concern. As far back as Carter could remember, she'd never been able to mask her emotions. She wore her heart on her sleeve, which was, in his opinion, both her greatest asset *and* her biggest downfall.

Carter looked longingly at the work that was only going to continue piling up before setting his pen down and blowing out a sigh. "All right, what's up?"

"Hmm?" Becca asked, the nonword almost reflexive, as she didn't even lift her eyes from her screen.

"Whatever you're doing over there on your phone, or whoever you called, must have gotten you worked up. What's going on? I need to pay somebody a visit while I'm here?"

Becca blew out a humorless laugh and finally met his gaze. "You better watch out, or I might actually take you up on that."

Carter's eyebrows hit his hairline, and he sat back in his seat, crossing his arms over his chest. "I didn't think I'd ever see the day when you'd want your big brother fighting your battles with a guy. But I'm here and willing, so you might as well put me to use."

Becca flashed him a grin. "And I still don't want you fighting my battles with any guys."

"No? Then what's this about?"

She studied him for a long moment, looking as though she were having an internal argument with herself. Finally she sighed and leaned back against the counter. "It's Dad."

A sucker punch to the kidneys would have been less surprising than hearing those words from Becca's lips. Initially, Carter had worried that coming here would excavate all the family issues they had. Would make him face head-on the underlying fear he'd always carried over turning into his father. But, save for the night Abby had come over for dinner, Carter and Becca hadn't discussed their father at all. And that was exactly how Carter liked it.

"What about him?" he asked, his voice hard.

Becca blew out a resigned sigh, her shoulders slumping. "Just hear me out, okay?" When Carter didn't respond, she probed. "*Okay?*"

"Just say whatever you've got to say, Becca."

"I haven't been able to get ahold of him."

Carter lowered his gaze and busied himself with the papers in front of him, making notes on the design changes Redmond had wanted for the latest mock-up. "I don't see why that's such a big deal. It *is* before noon, and you and I both know he hasn't slept off last night's alcohol stupor yet."

Becca's crutches thumped against the floor as she strode toward him before dropping into the chair next to him. "It's not just today. He hasn't returned my calls in almost a week."

"And that's unusual? He's not exactly a stellar communicator."

"This is different. We don't talk a lot, but when I call him, he answers or calls me back. Always."

Carter had absolutely no desire to name the emotion simmering beneath his skin, threatening to erupt at any moment. He'd known Becca still kept tabs on their dad because he'd attempted to talk her out of it nearly every time they saw each other. Because of those conversations, he also knew why she did it. She felt responsible for him—for a nearly sixty-year-old man, which was just another thing in the long list of items to resent his father for. A parent should look after their child, not the other way around. And what hurt the most was knowing exactly how different it would have been if Carter's mom were still alive.

He also tried to ignore the pang of guilt that had settled inside his chest. As the oldest, he should've been the one looking after their dad. But the moment he'd run from Heart's Hope Bay, he'd been running not just from a town, but also from a life that included an emotionally abusive father. He'd sworn he wouldn't look back. He certainly didn't intend to now.

"I don't know what to tell you, Becks. He's a grown-ass man, and he can take care of himself."

Becca rolled her eyes. "You know—probably more than most—just exactly how unrealistic that is."

"Maybe you should call one of his friends to check up on him. Oh, wait…he doesn't *have* any friends because he's a gigantic asshole, and he drove them all away, just like everyone else in his life."

"Look, normally I'd just go out there myself and check up on him. But getting around his run-down property isn't exactly going to be a cakewalk with these things," she said, gesturing toward her crutches.

Carter snorted but didn't bother to otherwise respond.

She reached out, resting a hand on his arm. "Would you go check on him for me? You know I wouldn't ask you to do this if it wasn't important and if I wasn't truly worried."

Carter closed his eyes and scrubbed a hand down his face, resigning himself for the inevitable because, yeah...he knew.

* * *

Heart's Hope Bay wasn't populous by any stretch of the imagination, but it was vast, the town limits stretching for miles along the Oregon coast. Since Carter's dad lived just on the outskirts of those limits, the ride there took a good twenty minutes, the entirety of which Carter spent with his hands gripped tightly on the steering wheel, his body rigid.

If he had it his way, he'd go the rest of his life without speaking another word to his dad. God knew they'd both be happier if that were the case. There was no love lost between them. And though it sometimes hurt to know that when his mom had passed away of cancer, he'd lost both his parents that night, he also knew he carried just as much distaste for his dad as his dad did for him.

Before his mom had died, Carter's and his dad's relationship had been strange in the way that teenage sons and their father's relationships naturally were. They were too much alike—or so his mom had told him— and that was why they'd constantly butted heads. That was also why Carter had made every effort to change himself, to work on the core of his personality. It may have made him more rigid and more focused, but if the other option was to turn into a drunk, verbally abusive asshole, he'd take the former.

It had killed him to leave his sister with their ill-fitted father, but in the end, it had been not just his sister's reassurance that she'd be okay, but also the promise he'd made to his mom before she'd passed away that he wouldn't throw away his future because of her inevitable death. Still, he'd felt tons of guilt in the weeks and months after he'd left for college. In the beginning, he'd called to check up on Becca every day, listening not only for what she said but also what she *didn't* say. Eventually, he'd come to realize the truth— that his dad wasn't a shitty father, period.

He was just a shitty father to him.

Carter rolled to a stop at the end of the gravel driveway, completely unsurprised at what he found at his childhood home. The yard was overgrown and unkempt, piled high with discarded junk better suited for the landfill instead of someone's front yard. But then again, when someone spent their days chained to a six-pack, there wasn't a whole lot of time for gardening.

He put the car in park, braced his hands on the steering wheel, and exhaled a long, slow breath. He'd stop in, make sure the old man wasn't dead, and then he'd leave. Five minutes, tops, and then he'd be out of there. And then he could put Becca's mind at ease and go right back to pretending he no longer had a dad.

After stepping out of the car, he carefully traversed the hidden path to the front door, avoiding the spare tires, upturned garbage cans, and rusted lawn chairs. He climbed the steps on the dilapidated front porch, testing the boards' stability before putting his full weight on them.

Hesitating only a second, he raised his fist and knocked on the door. He paused, listening for sounds of life inside the house. The low murmur of a television reached him outside. That didn't mean anything, of course. A TV playing in the background wasn't proof enough that his dad was okay, so he knocked again, louder this time, his fist pounding on the door.

"Dad?" he yelled, the words sounding bitter and sharp on his tongue. "Open up."

He waited another minute with no answer before exhaling sharply and reaching out to twist the knob, not at all surprised when it turned easily. The crime rate in Heart's Hope Bay was nearly nonexistent. And out here in the middle of nowhere, there was a better chance of lightning striking the house—four times—than someone breaking in.

He swung the door open and stepped inside. The stench of stale beer and rotting food was overwhelming, ripping a cough from him.

"Jesus," he said under his breath, contemplating lifting his shirt up to cover his nose.

It took a moment for his eyes to adjust to the darkness inside, and when they did, he felt like the air had been punched out of him. He hadn't been back here since he'd left for college. His childhood home looked so different, and yet entirely the same. The curtains that hung, blocking out every ounce of natural light, were the ones his mom had painstakingly sewn the last time she'd redecorated the living room shortly before she'd gotten sick. Their deep purple was darker than her usual tastes, but of course, when she'd been alive, they'd hung open all the time, bathing the room in sunlight. The once-pristine beige carpet was now mottled with stains visible even in the near-dark, and the floral couches were faded and threadbare, remnants of unknown substances dotting their surfaces.

And there in the corner, in the chair where his mom had slept the last few months of her life, unable to get a good night's sleep in her regular bed, was his father. His eyes were half-hooded, and he glared murderously at Carter.

"What the hell do you want, boy?"

It'd been more than ten years since he'd seen his father

in the flesh, and deep down Carter had silently hoped that somehow his own appearance would have changed drastically enough in the time that he'd been gone that he'd be no longer recognizable to the man who'd given him half his DNA. But as he stared at his father, there was no denying the family resemblance, even if Robert Hayes had done nothing to keep up his appearances. His hair was too long, the dark, greasy strands hanging limply, his face unshaven in a haphazard way. His cheeks were gaunt, but his stomach protruded from his frame. Good to know he still subsisted on a diet almost entirely of alcohol.

"I'm here to make sure you're not dead."

"Why the hell would you care?"

Carter barked out a laugh at his dad's petulant tone. Did he *want* Carter to care about it? He had a funny way of showing it, if so. "I don't, but Becca does. And since she needs at least one of the men in her family to not be a complete asshole, I'm here checking up on you because she asked me to."

"And you managed to show up? I'm surprised you didn't just bail from town again instead."

Carter's anger simmered just below the surface, and he clenched his hands into fists at his sides. He'd fought the voice in his head his entire adult life. The one that constantly told him he wasn't good enough, wasn't smart enough, wasn't talented enough to make something of himself. He'd like to think he'd overcome that since he'd been gone, but it had been an uphill battle, his demons something he still had to contend with more often than he'd like. But he had no intention of standing here and letting his father's bitter comments get under his skin.

"Yeah, well, I almost missed the house, what with all the trash you've let pile up outside. I'm sure Mom would be thrilled to know that you turned her garden into a junkyard."

Rage swept over Robert's features, his face turning a mottled red. "You don't come into *my* house and talk about *my* dead wife, boy! You left, remember? You went off to your fancy school to get your fancy degree and go on to your fancy career, but it doesn't mean shit in the grand scheme of things. You're a Hayes, and you got more of me in your blood than you ever did your mother. Don't ever forget that."

Carter couldn't deny the truth of that. Couldn't deny the shimmer of unease over turning into his old man that always sat just under the surface. Had, in fact, been why he'd left and hadn't returned. "That may be so, but Mom would only be disappointed in one of us, and I'd venture to guess it's the one who's drunk before noon."

"What the hell do you know about it? You abandoned us after your mom died! You don't have a right to come in here and speak to me like that. Who do you think you are? Might be a fancy architect with a big office and a nice title, but deep down, you're nothing more than a man who walked away from his family. Couldn't handle the responsibility. Couldn't handle when times got tough, and you bailed." His dad took a heavy pull from his beer can, then swiped the back of his hand over his mouth. "So I might spend my days buried in a bottle, but at least *I* stuck around."

The words landed like a grenade in Carter's chest, the shrapnel striking every inch of his body until he was nothing but an open wound. The words weren't a surprise. They weren't untrue, either, which was why there was no reason for his chest to feel like it had caved in on itself. While his dad's delivery was callous and harsh, meant only to wound him, there was no denying the truth in his words. Carter *had* left. He'd abandoned his family when they'd needed him the most. And it didn't matter that he'd made a promise to his mom before she'd died. It didn't matter that Becca had sworn she'd be fine on her own. Had gone behind his back and accepted his offer of enrollment at UNLV.

All that mattered was, in the end, he'd left. His dad might have been worthless—the kind of man who couldn't even look after himself, let alone his kids— but there was one thing he had going for him that Carter didn't.

He'd never run away.

Chapter Seventeen

Abby couldn't stop smiling—hadn't been able to for days. Her goal of opening her preschool was in reach, and she could see the light at the end of the tunnel. She had friends who loved her and whom she loved. And though she knew she shouldn't weigh Carter in that, she couldn't help but do so. There was no question that his being in Heart's Hope Bay was a contributing factor to her increased happiness.

Even so, she knew it couldn't last—that it *wouldn't* last. She had no grand ideas that Carter would suddenly change his mind—the mind that he'd had set since...well, probably since before they'd even started dating the first time.

Now that she knew exactly what he'd run from, she couldn't blame him. And she also wasn't naive enough to think that what they had now—no matter how great it was—would be enough to make him stay.

She'd just finished cleaning up in the kitchen from dinner when there was a knock at the door. She couldn't keep the smile from her face as she strode toward the front, eager to see Carter again, even though she'd just seen him that morning at drop-off. They'd been spending nearly every night together, and though she knew it was going to hurt in the long run, she couldn't make herself stop.

Grinning, she swung open the front door and greeted him. "Hey."

"Hi." Carter's single-syllable greeting was cold and hard, no warmth to be found. A smile didn't touch his lips like it normally did when he saw her.

Her brows pinched in worry. "What's wrong?"

"Nothing." A sledgehammer hung at his side, and he lifted it over his shoulder as he stepped inside the entryway. "I'm gonna tear down those walls today."

"Oh," Abby said, not bothering to hide the surprise in her voice. "Okay."

Without another word, he strode into the house and up the steps, Abby following behind with what might as well have been a giant floating question mark over her head. What the hell had happened to make him so...angry?

By the time she'd made it upstairs, he was already in one of the rooms they'd designated to expand for the three-year-old classroom, the large X on the shared wall between the two rooms proclaiming its destiny. Without pause, Carter lifted the sledgehammer and swung. The sound of it hitting the wall jolted Abby, the vibration rattling her teeth. It was a good thing it was bingo night and her grandma was out with her girlfriends; otherwise she'd wonder what the hell all the noise was.

Not knowing what to do or how to help—both in terms of Carter *and* the project—she busied herself with paint colors and flooring samples on her phone. After a bit, Carter rested the sledgehammer at his feet and reached back to grip the neck of his shirt, yanking it off in one smooth motion. Before Abby could even tease him or comment on the view, he went right back to work, his aggression and frustration showing in the taut lines of his muscles, the rigid cut of his arms and shoulders.

She wanted to go up to him, press her hand against his glistening back and ask him what was wrong, because this was definitely not normal behavior. But she could tell by his stance, the determined set of his jaw, and the focused squint of his eyes that he wasn't ready to talk, so she let him be, her heart breaking a little bit more at every swing of the sledgehammer and every grunt that fell from his lips.

It could have been minutes or hours later when he finally let the sledgehammer fall to the floor, his breath coming in quick pants as he lifted his discarded shirt and wiped at his face.

"Carter..." Her voice was quiet, the plea low, but he heard it all the same.

He lifted his eyes to meet hers, and, for once, he allowed her to see what he worked so hard to hide. With his shields forgotten, his eyes vulnerable, she couldn't ignore the pull to him anymore.

She walked to him, stopping only once she stood in front of him. The heat poured from his body and enveloped her as she reached up to brush strands of hair away from his face. She trailed her fingers along his jaw as she tried to read in his eyes everything he wasn't saying. But at the touch of her fingers on his skin, his lids fluttered closed, shuttering the only avenue she had to read him.

"What's going on?" she finally asked, figuring there was no use in guessing. The possibilities of his frustration were so vast that she had no hope of winning the guessing game. Was it work? Was it his sister? Was it something she hadn't even thought of?

Carter shuddered out a sigh and shook his head. "Nothing you need to worry about."

Abby snapped her mouth shut, her jaw clenching in frustration. "*Yes*, something I need to worry about. If it makes you feel like this, I want to know what's causing it. I thought we were...friends," she said, stumbling over the words even though they were true. Even though she knew better than to hope for something more. Apparently her heart hadn't gotten that memo yet.

"We are," he said, his voice barely more than a whisper.

She tucked her fingers into the waistband of his jeans and tugged him toward her, the move causing his eyes to snap open. "Then tell me."

He studied her for long moments, and she didn't pull away, hoping whatever he read on her face was enough to reassure him that he could trust her with his secrets. Because now, after witnessing his reaction, there was no doubt this was something he wouldn't normally share.

He swallowed, the sound audible in the quiet space around them. "I saw my dad today."

Shock reverberated up Abby's spine, and her mouth fell open. *That*, she hadn't been expecting. "Is everything okay?" she asked tentatively, even though she knew it obviously wasn't.

Carter breathed out a humorless laugh and pressed his thumb and forefinger to his closed eyes. "Well, he's not dead if that's what you're wondering."

Abby's eyes grew wide as she stared at Carter, trying to read the intention behind his words. "Was that a possibility?"

He let his hand drop from his face. "That's why I went there in the first place. Becca hadn't been able to get ahold of him in a while, and she was worried. Since she still can't get around on uneven terrain, she asked me to go and check on him in her place."

Abby held her breath, waiting for the other shoe to

drop, to hear what Carter had found when he'd visited his dad. While her eternal optimism *hoped* that they'd reconciled, his demeanor tonight proved otherwise, and she knew better than to hope. "Were you there for long?"

"Just long enough for him to let me know what a worthless waste of space he thinks I am."

"Carter..." she murmured, her hand pressed against the heated skin of his stomach.

Though want and need still thrummed between them, an undeniable force that always simmered just beneath the surface, her focus remained squarely on him and the emotions he seemed to be fighting to keep contained.

"Did he say that to you?"

"Not in so many words."

Abby's chest ached for him. "Is that what it's always been like between you two?"

Carter opened his mouth as if to speak, but then paused and studied her for a quiet moment. She hoped he wasn't reconsidering opening up to her. Because while this was undoubtedly painful for him, she couldn't deny the comfort that shot through her, warmth pouring over her like a soft summer rain, that he was willingly sharing this part of himself with her for the first time...ever.

He must have seen something in her expression because he lifted a single shoulder in a shrug. "He was always kind of a jerk, even before Mom died. We just... clashed. Whatever I did wasn't good enough for him. I wasn't smart enough, wasn't strong enough, wasn't fast enough. I was never *enough* for him. But I dealt with it, you know? I figured it was just one of those unlucky breaks—the kind of kid who didn't get along with his parents... or *parent* anyway. But then after my mom died, things got worse. He went from being just a jerk to being unnecessarily cruel. I think it built him up to tear me down. And considering he blamed himself for my mom's death, he had a lot of building up to do."

Abby's eyes filled with tears when she heard the anguish in his voice and couldn't imagine what it'd been like for him as a teenager, to lose one parent and then have the other cut you down. To tell you, in no uncertain terms, that their life would be better if you weren't in it.

She swallowed down the hard lump in her throat, realizing she *did* know what that was like after all.

Her mother hadn't made it a secret that she'd never wanted Abby. It turned out she and Carter's foundations weren't all that different, but the way they dealt with them were. Where he ran, flying as fast and as far from this place as possible, she'd grown roots, cultivating relationships and searching for the one thing neither of them had had.

Carter cupped her face, his thumbs brushing away the tears that rolled unchecked down her cheeks. "Don't cry. I'm okay. I'm okay," he said, firmer the second time.

She closed her eyes and shook her head, gripping his forearms as he pressed his lips to her forehead, then each of her eyes, her cheeks, the corners of her mouth, before sucking her bottom lip between his. She should tell him that it wasn't just him who felt this. That he wasn't alone. He wasn't the only one who'd been dealt a shitty hand in the family department and that he had the ability to make different choices for himself. But that was what he'd done, wasn't it? He'd made different choices. Different than his father had made, definitely, but also the exact opposite of her own.

But she didn't want to think about that now. Not when his hands were so soft against her face, his tongue so sweet against hers.

"I'm all sweaty," he murmured against her lips, and even that small space between them was too much.

"Don't care." She tugged his face back to hers and captured his mouth again, inhaled his groan—*reveled* in it—as he reached down to grip her bottom and hauled her up against him. Instinctively, she wrapped her legs around his waist and didn't question if he could see well enough to get them across the second floor and up the staircase to her room. She didn't care because he seemed to be as desperate to get lost in her as she was with him.

That desperation didn't stop when he set her down—in her en suite bathroom, she realized—and impatiently stripped her until she stood bare before him. He let loose a low hum of male appreciation as he worked just as quickly to remove his own clothes. Then he was reaching for something in his pocket before stalking to her, his hand cupping her bare bottom as he nipped her lower lip, tugging it between his teeth.

Without turning his face from hers, he reached toward the shower, his movements clumsy in a way she wasn't used to seeing from him, and turned the water on. As it heated up, so did their kisses, the full force of their chemistry reducing her to nothing but want and desperation. She clung to him, running her fingers along his sinewy muscles, the tips of her breasts brushing against the soft, downy hairs on his chest in a way that made her throb with need.

On a panting breath, Carter pulled back only far enough to meet her eyes, his dark and hungry. "Are you with me?" he asked, his voice sandpaper rough.

Without hesitation, she answered, "Yes."

Did he mean here, now, physically? Yes, a thousand times. The evidence of just how much she was with him was plain enough as he dipped his fingers between her thighs, his answering groan telling her just exactly how obvious it was.

And anything else he could possibly mean with that question, her answer was a resounding yes as well. She'd tried to fool herself into believing whatever this was between them was casual. That she'd be satisfied with anything he could give her. That since she'd walked in with her eyes wide open, the inevitable fallout wouldn't hurt as much this time around.

The trouble was, though, that this wasn't casual at all. And, as he carried them into the shower, braced her against the tile wall, and slid inside her, their eyes locked and their panting breaths in sync, it was more obvious than ever before just how deeply in they both were.

Chapter Eighteen

Two weeks later, Abby hummed to herself as she put the finishing touches on her signature charcuterie board. Tonight, instead of spending the evening with Carter, she was having Gia and Savannah over for a much-needed girls' night. It had been far too long since the three of them had gotten together outside of work—weeks, actually. Not since they'd shopped for Gia's baby registry. And the guilt over not seeing her friends other than at the Sunshine Corner—especially Gia when she was having a rough acclimation to her pregnancy—was eating at her. Something she'd rectify tonight.

They'd already made arrangements that Savannah would take care of dessert, and Gia had promised her homemade guacamole and salsa. That meant Abby was on sustenance detail. She filled her board with meats and cheeses, nuts and dried fruit, plus a couple spreads and honeys to go with the crackers and crostini.

But even as she was looking forward to an evening with her girlfriends, her thoughts kept drifting back to Carter.

Since the night he'd shared about his father, they'd been spending even more time together, and she couldn't say she minded in the least. Usually, he stayed the night at her house, slipping out in the early morning hours before her grandmother had awoken. They'd both agreed it was better that way—the fewer questions to answer and noses in their business the better. A couple of times, she'd gone over to Becca's place to help Carter watch Sofia if Becca was working a late shift or had errands to run. On those evenings, Becca would insist on Abby staying over—for her "convenience," obviously—but the smirk on Becca's face always spoke of something much more scandalous than mere accommodation.

When Abby and Carter had been teenagers, she'd known what they had was special. But back then, she'd been naive and inexperienced—both in love *and* in life. Now she was old enough to realize what they had together was unique. It was all-consuming and raw, an ocean current pulling her under. And even though she could swim, she wasn't sure she wanted to.

But she knew what she had with Carter, however perfect it was, was temporary. Just a pit stop on the road trip to her final destination of lasting love like she craved.

And, well, if that thought left a pit in her stomach and made her ache even more with a yearning that was all too familiar, so be it.

Once she was satisfied with the presentation of the charcuterie board, she glanced at the clock on the stove. She still had about fifteen minutes before the girls arrived, so instead of continuing to obsess about Carter, she settled in at the table in the breakfast nook, intent on using this time to put a dent in her email dungeon.

She opened the email tab on her phone and started clicking away. Spam. Spam. Junk mail, junk mail, junk mail. She could probably save herself fifty emails a day if she'd just unsubscribe from these incessant emailers, but who knew when she'd need a 20 percent off coupon for Old Navy?

On autopilot, she clicked the check marks next to each message bound for the trash bin, and then froze when the name of a sender caught her eye, the subject line making her pause. Her heart leaped into her throat.

New requirements for preschool licensing and approval

Ignoring the sudden pit in her stomach, she opened the email and held her breath as she started to read.

Dear Ms. Engel,

I'm writing to inform you of a new mandate that's been put in place by the state. Effective August 1, all preschools are now required to become accredited in order to be recognized by the Oregon Board of Education and to be approved for a preschool designation. Our hope is that by providing you the information now, there will be ample time to make any adjustments needed in order to be approved to accept students for the upcoming school year.

We apologize for any inconvenience this may cause. Please feel free to reach out with any questions.

Sincerely,

Mary Graves

The lump in Abby's throat only grew, her eyes automatically welling with tears. *Ample time?* In what world was there ample time to get this completed? It was already April, and in order to meet the various requirement deadlines for location inspections and staff training, she'd set a renovation completion date of June 30. Even that was pushing it a little too close to the beginning of the school year for her comfort. It only gave her two weeks of cushion based on the state's forty-five-day turnaround time.

Now, not only did she have to do everything she'd planned to in order to open in the first place, but she also had to go through the rigorous process of accreditation on top of it. If she hadn't had a home to renovate in order to make the space workable for a preschool, this wouldn't have been the end of the world. But as it stood now? She did a quick calculation, recalling what she could of the accreditation requirements and timing, and realized she'd need to have the renovations done by the first of May in order to move forward.

That meant she had weeks.

With the amount of work still needed, she couldn't see how she could shave off any time on the projects, especially without a full-time contractor completing the work. She was already on borrowed time with Carter. She wasn't sure when exactly he planned to leave, but she knew it was soon. It had to be. The six weeks were well up. Hell, the eight weeks he'd mentioned as cushion time depending on Becca's needs were up, too.

Hadn't Abby just been thinking how her life felt like a dream? Like everything was finally clicking into place? And now this. That dream dissolved and faded around her, turning to ash at her feet.

She blanched at the idea of having to tell the long list of parents that she'd no longer be able to offer preschool programming for their children. What would they do?

This was a choice parents made months in advance—sometimes a year or more.

And the fundraiser. *God*. They'd raised all that money for her and the preschool, and now it'd probably be another year before she had anything to show for it.

The back door opened, and Abby started, jerking her head up from her phone to find Gia and Savannah strolling in, their arms laden with food. They laughed at something as they strode inside, the trio long since past knocking at any of their houses. Abby turned away and surreptitiously swiped at her eyes, hoping they weren't red-rimmed and blotchy.

"I should *never* be allowed in the grocery store when I'm hungry," Savannah said without prelude, placing two overflowing bags on the countertop. She reached in and quickly pulled out an array of desserts—brownies, cookies, ice cream…that lemon layer cake that Abby would nearly sell her soul for. Thank God for that, because if there was anything that could cheer her up, it was definitely dessert.

She stood from the table and walked over to help, grabbing a few of the containers from Gia as she juggled them.

"Thanks," she said, smiling at Abby. Then in response to Savannah, said, "That's how I feel all the freakin' time."

"I think that's how we all feel." Abby placed the salsa, guac, and chips Gia had brought on the round table in the breakfast nook, smiling as her friend arranged them how she wanted them before removing the lids.

"Maybe so, but are either of you banned from going? I'm not allowed at the grocery store anymore. Marco's taken over that duty, because if I go, I end up with half of aisle six in my cart and absolutely no fruits or vegetables. And, apparently, babies need nutrients."

Abby didn't know what it said about her that she knew exactly what aisle six was and exactly what it contained. It was the snack aisle in their tiny grocery store, the chips spreading along one side and cookies of all types on the other. "I think you can do some of aisle six as long as you throw in an apple or two."

"That baby's going to be just fine—contents of aisle six and all," Hilde said as she strolled down the back staircase. "But I'm happy to help you girls with this spread if you're worried about it too much."

Abby rolled her eyes at her grandma's shamelessness in crashing their girls' night. "I don't think any of us are worried about it, but we can probably share."

Hilde sniffed. "Well, if you insist."

All three girls laughed as Abby carried the charcu-terie board over to the table and set it next to Gia's contributions. She turned back toward Savannah and eyed the spread of treats. "Should I grab something to put those in?"

Savannah snorted and shook her head, her arms already full as she strode to the table and unloaded everything on the surface without an ounce of grace.

"We're about to plow through these. I don't think we need something as formal as servingware."

With a laugh, Abby joined her two best friends and her grandma at the table, realizing just how much she'd needed this. She'd been spending so much time on the renovation that it hadn't left room for much else. Not only had she let her friendships suffer, but also the push she'd done for the renovations was going to be all for nothing. It'd be at least a year now until she was up and running...until she was bringing in revenue to help fund the renovation costs the fundraiser hadn't touched. Funds she'd pulled from her savings account. Still, she couldn't regret the time she'd spent on it, because it had been time spent in Carter's company. And she knew all too well just how tenuous that was.

"I wish there was a charcuterie battle on the Food Network, because I have no doubt you'd win," Gia said as she popped a cube of cheese into her mouth. "Look at this! I don't even want to eat it, it's so pretty. I mean...I don't *want* to, but I'm definitely going to."

"She's not wrong." Savannah loaded up her plate before Gia playfully slapped her hand away.

"Hey, save a little for the starving pregnant lady over here, feeding herself and the elephant inside her."

Abby snorted, grateful she hadn't yet taken a sip of the wine her grandma had poured them. She stared at Gia as her friend laughed good-naturedly while Savannah teased her, the pregnancy glow definitely not a myth, her bronze skin luminescent.

"Do you think you can do one of these for my birthday party?" Hilde asked, popping a crostini topped with goat cheese and honey in her mouth.

Abby shrugged as she dipped a chip in Gia's unparalleled guacamole. "I can ask Ben. I'm sure he'll be okay with it, but we'll probably need to have the rest catered there since he's letting us use the space for free."

Hilde waved her hand, unconcerned. "We definitely need to. We'll need something heftier than finger food, especially if they're going to be serving the umbrella drinks. Ben said if Mable danced on the tables again, he'd have to kick us out. I don't want to be booted from a bar on my seventieth birthday." She paused, tilting her head as if to consider it, then shrugged. "Eh...Maybe that wouldn't be so bad."

"You're my role model, Hilde. I hope you know that," Savannah said with sincerity and adoration. "Except I feel like I'd be the Mabel of the group. I think we all know these two wouldn't be caught dead doing that."

Abby and Gia shared a look of solidarity. Savannah wasn't wrong. The two of them would be the ones wrangling a drunk Savannah from the rafters.

"You're definitely the wild one of the group," Abby said. "Speaking of, I don't think I ever asked if you went out midnight surfing with your brothers the night of the fundraiser."

"Ugh, yes."

Abby laughed, raising an eyebrow at Gia across the table, who merely shrugged in response. Good, at least it wasn't just Abby who wasn't aware of what'd happened. "Why the ugh? Didn't you have fun?"

Savannah huffed, swallowing down her bite before taking a sip of wine. "I did, but I would've had a lot more fun if Noah hadn't gone. I don't even know why he was there—besides to irritate the hell out of me, of course."

"I don't know..." Abby lifted a shoulder. "I thought it was nice of Caleb to ask him to go to the fundraiser in his place."

"Oh, please. He just did it to schmooze my parents and piss me off. It wasn't like you thought my brother could come up from San Francisco for a single night anyway. Besides, my other three doofuses were there. I'm *certain* you didn't need a fourth."

Abby met Gia's eyes over the rim of her wineglass and could hardly contain her smirk when she saw her friend's matching one. They'd both agreed Savannah's distaste of her brother's best friend was a classic case of *doth protest too much*. Although there was no denying the animosity evident between them—on both sides—there was also no denying just how volatile of an emotion hate could be, and how much Savannah stoked those fires, whether intentionally or not.

"He went out with you guys?" Gia asked.

"Yep, for the sole purpose of getting on my nerves and constantly reminding me why I shouldn't be out there. Honestly, if I had a dime for every time that man was condescending or judgmental toward me, I could fly—on my private jet—to Bali every weekend."

"Sounds to me like he's a good one for you to ignore, my dear," Hilde said, patting Savannah's hand. "Perhaps he's picking because he likes whatever attention he receives from you when he does. So I say stop giving it to him. A flame only grows bigger if you stoke the fire."

Savannah huffed out a disbelieving laugh and shook her head. "There's definitely none of that going on, but you're probably right. He just irritates me so damn much, it's hard to ignore."

"Well, you're probably going to want to get a jump start on that, because I can almost guarantee he'll be at my birthday party, what with him being Mabel's grandson and all. She's been trying to set him up with a nice woman ever since his ex-wife abandoned him and Rosie." Hilde shook her head and made a gruff sound of distaste. "Poor little girl..."

Savannah opened her mouth to say something, and from the look on her face, Abby knew it was going to be something to spotlight one of Noah's negative attributes and no doubt the cause for his ex-wife's departure.

Before Savannah could say a word, Abby said, "Speaking of your party, do you have a guest list for me? I need to get invitations out this week."

"A guest list?" Hilde's tinkling laugh filled up the room, completely infectious. "Honey, this is going to be a free-for-all. If all of Heart's Hope Bay shows up, it still won't be enough."

Abby smiled, having already known taking on this party was going to be another full-time job. But now, with the preschool accreditation—not to mention Carter's inevitable departure—looming, the distraction couldn't have come at a better time.

Chapter Nineteen

Carter was knee-deep in the adjustments for the Redmond project. Today he'd managed to subsist solely on coffee and leftover pizza straight out of the fridge, too distracted to even take two minutes to warm it up. His attention was laser focused, his to-do list a mile long, so when his phone rang, he barely managed to peel himself away from the task at hand to check it. Distractedly, he spared the screen a glance, and then did a double take at the name illuminated there.

He fumbled with his phone and swiped to answer before it clicked over to voice mail. "Mr. Franken, hi. How're you doing?"

"Mr. Hayes," Stuart Franken boomed on the other end of the line, the command in his voice unwavering even through the phone. "Rumor has it you're not in Vegas right now."

Carter didn't even try to guess at how the man knew that. Franken was a heavy hitter in Vegas and had more connections than Carter could even dream of, which was exactly why he'd been on Carter's short list for maiden projects with his own firm. "You heard right. I had a small family emergency that brought me back to my hometown in Oregon."

"I see," he said, thinly veiled disdain present in his tone. "And when do you think this 'family emergency' won't keep you out of Vegas any longer?"

It was clear from the way Franken asked the question that neither family *nor* emergencies dared to distract him from his work, and he expected the same from those who worked with him. That should've bothered Carter, but all he could focus on was that he couldn't remember the last time he'd thought about leaving even in passing. It was a question that should have been at the forefront of his mind, but something he'd let slip into his subconscious at some point while he'd been back.

With startling clarity, Carter realized Becca hadn't used her crutches in more than a week. Though she was still a little clumsy getting around with her boot, she *could* get around. And because of that, she no longer needed him there to help her with the day-to-day things that were too challenging to complete while using crutches.

He swallowed down his irritation—both at his sister for not mentioning her improving circumstances and at

himself for not seeking out answers in the first place—
and cleared his throat. "Very soon. I'm thinking I
should be back in Vegas by late next week."

Even saying the words had bile rising in his throat.
Where once he would have been thrilled to go back
to Vegas, a boulder now sat in his stomach over the
thought of leaving Heart's Hope Bay. In the two
months he'd been back in his hometown, he'd managed
to slip seamlessly once again into small-town life. A
life where he got to see his sister and niece every day.
Where he didn't have to be surprised at how much
Sofia had grown between their infrequent visits. Where
he could help Becca with the inconsequential but
difficult-to-deal-with situations that frequently arose
for a single mom.

And then there was Abby, his—at one time—once-
in-a-lifetime. Maybe *still* his once-in-a-lifetime.

"That's good to hear," Franken boomed. "Because
I'm just about ready to move forward with that project
we talked about last year. You're at the top of my list
for this one. I recall when we last spoke that you were
looking to branch out on your own..."

The unspoken words at the end of Franken's sentence
were enough to jolt some sense into Carter. This project
of Franken's was exactly the size and scale that could
put a firm on the map. One that could put *Carter's* firm
on the map.

This was an unheard of chance for a brand-new firm,
an opportunity that didn't come around every day. And

it had practically fallen in his lap. No, that wasn't true. In the years he'd been in Nevada, he'd put blood, sweat, and tears into cultivating relationships with the Vegas elite. He'd made a name for himself in the area with the jobs he'd completed, making sure the heavy hitters knew what kind of worker he was, how dedicated and creative and innovative he was. How *indispensable* he was.

Regardless of how the opportunity came to him, it *had* come. He'd be a fool to dismiss it, even if it meant he'd have to stamp a final date on his time in Heart's Hope Bay.

Ignoring the knot in his stomach, he said, "You recall correctly. Why don't we schedule a meeting when I'm back in town to discuss this further?"

"That's what I like to hear," Franken said, his smile coming through across the line.

After Carter threw out a few dates and the two of them settled on one before saying their goodbyes, it was all he could do to ignore the incessant voice in his head, reminding him of what Abby was to him... could still *be* to him.

He didn't know if it was luck or misfortune that had not one but *two* once-in-a-lifetimes presenting themselves to him at the same time. Two incongruent once-in-a-lifetimes, at that. It was a cruel twist of fate that he'd have to choose between the two of them. But he'd had his chance with Abby—their relationship had already run its course many years ago—and this... what they had now? It was just a bonus. What he had waiting for him in Vegas was exactly what he'd been striving toward his entire adult life. Because of that, the choice was a no-brainer.

Even still, he couldn't stop the voice in the back of his head warning him this was a bad decision...the tiny whisper that questioned whether or not he'd chosen the right one.

* * *

By the time Becca had gotten home from work, Carter's frustration had been simmering for hours. Never mind the fact that he was a fully grown man who was capable of seeking answers when he wanted them. The trouble was, he *hadn't* wanted them. Because of that, it was a hell of a lot easier to place blame for his preoccupation with his make-believe and completely temporary life here at Becca's feet than it was to take that responsibility on himself. Besides, if it was Becca's fault, that meant it didn't have anything to do with a certain redhead who'd managed to steal his heart not once but twice.

He waited only until Sofia was preoccupied with *Sid the Science Kid* before he stalked into the kitchen where Becca was preparing dinner. Keeping his voice hushed so as not to interrupt Sofia, he demanded, "Why the hell didn't you say anything when you swapped out your crutches for a boot?"

Becca twisted back to stare at him, her brow pinched in confusion. "What?"

Carter gestured to her ankle. "*Your boot.* You've been wearing it for at least a week, and you didn't say a damn word. You know I was only staying as long as you actually needed my help, and you clearly don't anymore. I have to get back to Vegas."

She opened and closed her mouth several times before shaking her head and tucking her dark hair behind her ear. "But I thought...You just seemed so happy here."

Carter barked out a humorless laugh. "I know you're not that naive. You can't honestly think a few weeks of happiness are enough to totally rewrite my plans."

She rolled her eyes. "And I know you're not that dramatic. You're a single guy who has no ties to Vegas. Your family is here."

"And I have absolutely zero interest in seeing a third of those people ever again."

Becca braced herself on the counter as she crossed her arms over her chest. "Yes, Carter, I know you hate Dad. But what about me and Sofia? She's going to be changing so much in the coming years...Do you really want to miss that?"

"Oh, come on, Becks. Don't guilt me into this. That's low, and you know it."

She held up her hands in surrender. "Fine, take us out of it completely. What about Abby? What about

Marco? He's been begging you for ten years to work with him, so you've already got a job waiting."

"Yeah, I've got a *job* waiting," Carter said through his teeth, his anger and frustration getting the better of him. "I want more than just a job. That's what I've been working toward—my own firm. You know that's something I can't have here."

"And is this arbitrary goal worth your happiness?"

"Who says I'm not happy in Vegas?"

Her only response was to raise a single eyebrow as she continued to stare at him.

Carter scrubbed a hand down his face and blew out a long-suffering sigh. "Look, I get it. I'd love to be closer to you and Sofia." So long as that *closer* didn't happen to be in the one town he couldn't get away from fast enough. "But that's not in the cards right now. You know this has been my plan for years. I'm not just going to throw it away."

"But you're willing to throw everything else away? Everything that's here waiting for you?" She sighed, shaking her head. "Look, I just want you to ask yourself one thing and then I'll leave it alone. Deal?"

He gestured for her to get on with it already.

"Is owning your own firm in Vegas truly what you want? Or is it a spiteful response to all the bullshit Dad says to you?"

He opened his mouth to respond, but his words were caught in his throat. *Was* he doing this just to spite his father?

No. Absolutely not... This was what he wanted. The spiting part was just a bonus as far as he was concerned. But even if he was, so what? It didn't matter. It wouldn't change the fact that Carter still felt claustrophobic here like he had when he'd lived at home with his father. Heart's Hope Bay and the well-meaning people in his life would always suffocate him in a way that made him itch to flee. Wouldn't they?

Whether or not he had a job waiting for him here... whether or not his sister and niece were here... whether or not the woman he'd come to love yet again—or maybe still?—was here, he couldn't be. It was as simple and as complicated as that.

Clearing the emotion from his voice, he said, "I'll stick around till your checkup, but don't expect me here past next week. Tonight, I'm booking my ticket home."

He ignored how that single word—*home*—felt all wrong on his tongue. Ignored how his heart screamed at him that another place had taken over that moniker. He had no idea if he was doing the right thing, but he did what he'd done since he'd left the first time. He relied heavily on his goals to guide him through to the next phase in his life. Without them, without any direction at all, he was no better than what his dad had accused him of being—just a failure of a man who'd abandoned his family. And if he didn't succeed in the goal he'd set for himself, what had it all been for? Just so he could come crawling back and end up in exactly the same place he'd started in? If that happened, who knew how long it'd be before he turned into his father. Before he resented the people in his life and lashed out at them because of it.

He couldn't do it. He *wouldn't*. From the minute he'd received the call from Becca that she'd been in an accident, his plan had been to stay only as long as she needed him and then get back to his regular life. And that was exactly what he intended to do.

Chapter Twenty

✺

"It's starting to look pretty good here," Carter said as he drilled in the last piece of drywall for the room, finishing the portion of what would no doubt be a multistep process, just like all of them seemed to be.

Abby breathed out a laugh and looked around. Maybe to a professional's eye, it was starting to appear near complete. But to her untrained eyes, all she saw was unfinished walls, missing trim, faded and scratched hardwood floors that still needed to be refinished, and about a thousand other tiny things she couldn't even begin to think about lest she break down and start crying right there in front of Carter.

She'd had a couple days to let the inevitability of the email settle. But even with the days' padding, the predetermined outcome of her preschool still stung. A pit in her stomach had been her constant companion since she'd opened the message, and she didn't foresee that disappearing anytime soon. And even though she worried the work they were putting in now would be all for nothing, she still had to try. Which was why she'd agreed when Carter said he could come over tonight to work on the space.

This week, their schedules hadn't meshed very well, and they'd once again gone back to spending their nights apart. She didn't know what was going on on his end, and she was too scared to ask, afraid he'd put voice to her worries that his time in Heart's Hope Bay was up and he was leaving soon. After the blow regarding the new preschool requirements, she wasn't sure she could handle another one right now.

"If you say so," she mumbled, unable to put any of her normal cheer in her voice. She'd been faking it for days, too raw inside to have sought out advice over the situation she found herself in, and she was exhausted.

Carter slid his eyes to her, cocking his head to the side and studying her. After a moment, he said, "It's already pretty late, so I'll start mudding the drywall tomorrow."

Before she could answer one way or another, he swore under his breath. "I can't tomorrow. Sofia has a dance recital, so I'll be busy with that. But how about the day after tomorrow?"

Abby swallowed down her disappointment. After all, what was another day when she was already going to miss the deadline? "Okay. And then we can start painting?"

Carter chuckled quietly and shook his head as he packed up his tools. "No, not for a while yet. The drywall mud needs to cure for at least twenty-four hours between each coat, and I'd like to put three coats on."

Her shoulders slumped. The days just kept racking up, extending her already challenging timeline. "And how much longer do you think after that?"

He shrugged and glanced around the space, surveying it. "You're probably about halfway done."

The words hit Abby like a brick, expelling all the air in her lungs. "Half... *halfway*?"

Carter seemed to finally register the note of panic in her voice, because he came over and cupped her shoulders, brushing his hands up and down her arms. "Hey, it's not that bad. Halfway will put you at five or six weeks to go, give or take." He cringed, seeming to realize something. "At least, if you're able to hire somebody else to come help you out. I wish I could stick around to see the finished product."

His comment was like a bucket of ice water dumped over her head. Of course she'd known all along he wasn't going to be there when the preschool was finished, but somehow, in the weeks he'd been helping her, she'd managed to delude herself into concocting a fantasy that differed from reality. But he'd just set her straight about that.

She couldn't think of anything to say. And even if

she could, she wasn't sure any sound would actually come out. So she pasted on what she knew was a tense smile and stepped out of Carter's grasp. He was leaving—he hadn't told her when, but she knew now it'd be sometime very soon—and she needed to get back to how it used to be since she wasn't going to have him to turn to.

He cleared his throat, no doubt picking up on the sudden tension in the room, and seemed to force out a laugh, an obvious attempt to change the subject and lighten the mood. "Marco's sure been worked up lately."

Only half listening, she put all of her attention into the paint samples spread out before her so she wouldn't cry. "Oh yeah, he's got a project he's working on?"

Carter snorted. "No, I mean, he seems to be nearly as obsessed with preparations for the baby as Gia is."

By the lighthearted tone of Carter's words, Abby could tell he'd meant it to be humorous...playful. But what was funny about starting a family? About being there for your wife when she was having a tough time going through something neither of them had anticipated or experienced before?

Abby glanced at him over her shoulder, her brow furrowed and her head cocked. "Why wouldn't he be?"

Carter slipped a hand in his front jeans pocket and lifted a single shoulder in a shrug. "Well, you know..."

She turned around to face him completely, her arms crossed. "No, I don't. Please elaborate."

He glanced to the side before meeting her eyes again. "I just mean he's supposed to be a career guy... like me."

There was too much to unpack in that single sentence, and she didn't know where to start, the heaviness of unspoken words seeming to hang in the air between them. "What does having a career have to do with having a family? They're not mutually exclusive."

"To me they are. My career is my life." Seeming to resign himself, Carter blew out a deep sigh and lifted his hands before dropping them back to his sides. "I don't want to get married. Or have kids."

Abby froze, her heart in her throat. While they'd never specifically had this discussion before—after all, what teenager did?—she'd assumed they were moving from casual to something more. She hadn't hidden her desire for a family, even back then. And all that time, while she was waxing on about the family life she'd desired, he was sitting back...in judgment? In distaste?

What he wanted—or didn't want—shouldn't have any bearing on her. Carter wasn't sticking around, and she knew that. But there was still a tiny part of her that had been hoping, and that flicker of light was snuffed out completely at his words.

After several tense, silent moments, he said, "Come on, Abby. You're not really that surprised, are you? I mean, I haven't exactly had a picture-perfect family life. Look at how well it turned out for my dad."

She shook her head, still speechless...completely unsure what to say. Abby didn't know Carter's dad, not really. But she knew *Carter*, and he was a good man. He was responsible and caring...hardworking and loyal and loving. Doting to his niece. There wasn't a single doubt in her mind that he'd make not only a great husband but also a great father.

"Besides," Carter said, "things are going to start rolling as soon as I get back to Vegas, and I won't have time for any of that anyway."

The cold detachment in his voice shook Abby out of her stupor, and her frustration amped up. Was him not wanting a family a new development? But that didn't make sense...Not when he'd cited his dad as the reason family life wasn't for him, and Abby now knew those two had had problems since she and Carter had been dating the first time.

"Is that...is that why you broke up with me after graduation?" she asked, her voice wavering the tiniest bit. She swallowed and cleared her throat, steeling herself to ask what needed to be asked. "You told me it was because we wouldn't be able to make the long-distance thing work, but that wasn't it at all, was it? You bailed because you couldn't handle what I wanted." Abby didn't even attempt to tame the accusation, too hurt to do anything but hurl the words at him.

He snapped his mouth shut, the muscles in his jaw

tight and bunched. "I can handle it just fine. I just don't want to."

She breathed out a humorless laugh and shook her head. "You're not the man I thought you were. Instead of facing your demons head-on, you run away every time, just like your dad said you do."

It might have been the cruelest thing Abby had ever said, and she regretted the words as soon as they were out of her mouth. Wanted to catch them in the air and stuff them back inside, but life didn't work like that. Words were powerful, beautiful, sometimes cruel things. And they did exactly what she feared they would—it was gasoline on the sparks between them, igniting into an inferno.

"Not all of us have been obsessed with having a family since we were *three*, Abby," he snapped, his voice cold and harsh. Something she'd never heard from him before. "You never shied away from telling me that. You also never *once* asked what I wanted—you just assumed—so don't pretend like this is all on me."

She opened her mouth to deny it, but she couldn't. He was right—she hadn't ever asked him if the life she wanted was something he did as well...hadn't discussed what he saw for his future. She'd been too focused on her own.

Even if she could have responded, he didn't give her a chance to. "What was I supposed to do? Put all my dreams aside because of what you wanted? Stay here in this tiny town and turn into the lowlife deadbeat my dad always said I'd be? Get stuck here just like him? Marriage and kids aren't the answer to everything. Do you honestly think that will make up for the fact that you're all alone in the world except for Hilde?"

Getting hit by a bus would've been less painful. She exhaled sharply, drawing her hand to her abdomen as if that would help the ache blooming there. It was one thing for him to have lied by omission regarding what he did—or didn't—want, but to have him betray her like this...to have him toss back her worst insecurity—the one thing he *knew* she felt troubled by—was callous. Beyond what she'd thought Carter capable of.

Fighting to steady her voice, she said, "And what about you?"

"What about me?"

"Do you honestly think that a fancy job will keep you warm at night? Will it bring you soup when you're sick or send you birthday cards? Will this *amazing* career grow old with you?"

"You're still not listening to me!" he yelled. "I never once said I wanted those things. That's all you, Abby. I'm perfectly happy without them."

Without *you*, he might as well have said.

She laughed bitterly. "Oh please. Can you tell me even one single person whose greatest dream in life was solely to *work*? What about retirement? What will you do then, all by yourself? After you've wasted your life away doing nothing but striving toward goal after goal? Or do you plan to work until the day you die? Quite the American dream. You'll sure show your dad then."

He stared at her for a long moment, the anger and frustration clear on his face. But beneath it was the underlying hurt he was trying hard to hide. "You don't know what you're talking about."

And then, without another word, he grabbed his tools and stormed past her and down the steps, the front door slamming in his wake only moments later.

Not bothering to hold back her tears any longer, she slid down the wall until her butt hit the floor and rested her forehead on her bent knees, crying harder than she could remember. Through her tears, everything she'd been holding inside poured out of her. How she was letting down the parents of her preschoolers. Letting down the friends and employees who counted on the Sunshine Corner for their living. Then the barbs Carter had thrown at her repeated in her mind, over and over again until they were all she could hear.

What he'd said was cruel and unnecessary, harsh words hurled when he'd been backed into a corner, but she couldn't say they weren't true. The reason she wanted a family was precisely because of the one she'd never had. She was just as bad as he was, too focused on a goal to let anything else get in her way.

Perhaps it wasn't the men of Heart's Hope Bay who were the duds. Maybe she'd driven them all away with her tunnel vision, too fixated on what she wanted to even consider someone else's needs. No wonder she hadn't found someone to share her life with. It was the cruelest twist of fate—that her overwhelming focus on the one thing she wanted could be the exact reason she wasn't getting it.

Chapter Twenty-One

Abby had thought that her one great heartbreak had been the first time she and Carter had broken up back in high school, but now...this? It superseded prior events without comparison. And the ironic thing was, this time, they hadn't even been a couple.

She felt so stupid, so naive and childish that she'd concocted this fantasy life in her head. One created with a man who apparently never wanted to be there in the first place.

It was their weekly art day, so everyone was at the Sunshine Corner. Gia, Jenn, and Savannah had all been staring at Abby with some form of concern nearly the entire day. Even Ollie had gotten in on the action, sticking close to Abby's side as if he could sense her sadness. She hadn't wanted to spill about what happened with Carter, but she hadn't needed to.

Savannah had taken one look at her that morning, and she'd known something was wrong. She'd breezed into the house before dawn, like always, had taken one look at Abby, and narrowed her eyes while demanding, "What the hell did he do?" without so much as a hello.

Abby had merely shook her head, because she knew if she detailed the events of last night, she'd start crying all over again. And, though she should've been all cried out after the night she'd had, that wasn't the case. She didn't want to tempt fate. Besides, red-rimmed eyes and tear-streaked, blotchy cheeks weren't exactly the face of a business called the Sunshine Corner, so she figured it would be prudent to keep a lid on it.

Even so, Savannah had persisted the rest of the day. Had, in fact, coerced both Gia and Jenn to get in on the action as well, each of them trying to make her spill with subtle questions meant to get her talking. Abby had held strong all day, but now as the evening was wearing on, their six o'clock closing time ticking closer and closer, her resolve was crumbling. The only kids left were the Jensen twins, and once they were gone, there'd be nothing for Abby to hide behind.

"It'd be better to just get it over with and tell me now. You know, while there are witnesses, since I won't fly off in a rage and go after him if I have to take care of these kids," Savannah said, her tone far too casual for homicidal rage.

Abby didn't know if it was the long day, or the way

her friends all looked on with concern that made her realize Carter had at least been wrong in one thing last night—she wasn't all alone, save for her grandma. She had these amazing women in her life, who felt like family to her. Who cared about her and had her back, every day, without question or hesitation. Women she could count on to support her and to hold her up when it felt like she could barely stand on her own.

Because of that, her walls crumpled, along with her shoulders, the words flooding past the dam she'd erected to keep them locked inside. "I don't know where to start…"

Savannah spun around and dropped to the floor, scooting close to Abby's side. "Start at the beginning. Was it something he said?"

Abby looked down as she petted Ollie's head where it rested gently in her lap as she sat on the floor. "Kind of… Carter was poking fun at Marco—"

"He *what*," Gia interrupted, her once worried expression transforming into anger in a split second. Those pregnancy hormones were no joke.

Glancing up, Abby shook her head. "He wasn't doing it to be mean. He just… he said that he thought Marco was a career guy like him."

"What does that mean?" Jenn asked, her brow furrowed.

"It means he thinks everyone is an emotionless ass." Savannah barely managed to muffle the last word in deference to the three-year-old ears across the room.

Abby swallowed down her nerves and continued petting Ollie, unable to meet any of her friends' concerned stares. "He told me he's never wanted to get married or have kids."

She looked up in time to see the three other women exchanging glances, and Abby's cheeks heated, her embarrassment over that confession nearly overwhelming. God, she was a *fool*, and now she wasn't even a fool in private.

"And you thought that was in the future for you guys?" The quiet but confused question from Gia only made Abby's cheeks flame hotter.

Hearing it come from her friend just reinforced how stupid it was that she'd thought it in the first place. After all, only someone who was so laser focused on having a family would start planning one with a man who wasn't even sticking around. With a man who didn't want it in the first place.

"I know it's dumb," Abby said, "and I feel like an idiot for it. I feel so *stupid*. Especially when he's apparently never wanted it. I was fine with casual, until I wasn't. And I guess I just assumed he was feeling the same way. And you know what the first three letters of *assume* are.... God, I'm so stupid." She couldn't bring herself to tell them what he'd thrown in her face last night—that she'd never even asked—too ashamed to do so. "Do you know how many guys I sent away because I held them up to his standard? And he never wanted me in the first place."

"That's not true," Savannah said firmly. "He may be a lot of things—like a selfish prick—but there's no mistaking that he wanted you, Abby. Then and now." She wrapped an arm around Abby's shoulders and tucked her into her side.

Abby shrugged. "Maybe. But it doesn't matter. He's leaving anyway, and I was an idiot for pretending otherwise. I just let it get me down, especially on top of everything else."

"What do you mean?" Gia asked. "What else?"

Abby pressed her lips together and shook her head. She hadn't meant to let that slip. She thought she'd have a bit more time...could stretch it out, at least until she figured out what to say to her friends, but it was no use keeping it a secret any longer. After all, they'd find out soon enough anyway. "I got an email last week from the state."

"Okay...," Jenn said, dragging the word out in a clear question as all three of them stared at Abby, their brows drawn in confusion.

Abby swallowed down her nerves and closed her eyes, unable to watch the looks of disappointment, frustration, and hurt that would no doubt cross her friends' faces. "They changed the requirements for preschools. Before we can receive a preschool designation and begin accepting students, we have to be accredited now. And with the renovations that still need to be done, it's not going to happen. There's no way we can open on time." She opened her eyes to the stunned faces of her friends. "We'd have to have a dedicated full-time contractor, probably a team of people. And, even with the fundraiser, I don't have the money for that. Even if I did, I already know the two contractors in town are booking out for months."

Saying it aloud made it all real, and Abby couldn't stop her tears from falling, forgoing the composure she'd been working hard to maintain. She'd goaded Carter last night about his plans and goals, how they ruled his life, but she'd been living her life by those same principles. The only difference was that their outcomes were incongruent. She wanted a family, both a family she created with someone she loved and her family at the Sunshine Corner. And now it felt like both goals had been shredded, ripped up into a million tiny pieces, unable to be put back together again.

Savannah made a gruff noise of commiseration in her throat and hugged Abby tighter, whispering under her breath all the things she'd do, not only to Carter, but also to the State Board of Education. Her words were hushed so as not to carry to the two children still in the space, but they rang out loud and clear for Abby.

She closed her eyes and finally allowed herself to truly break, and to do so surrounded by the comfort of her friends. She felt Gia's arms come around her, too, and then she was engulfed in honeysuckle—Jenn's preferred scent—suddenly surrounded by the family she'd made for herself. Not the one she'd spent her whole life wanting, but the one she needed the most when it counted. While they rocked her and held her tight, she let herself cry for the other family she wasn't sure she'd ever have.

The scene was so reminiscent of the first time Carter had broken her heart—except now Abby had two additional people there to support her and hold her up—that the embarrassment she'd felt earlier reared its head once again. How had she allowed this to happen to her, not once, but twice?

"It'll all be fine, Abby. We'll figure out something. Maybe..." But Savannah didn't continue, clearly out of ideas, much like Abby had been.

"Maybe Burt would like an exclusively commissioned painting of his family?" Gia said. "I could use that to sweet-talk him into shuffling you to the front of his commitments."

Abby took the tissue Jenn offered her and dabbed at her eyes as Ollie gave her a kiss on her arm. "Burt's getting a divorce, remember? And as amazing as your paintings are, I don't think he'd work at cost for one."

"Look, even if it takes another year, that's okay. We'll still be here. And the parents who put their kids' names down..." Savannah trailed off, seeming to realize what Abby had during one of her many solo brainstorming sessions—that at least half of the parents who put their kids' names down wouldn't *have* kids in preschool next year. Savannah waved a hand in front of her face. "Whatever. We'll find more parents. You *know* this is *the* place in Heart's Hope Bay to go.

This is where parents want to send their kids because it's the best."

Abby hoped Savannah was right. It was true that they always had kids on their waiting list, parents hoping something would happen to cause a slot to open up, so maybe they wouldn't have any issue filling those spots whenever they were able to open.

"And I *hate* Carter for doing this to you in the same week," Savannah said. "He's a complete ass. But you have us. And we're better than a stinky boy anyway, aren't we? Except for Ollie, of course." Savannah cooed at the dog, bending to press their heads together and scratching under his chin. She received a lick on the nose for her efforts.

Through her tears, Abby forced out a chuckle and nodded, even if it felt all wrong. She loved her friends, loved that they'd pulled together to support her when she needed it, but... she loved Carter, too. There was no more denying that, and that only made her tears fall faster.

Vaguely, she registered the doorbell ringing and Jenn shuffling the two remaining kids out to the front, leaving her, Savannah, and Gia huddled together as Abby cried.

She didn't know how long the four of them sat there, Gia's and Savannah's arms around her with Jenn's hand resting on Abby's knee right next to Ollie. They whispered words of encouragement interspersed with rants about what a jerk Carter was and the nerve of those people at the state. None of it seemed to help as much as just knowing she had these women to lean on when she needed the support.

Sometime later, Hilde came into the great room to find the four of them huddled together, and she rushed over, hands hovering in midair. "What's going on here? What's wrong?"

Abby just shook her head, unable to bring herself to tell the whole story again, too exhausted to relive it so soon after she'd spilled her guts the first time. Instead, Savannah gave Hilde a very condensed version of the events, tossing in some colorful swear words to liven up the retelling.

Once Savannah had finished, Hilde huffed and held out another tissue for Abby, a scowl on her face. "It sounds like you've had one hell of a week, honey. I can't do much about that email or those ridiculous new requirements, but I *can* do something about Carter, especially since this is all my fault."

"Grandma," Abby said. "How is this all your fault?"

"If I hadn't done that love spell for you after your last blind date, none of this would've happened."

Abby smiled and shook her head. "I think this was inevitable with or without your full-moon ritual."

"Well…" Hilde sniffed and crossed her arms. "I'll be damned if I give that boy a single slice of cake if he has the nerve to show up at my birthday party."

For the first time in days, Abby genuinely laughed. Yes, it was laughter through her tears, but sometimes baby steps were good enough after the week she'd had.

Chapter Twenty-Two

✸

Abby had never been more grateful for her grandma still wanting to celebrate every birthday, even at seventy, than she was this particular year because it meant she had something to focus on besides all the turmoil in her life.

A week had passed since she'd last seen Carter, almost two since she'd gotten the email from the state, and she was no better off now than she'd been in the first place. She still had no answers as to what she'd do for the preschool. And since her and Carter's fight, he hadn't been back to help with anything. Luckily, Google was on her side... and so were her friends. They'd stayed late nearly every night, working to finish the drywall. The walls may not have been as clean or as seamless as a professional would have done it, but at this point in time, Abby didn't have many options left, so she certainly wasn't going to be picky.

Once again, the town of Heart's Hope Bay showed up at Last Call for one of the Engel girls. But this time, the only money they were asked to give was in the form of buying umbrella drinks for Hilde.

Across the bar, her grandma laughed uproariously, clapping her hands in delight as a scantily clad man performed a singing telegram for her and the Bridge Bunch. Abby didn't need two guesses to figure out who had arranged that. Mabel had always been the trouble-maker of the group.

She couldn't help but grin in response to her grandma's joy, thrilled to see her thoroughly enjoying herself and relieved that her own smiles had been coming a little easier every day, one currently stretched across her mouth. Her grandma seemed to be having a fabulous time—at least when she wasn't scowling at Carter from across the room.

Abby had no idea what would possess him to show up at the event tonight when he hadn't even been dropping off or picking up Sofia from the Sun-shine Corner, but she couldn't concern herself with it tonight. She was busy making sure the hors d'oeuvres were continually stocked and that everyone was having a good time…most of all, her grandma. And well, if her grandma wanted to give Carter the stink eye every other minute, who was she to stop her?

"Oh, thank God you're free," Savannah said in

obvious relief as she gripped Abby's arm. "I promised Gia I'd stick to her side tonight, but the group she's hanging out with is talking about nothing but babies. How much they pee, how much they poop, what color it is and what the different colors mean…"

"You're really selling me on this," Abby said dryly.

"I don't have to sell you on it."

"No? You thought you'd just drag me into this fun time?"

"Best friends suffer for each other," Savannah said matter-of-factly, and Abby couldn't help but laugh.

She hadn't had a chance to say hi to Marco or Gia since the party had started, so she allowed Savannah to lead her by the arm to where the group stood in a loose circle, laughter ringing out.

"Seriously, though. Breastfeeding poops are the *worst*." Susie, who'd graduated a year ahead of Abby and Savannah, laughed. She cocked her head and studied Gia. "You *are* going to breastfeed, aren't you? You know it's best for the baby."

Abby snapped her teeth shut so loud, Savannah must have heard it, as she gave her a look out of the corner of her eye. Abby ignored her, instead focusing all her efforts on keeping her mouth shut. This wasn't her circus or her monkeys. She wasn't a mom—didn't know if she'd ever *be* a mom. But she did know kids, and she did know women. And she knew that no matter how that baby got fed, as long as it was fed, it was going to be just fine. She'd never noticed until Gia had gotten pregnant just how judgmental and catty other moms could be. Abby was tired of it, so she couldn't imagine what Gia felt. But this was Gia's battle, and Abby didn't want to presume to talk for her friend, so she kept quiet.

Savannah, on the other hand, had no such qualms. "I'm not really sure why that's any of your business, Susie," she said in a saccharin voice, blinking innocently as she cocked her head.

The other woman sputtered and held up a hand to her chest in mock offense. "Well, excuse me. I was just curious."

Gia shot Savannah a grateful smile before turning her attention back to Susie. She opened her mouth to speak, but Marco cut in before she got a word out.

"Actually, we're going to do a combination breast and bottle, so I can help out in the middle of the night." He slung an arm around Gia's shoulders and tucked her into his side, glancing down at her with a fond smile. "I don't want her to have to do it all on her own."

Abby cringed internally, hoping beyond everything that Gia had taken her advice and talked with Marco about this. But from the slow, calculated way Gia turned her head to face her husband, quiet fury lurking just under the surface, Abby knew that was a futile hope.

With a fake smile plastered on her face, Gia said, "Oh, we decided that, did we?"

Marco seemed to pick up on the tension in his wife's voice at the same time as everyone else around the circle. Without a word, the group dispersed as subtly as possible, but Abby and Savannah stayed, flanking Gia as she stood off against Marco. Abby was only distantly aware that Carter had come up at some point and now stood behind Marco, his brows drawn down as he watched the scene unfold.

"Seriously? We're discussing this *again*?" Marco said. "I thought we hashed this out the last time we were here."

"Just because we stopped talking about it does *not* mean we hashed it out. Unless, of course, you're fine with the decision that *I've* made, which is to breastfeed exclusively."

Marco groaned and ran his fingers through his hair. "Why would you do that? All I want to do is help. I don't want you to be exhausted. And from everything I've read, you could spend more than half your day just feeding the baby! They typically breastfeed every two hours, and that's from beginning to beginning, so who knows how much time you'll actually have to sleep. If we give the baby a bottle too—"

"I assume," Gia cut in, "if you're so well read, that you'll know if we give the baby a bottle too early, they could develop nipple confusion. Is that what you want? Do you want the baby to not take my nipple?"

Well, this was swiftly moving into uncomfortable territory. Abby exchanged a look with Savannah, the other woman's eyebrows raised as if to say shit was getting real. If Abby was at all concerned with paying

Carter any attention, she would have glanced his way to see what his reaction was to this conversation. Since she couldn't possibly care less, she forced herself to stay focused on the couple, only vaguely aware of Carter's stiff shoulders.

Marco reached for Gia's hand. "Are you seriously talking about your nipples in the middle of Last Call in front of every resident of Heart's Hope Bay?"

Gia jerked her hand out of Marco's grasp. "*That's* what you're worried about? We're discussing something serious about our baby, and you're worried about people hearing that I have nipples? *Newsflash*," she yelled to the room, "I have nipples!"

Okay, maybe it was time for Abby to step in. She had no problems cutting off her friends when they'd had a few too many drinks, and this was no different. Gia had just been shot with pregnancy hormones instead of liquor. "Do you think—"

"Oh, that's great. That's very mature, Gia," Marco said, his voice hushed. "You act like I'm saying I want to give the baby a sippy cup of milk on the first day. All I'm suggesting is that you pump and let me supplement with a middle-of-the-night bottle."

"And all I'm asking for is that you trust me and the research I've done on this. I don't want to introduce a bottle too early on."

"Yeah, well, I want to have some bonding time with my kid. Is that so wrong? You're being ridiculous again."

Gia stood perfectly still for three seconds, her gaze never wavering from Marco's, and then she spun on her heel and stormed out of the bar without sparing Marco a backward glance. He groaned and jogged after her, not paying them any attention.

Abby turned to Savannah. "I'm gonna check and make sure she's okay. Can you just…" Abby gestured around the space.

With a nod, Savannah said, "Yeah, go ahead. I'll make sure everything runs smooth. Give her a hug for me."

Abby strode after her friend with a single-minded focus to make sure she was okay. Which was the only logical reason she didn't realize Carter had joined her until suddenly the door opened in front of her. He stood next to her, his arm outstretched over her head as he held the door open for her.

She jerked her gaze away from his, not wanting to get snared by his eyes. "Thank you," she said stiffly, and strode outside. The streetlights had just come on, the fading sun casting a soft glow over the nearly full parking lot.

Her rushing was all for naught as Abby watched Marco and Gia both climb into their separate cars, Gia having driven over straight from work. Their departures were quiet. No roar of engines or squealing tires. But she knew there might as well have been for what was no doubt awaiting the couple when they arrived at home.

Abby blew out a long breath and tucked her hair behind her ear, wanting desperately to turn around and stroll straight back into Last Call but also knowing that was the childish way out. Regardless of any lingering embarrassment she still felt, she didn't want Carter to leave again—maybe for another ten years—with their last conversation having been a fight.

He cleared his throat, and she braced herself before turning to look at him. He stood there, his elbow bent and hand cupping the back of his neck, as he studied her out of the corner of his eye, looking delicious and a little bit ragged at the same time. Good, it wasn't just her, then. "Think they've got us beat on the fight?"

A smile quirked up the side of her mouth. "Maybe if we were scoring solely on awkward points."

With a laugh, he shook his head and dropped his hand, tucking it into the front pocket of his jeans. "I never thought I'd have to say this, but I don't ever want to hear Gia talk about her nipples again."

Abby's shoulders loosened from the stiff posture she'd been holding, and she laughed along with him. "I'm pretty sure everyone in Last Call would say the same thing. And if I know Gia, she's going to be completely mortified tomorrow."

"Yeah, well...sometimes stupid things are said in the heat of the moment that you wish you could take back."

She met his eyes in the fading light of the setting

sun and read the sincerity in his gaze. "I may also be familiar with that..."

He blew out a deep breath and turned to face her fully. "I know this probably isn't the best time since it's your grandma's birthday party, but I was hoping we could talk."

Her stomach soared and plummeted at once, hope and dread clashing inside her. But instead of running away, she metaphorically pulled up her big girl pants and nodded, steeling herself for what was to come.

Chapter Twenty-Three

Carter hadn't realized just how much tension he'd been holding over the past week until Abby had agreed to talk. A talk that would be bittersweet at best. But even though none of the circumstances surrounding their fight had changed, that didn't mean he wanted to leave on bad terms. He'd spent the past ten years completely cut off from someone who'd once been his best friend. He didn't want to spend the next ten facing the same fate.

After watching Gia and Marco drive off, he and Abby had stayed at Last Call for another half hour, letting the party wind down naturally until Abby had felt comfortable enough to leave early. As for Hilde, from the looks she'd been shooting his way all night, it was crystal clear that he hadn't been welcome there in the first place, so he was all too ready to make his departure.

After they'd said their goodbyes—separately—he followed Abby home, reminding himself why this conversation was necessary, and why, despite how much he wished otherwise, they needed to figure out what they were doing, was it making a clean break... or not.

He parked behind her in the driveway, pulling into Hilde's spot—his own personal insurance so he wouldn't chicken out and end up back in Abby's bed again.

She didn't so much as glance back to make sure he was following her, and he'd give just about anything to know what she was thinking in that moment. Was she trying to find a way to make this work with them like he'd been doing? Or was she ready to throw in the towel, having no interest in being with a man— *just* a man—who wouldn't give her the family she so wanted?

She stepped into the quiet, empty house, flipping on a light before she hung her keys on the hook by the back door. Tension hung heavy in the air, but he ignored it as best he could as he followed her inside and shut the door behind him. As easy as it'd be to bury his head in the sand, to ignore their fight and go about his life as if nothing had ever happened, their relationship—their *friend*ship—meant too much to him to leave it broken.

Abby shrugged out of her cardigan, leaving her in a dark green sleeveless dress, making her fair skin glow even under the harsh kitchen lights and awakening parts of himself that he'd just as soon stay sleeping. He stuffed his hands into his jeans pockets to keep from reaching for her, his body aching to feel her silky smooth skin under his fingertips, even just once more. But he knew nothing good would come from them sleeping together again. Nothing good besides the obvious, anyway. And as amazing as *the obvious* was, it wasn't nearly enough to jeopardize whatever friendship they could salvage.

"Do you want something to drink?" she asked.

The formal question only reminded him exactly how far they'd fallen. Had it really only been a little over a week ago when he'd pressed her against the counter and feasted on her neck while her grandma had been out with her friends? They'd spent the evening working upstairs, and before they'd known it, it had been nearly nine and they'd missed dinner. They were both exhausted and starving, but it'd been too late to order takeout from anywhere, so they'd scavenged. He'd wowed her with the one dish he'd managed to perfect while he'd been staying at Becca's—grilled cheese, Sofia's actual favorite. And then, when there was nothing left on their plates but crumbs, he'd wowed her with something else entirely.

Even though that night hadn't been that long ago, it felt like a lifetime. Now it seemed like they were back exactly where they'd been when he'd arrived, all avoidance and stilted conversation, and he hated it. He wanted to laugh and joke with her, wanted to vent to her about the constant edits from Redmond, wanted to hear about whatever hilarious thing Sofia or one of the other kids did at day care that day. He wanted to carry her upstairs, lose himself inside her body until they both saw stars, and then hold her in his arms as they drifted off to sleep.

But that was no longer in the cards for them.

He cleared his throat. "I'm good, thanks."

Abby nodded, her lower lip caught between her teeth as she studied him with apprehension. An expected expression, even if he hated it.

He sighed and ran a hand through his hair, knowing this wasn't going to get any easier, so he might as well get it over with. Rip it off like a Band-Aid so they could move forward with the next aspect of their relationship...whatever that looked like.

"I wanted to talk to you about last week. Look, Abby, the things I said...the way I spoke to you—it wasn't okay." He put as much sincerity as he could in the words, desperate for her to believe every ounce of his remorse. There'd been many times in his life where he'd wanted to go back and do things over, but none as much as that argument between them.

She pressed her lips together and gave him a small nod. "You weren't the only one...I said some pretty hurtful things, too, and I'm sorry."

Shrugging, he pretended as if her words—so much like his dad's—hadn't affected him as much as they had. "Hurtful, maybe, but not untrue."

He *had* bailed—on his family, on his friendships, and on this town. But back then, he hadn't been able to picture a way to heal, to *grow*, without fleeing. Hell, he still couldn't.

"I suppose this was coming all along," she said. "There's no way we could've ever made this work...right?" The longing in the last word, like she was hoping he'd tell her otherwise, nearly had him reconsidering everything he thought he wanted. Was a career really all that important to him? After all, like she'd said, his job wouldn't keep him warm at night.

But he'd spent his entire adult life working toward this goal, and he didn't want to abandon it. Without achieving that goal, what would he be?

"Yeah," he said quietly, and hated himself a little more when her eyes lost a bit of their sparkle.

Tentatively, he walked toward her, not stopping until he was close enough that he could reach out and touch her. Despite their nearness, he held back, unsure of the reception he'd receive and knowing how much it'd crush him if she pulled away. "This is going to sound pretty shitty of me, but I'm really glad Becca broke her ankle."

Abby breathed out a laugh, her smile brightening her eyes in a way that made them shine. "I'll deny it if you ever repeat this to her, but I am, too."

Slow enough so she could push him away if she wanted, he reached out and cupped her face, sighing in relief when she allowed his hands to touch her skin. He brushed his thumbs against her cheeks, trying to memorize every bit of her he could in their nearness. How silky her skin was under his hands, the wispy flyaways at her hairline that just kissed her forehead, and the tiny flecks of gray in her eyes.

"I've loved spending this time with you, and I wouldn't change it for anything," he said, meaning every word. It didn't matter that his goal had been pushed back. That he'd have to bust his ass even harder to have everything ready in time to take on Franken's project, assuming their meeting went well. He was just grateful they'd had this time together. "Getting to know the woman you are now, layered on top of the girl you used to be... the girl I fell in love with... is something I never knew I needed."

Her eyelids fluttered closed, and she exhaled sharply. "Me too," she whispered as she reached out and rested her hands on his waist. Their eyes locked, hers searching for something he wasn't sure he could give her. Finally, she gave him a sad smile. "But no matter how much we've enjoyed these past two months, it doesn't change anything."

Even though she didn't ask it like a question, he answered anyhow, shaking his head as regret sat heavy in his stomach. "Right. Our paths are just too incompatible. We want different things, Abby, and I couldn't live with myself if you ended up resenting me for not giving you what you need."

Since their fight, he'd turned over a hundred different possibilities in his head, trying to find a way they could make this work. He had no intention of ever moving back to Heart's Hope Bay, and he knew it'd take an act of God to get her to move to Vegas. But people successfully did long-distance relationships all the time. Why couldn't they be one of those couples?

But no matter how he worked it out in his mind, he always got hung up when he imagined what their life would look like five or ten or twenty years down the line. When it was just the two of them, living in separate cities, not married, Abby never realizing her dream of having a family and kids of her own. All because he was a selfish bastard who couldn't give her what she needed. Who *wouldn't* give her those things.

She nodded, the soft smile on her face doing nothing to mask the sheen of tears in her eyes, and if he hadn't already broken his own heart with his choice, that would've done it. "At least this time we can stay friends, right?"

He gripped her tighter and pulled her close, resting his forehead against hers. Closing his eyes, he whispered, "Always."

And then he did what he promised himself he wouldn't. He tilted her face up to meet his and pressed his lips to hers, attempting to memorize every second. Instead of leaving it at that... instead of backing away after a quick, chaste kiss, he took it a step further than he should have and swiped his tongue against her bottom lip. He swallowed her soft moan, memorizing the exact cadence as he tasted her for what he knew would be the last time.

Chapter Twenty-Four

A couple days later, Carter met Marco at Last Call for a beer. It was later than they originally planned to meet, but seeing as how this was Carter's last night in Heart's Hope Bay, he hadn't wanted to miss a second with Sofia, so he'd waited to leave until she was in bed for the night.

They hadn't been there more than five minutes before Marco had talked him into a game of pool. Carter tried to block out the last time he'd been there, doing that very thing, but it was no use. The memories from that night with Abby were too fresh, too overwhelming for him to have any hope of doing anything but be lost in them. Had that really only been five weeks ago? It felt like a lifetime had passed since the night they'd stumbled upstairs into Abby's room and had finally given in to the irresistible connection between them.

But thinking about Abby wasn't going to do him any good, as he'd proven to himself over the past week. He was leaving tomorrow, and no amount of wishing or hoping was going to change that. He had plans and goals, and he had to prioritize them right now.

As much as he was tempted to draw this out...to stay another day or two if only to soak up time with the people he loved, it wasn't an option. His meeting with Franken was first thing Monday morning, and he wanted to get back to Vegas with a couple days' cushion so he could get in the right mindset and prepare for what would ultimately be the most important interview of his life. If he nailed it, he wouldn't need that final promotion he'd had his eye on and could skip straight to his ultimate goal.

"So you're really leaving, huh?" Marco asked, standing off to the side as Carter took a shot.

Carter glanced at him and stood to his full height, raising an eyebrow. "Did you think I was lying when I said I was only here temporarily?"

Marco laughed, the booming sound something Carter hadn't even realized he'd missed in the time he'd been gone. "Nah, man. It just looked like maybe some things had changed."

"Nope, no changes here." Unless he was talking about the invisible vise around Carter's heart that he couldn't seem to shake. "Still have a job waiting for me in Vegas. I actually have a meeting scheduled with a heavy hitter on Monday. He's got a project that could put my own firm on the map."

"No shit! That's fantastic. I'm happy for you. Well, as happy as I can be since now I definitely won't be able to lure you over to our side."

Carter chuckled and shook his head, bending to line up another shot. "You're relentless, you know that?"

"Or as my wife likes to call it, a pain in the ass."

He missed and stood, letting Marco have the table. "Speaking of your wife...how are things?"

Marco blew out a heavy breath as he leaned over the table, pool cue drawn. "I don't know, man. It's weird. We're fighting all the time, and it's about stupid shit, you know? I mean, we've always fought hard, but we make up hard, too, and the fights never last for more than a day. But now it feels like we've been in a never-ending one for months."

Carter cringed. "I'm no expert on women—certainly not wives—but could it be that what you think isn't a big deal *is* a big deal to her?" He scratched his jaw and lifted a shoulder. "If there's one thing I learned growing up with a sister it's that she and I ultimately care about different things."

After missing his next shot, Marco stood and wrapped both hands around the top of his pool cue. "You're probably right. I just...I get so frustrated. When I try to talk to her about this, she doesn't want to hear anything I have to say. I get where she's coming from, but there's got to be a compromise there somewhere. I don't want our family to be a carbon copy of the one I grew up in." Marco seemed to anticipate Carter's rebuke before he could speak a word, and he held up a hand. "You don't have to remind me—I know my family's great, and I love them. They've always supported me and provided for me. Some may even say they smothered me a little too much with love."

Carter chuckled softly. "Your mom spread that love around, too—don't forget that."

"She's good at that. She's good at a lot of things, which is probably why my dad just let her do it. But that's the thing—she did it *all*. And as much as I love my dad, you know I don't have a real close relationship with him because he wasn't there for us in the thick of things. That was my mom. She's always been the rock. But I don't want the family Gia and I have to be like that. I want it to be an equal partnership where we're both there. I don't want to just be a babysitter, you know? That's my kid, too."

It was hard not to feel an ounce of jealousy toward the kind of family Marco was talking about, because it was something Carter hadn't had in so long. His mom had been like Marco's, too. Had taken on nearly all the child raising and household responsibilities. And then she'd gotten sick and things began to deteriorate. She'd been their rock, the foundation upon which their family was built. And then when she passed away, the entire thing crumbled around them without her.

"Have you told her this?" Carter asked.

"Yeah. You were there at Last Call both times. I tried telling her, but she won't listen."

He stared at his friend for long moments, dumbfounded, before finally saying, "You're an idiot."

"No doubt," Marco said without hesitation.

Carter snorted and shook his head, setting his beer mug down on the tall table they'd commandeered off to the side. "Now remember, I'm not a marriage expert, so take this with a grain of salt. But it seems to me that you might have a better reception with your wife if you approach this when neither of you have been screaming in the past hour. Wait until tempers have cooled, and you can both think clearly. Then you can have an actual, productive conversation."

Marco eyed him skeptically over the rim of his beer mug. "You think we just need to talk it out," he said, doubt ringing clearly in his tone.

Carter lifted a shoulder. "I'm sure it wouldn't hurt if you brought her some flowers, too, or maybe some chocolate. Or whatever she's been craving—if pregnancy cravings are actually a thing."

Marco tossed his head back, his booming laughter raining down. "Oh, it's a thing. You have no idea how far I had to drive the first time it happened, because every place around here was already closed for the night. But it didn't take long for her cravings to shift into a pattern, so now I just keep extras stocked in the basement. She hasn't gotten wise to it yet because I've cut her off from going down there."

"Why? Is that where you hide the bodies?"

Marco attempted a scowl but ruined it when he chuckled. "Watch out or you might find out. Nah, I'm building a rocker for the nursery so we've got somewhere to sit for middle-of-the-night feedings—as long as she'll let me help—and I want it to be a surprise."

Carter marveled at the genuine happiness that radiated from his friend when he talked about the surprise addition to their family. There was no doubt Marco was completely invested in this kid, even though it hadn't been in the plans for them yet.

"Well there you go." Carter glanced at his watch, noting the time and that the stores in town had long since closed. "Maybe you can sneak downstairs and grab something from that stash tonight before you talk."

"Good idea. Hopefully the girls have set up in the living room for the night—then there'll be no sneaking needed. I can just slip in the back door and head straight down."

"The girls?" Carter asked, attempting to school his voice into bland interest, but from the smug look Marco shot him, he hadn't been very successful.

"Yeah, Savannah and Abby came over tonight for an impromptu girls' night. Speaking of talking shit out, maybe you should come with me."

Carter pressed his lips together in what he hoped passed for a smile, tense as it was, and shook his head. "Been there, done that. Abby and I talked, and we're good now."

Marco's eyebrows hit his hairline. "*Good*-good, or good-nice-knowing-you-see-you-in-another-ten-years-good?" The blatant sexual innuendo from his first *good* was hard to ignore, and Carter's smile wasn't quite so forced anymore.

"That first 'good-good' was damn near filthy, man. You do realize that, don't you?"

"I do indeed." Marco shot him a blinding smile before lifting his mug in Carter's direction. "And you're avoiding the question."

Carter sighed and turned his back on the pool table, leaning up against it. "Somewhere in the middle?" He said it like a question, even though he knew that was exactly where they were.

He and Abby had been on each extreme, and they couldn't make it work either time. He just hoped they could find a lasting relationship now that they'd landed somewhere in the middle.

Marco stationed himself at Carter's side, both of them facing the thin crowd at the bar tonight. "Look, man, I'm not trying to get in the middle of whatever you guys have going on. You're adults and you can handle it."

"But..."

"But, you're the most driven person I've ever known, and I know those goals guide you. I just don't want you to regret your choices five years down the line. Life is what happens when you're busy making other plans, and you excel at that distraction." He reached out and clapped a hand on Carter's shoulder, squeezing lightly. "Take it from me—sometimes the best things we never knew we needed are the ones that just fall into our laps. But you have to be willing to break from the plan and run with them."

* * *

When Abby and Savannah had arrived at Gia's house, their arms weighed down with enough ice cream to feed an army, she'd never been more grateful for the close friendships she'd cultivated with these two amazing women. Two amazing women who were ready to drop everything in deference to an emergency girls' night.

A couple hours prior, at evening pickup, Becca had casually mentioned that tonight was Carter's last night in Heart's Hope Bay. At the time, she'd worked hard to maintain her composure, not allowing her true feelings to show on the outside, but beneath the surface, she was reeling. Heartbroken that Carter's time in their little town was truly over. Of course, she'd anticipated this from the beginning. From the very first day he'd showed up in town, she knew it wouldn't be lasting. But knowing it and seeing the reality of it were two very different things.

Savannah had been within earshot, and without giving Abby the option of arguing, she had called for an emergency get-together. Abby knew better than to argue. Besides, she needed this night as much as Savannah thought she did, because without it...without the support of her friends to lean on...she'd be spending the evening doing exactly what she was now—sitting on the couch, face-first in a carton of ice cream—except she'd be doing it all alone.

And as it turned out, Gia needed the support just as much.

"So what happened after you guys left Last Call the other night?" Savannah asked.

Gia blew out a breath and dropped her head back to rest on top of the couch cushions. "Nothing."

Abby and Savannah shared a look over Gia's head before Savannah said, "Nothing?"

"Nope. I beat him home, and by the time he got inside, his pillow was on the couch and I was locked in the bedroom."

"That's...definitive," Abby said hesitantly, unsure how well Gia would receive any sort of advice.

But Gia answered that question in the next breath when she groaned. "I know. It was stupid, wasn't it? If we'd just talked then, we probably would have figured it all out. But I just get so *mad* when it's in the heat of the moment. And it's not even anger, really, it's hurt." Gia's voice cracked on the last word, and both Savannah and Abby immediately wrapped an arm around their friend, making a Gia sandwich.

"Oh, sweetie," Abby murmured. "I don't want you to be upset anymore."

"I don't want to *be* upset anymore. I hate that this

time—which is supposed to be magical—is filled with tension and arguments and frustration. I want to be happy with him. I want to talk with him about what's going on and what I'm feeling without fear of him swooping in and making a decision for me."

"Ugh, men are the worst at that," Savannah said. "My brothers try to do it to me all the time."

"They really are. I get that he just wants to fix everything all the time, but sometimes I don't need that. Worse is when he dismisses me and the research I've done and the work I've already put in and comes up with what he thinks is the best solution. Like with the breastfeeding thing…If he would stop and listen to me, he'd know that I'm not against pumping and bottle feeding *eventually*, but I want to make sure the baby is firm with exclusive breastfeeding first. And if he'd just listen for two minutes instead of questioning everything and thinking that he knows best, this all could have been avoided."

"Well, it sounds to me like he's suffering from a case of Men Are Dumb." Savannah dipped her spoon into her pint of ice cream. "Honestly, they are *all* afflicted by it."

Abby laughed, unable to deny the truth of that. Although the one man she was basing her assessment on just happened to be Carter, and he just happened to be breaking her heart at the moment, so she may not have been the most reliable witness.

"I've just been trying so hard to figure out a way

through the situation that we didn't plan for," Gia said into her ice cream. "Everybody tells me I just need to go with the flow more. That's not how I work! When chaos gets thrown my way, I want to have Plan A, B, and C ready if I need it. And I think, considering these circumstances, I'm doing pretty good."

"Of course you are!" Abby said reassuringly, rubbing a hand up and down Gia's back. "I know Savannah isn't going to get this because she doesn't even like to plan what she's having for dinner—"

Savannah laughed, completely unoffended because it was the truth.

"But having a plan makes us feel more in control." Abby didn't want to admit the reason she felt she needed that plan in the first place—that life with her mom had been chaotic and ever-changing, and always having a plan helped her mitigate that. Yet while it had helped her make it through her life thus far, she also hadn't obtained what she'd planned for—a family of her own. A perfect husband and a dozen perfect kids.

And even though she was only twenty-nine, she couldn't help but wonder if that was something she'd ever have in her life. After all, how many once-in-a-lifetime loves did a person really get? She'd already had two. With the same person, true, but at different points in their lives. She didn't know how realistic it was to think that she could ever have that with somebody else. But more than that, she wasn't sure she even *wanted* that with someone else anymore. Not when she feared she would be constantly comparing that person to Carter and comparing their relationship to the blink of time she and Carter had shared when he'd been home.

Tears stung the backs of her eyes, and she blinked hard to keep them at bay. She'd already cried enough this past week, and she was damn near dehydrated.

Even without her plan coming to fruition, she had to admit she'd done well with the cards she'd been dealt. She had an amazing career she loved and got to spend the days with kids who may not be her own, but who she loved all the same. While, true, her mom couldn't be bothered to be a part of Abby's life, her grandma loved her enough to make up for anything she may have been lacking. She wouldn't trade that for the world.

And her friends? She looked at them, laughing as Savannah bemoaned another tense run-in with Noah, and felt a tug on her heartstrings. She loved them, wholly and completely. More so, even, than many people loved their blood families. She realized then that forging a bond as strong as the three of them had was more powerful than a "real" family could ever be. They hadn't been forced to be with each other—they'd *chosen* each other. They'd stuck it out together through fights and disagreements, arguments and frustrations, not because they had to, but because they wanted to. So if she ended up being an eighty-five-year-old spinster, she'd be okay as long as the friends she'd collected along the way were still by her side in the end.

"You're awfully quiet over there, Abby," Savannah said with a raised eyebrow as she dug into her mint chip ice cream. "I think we've scared Gia into talking to Marco tonight, but what about you?"

"I'm not sure talking with Marco will solve my problems."

Gia laughed and slapped Abby's knee. "You know what she means."

She did. But unfortunately, Abby already knew a conversation wouldn't be the answer for her. At least not in the way they meant. She and Carter had had that conversation—the first one in which Abby had actually listened to him and his wants and needs. She felt sick that it'd taken so long for her to do so, and she wished she could go back in time and tell her younger self to pay attention to what other people needed and actually listen to their answers instead of plowing ahead with tunnel vision focus on her own goals. Maybe knowing that would've changed the outcome of her and Carter's relationship. Maybe it would've preserved it.

Abby was saved from voicing any of this by the back door opening. She met Savannah's gaze and tipped her head toward the door, eyebrows lifted in silent question.

Savannah nodded and pushed to stand. "Sounds like that's our cue."

The three of them strode into the kitchen, capping their empty pints of ice cream before tossing them in the garbage. Savannah hugged Gia before turning her over to Abby and grabbing her purse off the counter.

Abby squeezed her friend tight and whispered, "Now's the perfect time to talk. Neither of you are mad, you just had a pep talk from your girls, and you're fueled with ice cream."

Gia laughed and nodded, pulling back and dropping her hands to rest over the tiny baby bump that had just begun to appear. "I'll let you know how it goes."

"It's going to go great," Abby assured her as she and Savannah gathered their things.

They'd made it to the back door just as Marco ascended from the basement, jerking to a stop when he saw them in the room. "Oh, uh...evening, ladies."

Abby glanced down, noticing the box of chocolate-covered cherries Marco carried, something Gia had been craving nearly nonstop during her pregnancy, and smiled. Maybe Marco's time with Carter had been equally productive, and Carter had knocked some sense into his friend and sent him home with instructions to talk.

It seemed both she and Carter were good at helping their friends. She only wished they'd been as good doing it with each other.

Chapter Twenty-Five

✺

It felt weird to be leaving Heart's Hope Bay with only the single suitcase Carter had packed in a rush to get to Becca. He might have only been in town for a couple months, but it felt like his life had irrevocably changed in the time he'd been there. He just didn't know if it was for the better.

He set his suitcase by the front door, his heart breaking when Sofia ran over to him and threw her arms around his legs.

"I don't want you to leave, Uncle Carter! I want you to stay. You're my favorite." Emotion shook her voice as fat tears rolled down her cheeks.

He squatted down to her level and wrapped his arms around her small frame, gathering her close. This time with her had been something he'd never thought he'd have, and what he'd told Abby the other night about him being glad that Becca had broken her ankle hadn't just been because of the time he'd gotten with Abby. Since he'd been back, he might have had to deal with unsavory things like his father, but he also got bonus time with his sister and his niece. Time that would have taken him years of weekend visits and summer vacations to account for. So while some parts of his stay here had been painful, the trip as a whole hadn't been nearly as challenging as he'd thought it would be. The good far outweighed the bad.

He placed his hand on Sofia's back, rubbing soft circles. "You know something? You're my favorite, too."

She just tightened her arms around his neck, unwilling to let go.

"Your mom and I have already talked about when you guys can come visit me again. I don't know if you remember, but my condo has a pool."

Sofia sniffed, pulling back and swiping her hand across her nose, her eyelashes glittering with unchecked tears. "It does?"

"Yep. And it even has a slide."

Sofia's eyes lit up, her emotions flipping like a switch, happiness erasing the sadness in a blink. If only it was so easy for everyone. "Slides are my favorite!"

"Then you're going to have a lot of fun when you guys come visit me."

"Why don't you grab the picture you drew for Uncle Carter, bug?" Becca said.

Sofia's eyes grew wide, lighting up as she smiled

before running down the hall to her bedroom. Carter stood and had to force himself to meet his sister's eyes, not wanting to see the sadness or disappointment he was sure would be there. Bracing himself, he met her gaze straight on and was surprised to only see the former, despite her holding out hope that he and Abby could have something more permanent.

"Even though you leave your clothes in the washing machine for days at a time and never rinse out your crusty bowls, I'm still going to miss you," she said.

Grinning, he hooked his arm around her neck, tugging her to him as he pressed a kiss to the top of her head. "Admit it—you love me."

She glanced up at him and rolled her eyes at the same time she pinched his nipple and twisted.

"Ow! What was that for?"

Her smile only grew. "I wanted to show you just how *much* I love you."

"Next time do it with a little less twisting, yeah?"

"Uncle Carter, Uncle Carter!" Sofia ran down the stairs, clutching a piece of paper as it flapped in the breeze. "I made this for you to put in your office!"

Once again, Carter squatted to her level and accepted the picture she offered him. She'd been getting better at drawing, especially since the weekly art classes Gia taught at the Sunshine Corner, so Carter was able to just barely make out what he assumed were four people standing in front of a large blue square he figured was meant to be a house. The bright yellow door gave it away as the Sunshine Corner. She'd written her name in the bottom corner, and it was seeing those shaky, imperfect letters that nearly undid him. Knowing just how much it would change in the months and years ahead, and knowing that the only time he'd see that change would be once a year in cards, broke his heart.

He cleared his throat from the unexpected emotion that had crept up on him. "Wow, this is really good."

She beamed at him. "It's me and Mommy and you and Miss Abby at the Sunshine Corner." Sofia pointed to each object in turn. She hooked an arm around his neck and pressed their heads together as they gazed at the picture. "Put it in your office so you can see it every day and 'emember us."

God, just when he thought this couldn't get any harder, this sneaky little three-year-old wormed her way into his chest and poked around inside with a sharp stick, prodding at all his soft spots. He was going to have to make a more concerted effort to either come back and visit them more or fly them out to him, because he didn't know how, after spending two months being a part of their daily lives, he could go back to only seeing them twice a year at most.

He opened his mouth to ask Becca if she'd come to Vegas later in the summer, but snapped it shut when he realized that taking time off for family was about to be a luxury he would no longer be afforded. His appointment with Franken was on Monday, and he anticipated things moving very quickly after that. He had so much to do, so many plans to put in place before he'd be ready to open, and since he was still working at Mosley & Associates, his free time was going to be a thing of the past.

Giving Sofia one last hug, he thanked her for the drawing before standing and hefting his suitcase. "I'll call you when I get to Vegas and let you know I made it home okay."

Becca nodded and opened the door for him, holding Sofia's hand. "Thank you. For everything," she said, sincerity ringing true. "Don't get so busy you can't come back to visit us, okay?"

He managed to keep his cringe to himself, but just barely. She knew him too well, and knew exactly who—or rather what—their competition was. Well, he was just going to have to figure out a way to make it back here to see them. He had to. Their newly enriched relationships were too important for him not to.

Of course, more trips back here meant an increased chance of running into Abby again. He'd lasted little more than twenty-four hours before seeing her again this time and knew the same fate would greet him every trip back home. While he planned to stay in touch with her, there was a big difference between exchanging texts once in a while or calling every so often and coming face-to-face with each other.

He couldn't stand the thought of seeing her with someone else. Even though he told her he'd wanted her to have the life she'd dreamed of—one with a husband and kids of her own—facing the reality of that was going to be devastating, especially knowing how different things could have been between them.

* * *

Driving away from Becca's house was one of the hardest things Carter had ever done, and considering the life he'd lived thus far, that was saying a lot. He gripped the steering wheel as he passed the *Welcome to Heart's Hope Bay* sign, the breathtaking views of the ocean to his left not even a match for the thoughts currently occupying his mind.

If he was doing the right thing, why did it feel so absolutely shitty? Like he'd ripped out his heart from his chest and left it sitting in the center of town with a kind, compassionate, loving woman who'd stolen it at sixteen and then again at twenty-nine. None of this felt right, but how could he change it? He'd already committed to this path, and if he backed down now, he'd be everything his father accused him of, wouldn't he?

He was only fifteen miles out of town when the faintest hint of smoke drifted up from under the hood of his rental car. Carter lifted his hands from the steering wheel to read the gauges, but he might as well be reading a cookbook in Japanese. He had less than zero knowledge about cars, but he *did* know the temperature gauge was definitely not where it should have been, and the smoke now billowing from the hood told him the same. He groaned, slamming his hand against the steering wheel as his car finally sputtered to a stop along the side of the road.

Like he needed one more obstacle in his path back to Vegas. He was already on tenuous ground, his determination to leave chipped away little by little with every mile he traveled away from Abby, the abyss in his chest growing wider with each passing minute.

The stretch of highway leaving Heart's Hope Bay was practically deserted—he'd only passed a handful of cars in the time since he'd left, which meant he was on his own. Probably for the better, all things considered. He needed to get used to that again since he was currently on a one-way track to solitude, all thanks to his own doing.

During his time in his hometown, it'd been so easy to fall back into old patterns, accepting help from the people he loved and cared for, and offering it just the same. But as soon as he stepped on that plane out of Oregon, things would take a sharp turn back to the status quo. Sure, he had friends in Vegas, but they were more of the *let's grab a beer after work and BS about nothing* variety and less of the *my car broke down on the side of the road and I'm having a bit of an existential crisis* variety.

Grumbling curses, he climbed out of the car and kicked the front driver's side tire as if that would do him any good. He grunted as pain radiated up his foot, the cadence of his favorite four letter words only intensifying. Blowing out a frustrated breath, he limped to the passenger's side of the car, near the guardrail that protected him from the crashing ocean waves below, and braced his hands as he stared off into the distance.

He'd always been a bit cocky in that he'd always had his life figured out, but that had fallen by the wayside recently. His life had become confusing, and suddenly the goals he'd been working toward his entire adult life were starting to seem like not enough. Lately, he couldn't picture his successes without also picturing what those successes would cost him.

He picked up a stray rock and hurled it into the ocean, channeling all his frustration in the throw, and watched with little satisfaction as the palm-sized rock disappeared like a speck into the vast, crashing water below.

"A lot of good that did me," Carter grumbled.

Well, so far, hitting a steering wheel, kicking his tire, and hurling a rock into the ocean hadn't made him feel any better, nor had it provided him any answers. Maybe…just maybe…this was an ache that physical aggression couldn't relieve.

He hung his head and braced his hands on the rail as a gust of wind swept over him, stirring his hair around his face. A flash of white out of the corner of his eye caught his attention, and he turned in time to see Sofia's picture lifted on the breeze, the wind sweeping it up and out through the open car window with ease.

Heart seizing, he lunged for it, slipping on some stray rocks as he tried futilely to catch it. He fumbled for it twice, missing the floating paper by mere centimeters each time as panic climbed up his throat. He absolutely couldn't lose the last thing his niece had given him, not when he didn't know when he'd see her next.

Finally, on his third try, he caught it, the once pristine paper now crumpled in his grasp, but crumpled was better than lost entirely. Collapsing back against his car, relief washed over him as he pressed the drawing to his chest. If this picture had managed to be swept off to sea, he didn't know what he'd do.

And how sad was that? He glanced down at the drawing—one that depicted his family...his *true* family. Though losing it would hurt, it had nothing on the pain he was about to inflict on himself and the people he loved.

What the hell was he *doing*?

He didn't want to leave. Not Oregon, not his sister or niece or friends. And certainly not Abby.

He wasn't going to be content trapped in a stuffy office all day, looking out over the Vegas skyline, surrounded by white walls save for the single picture his niece had drawn for him. He wanted to be *living* that picture, every day of his life. If his time in his hometown had shown him anything, it was that he didn't take after his father. He was so much more than Robert Hayes ever was or would be, and he needed to stop comparing himself to someone with whom he shared DNA and little else.

Fear and imagined judgment had no place in his life, especially when it was keeping him from the woman he loved and all the dreams he hadn't been sure he'd be able to provide. But his two months under the same roof as a three-year-old was all the proof he needed that this wasn't beyond his capabilities. He was patient with Sofia—fun for the most part, stern when necessary, but loving always. Would a family of his own really be any different, especially if he had someone as kind and nurturing as Abby by his side? They'd make a great team, both using their upbringings, not as a roadmap for how to raise their own kids, but rather how *not* to.

He clenched the picture in his hand, curling his other around the guardrail as he inhaled the salty ocean air. Realizing he'd made his choice a long time ago, and his subconscious had been trying to tell him that in a thousand different ways. He'd just been too stubborn to listen.

Choosing Abby and Heart's Hope Bay meant sacrifices. His dream of owning his own firm would no longer be a possibility, but as he closed his eyes and pictured Abby's smiling face, her fiery, sunkissed hair swirling in the breeze, he didn't care about what he was giving up in order to stay. He'd make a thousand sacrifices if it meant he got to grow old with her. He'd had enough heartache in his life. He wasn't going to inflict any more on himself. He'd take the happiness that had been dropped into his lap, hold on with both hands, and never let go.

Taking one more deep, calming breath, he folded up Sofia's picture and tucked it into his wallet. He pulled his phone from his pocket and navigated to Becca's contact information just as a car rolled to a stop behind him. He lifted his hand to block out the glare of the sun off the hood and saw the last person he thought would ever pull over to help him. Especially given how he'd left her granddaughter. But there was no mistaking the scowl Hilde shot him as she stepped out of her car and slammed her door.

"Huh. I thought for sure this would take another day or two," she said, glancing to the smoke billowing from his hood. "Looks like my spells are getting more powerful."

Carter's eyebrows hit his hairline as he glanced from his broken-down car to her.

She merely shrugged. "Knew you just needed a gentle nudge to figure out what was best. Or, really, more of a shove." She tipped her head to her passenger's side door. "You going to get in or what?"

Chapter Twenty-Six

As much as Abby had needed time with her girl-friends last night, she also needed time by herself to sort through everything. She'd been able to put on a brave face throughout the day, her kids at the Sunshine Corner making that easier than she thought possible. But once everyone was gone, things got lonely.

In the past seven weeks, since Carter had started helping Abby with the preschool renovation, she'd gotten used to his company nearly every night. And now it was suddenly gone. It reminded her a lot of how she'd felt in the days and weeks following their split after high school. When, suddenly, one of her best friends was no longer there. She'd gotten through it then with the help of Savannah. She figured she'd get through this one much the same. The only difference was while she'd only had two months with him this time as compared to two years, the loss felt even more overwhelming.

But that made sense, didn't it? Because at eighteen, she'd had no idea just exactly what she was losing. And now at twenty-nine, her eyes had been opened. She no longer held delusions of her prince waiting for her. Because that prince—her true one and only—had slipped through her fingers once again.

In the family room, she curled into the corner of the couch and rested her bowl of popcorn sprinkled with peanut butter M&M's in her lap, settling in for a night of *Gilmore Girls* reruns. She'd seen the series in its entirety at least five times already. But what was once more? It was her happy place and if she ever needed that happy place, it was now.

Nearly halfway through episode two of the first season, her grandma poked her head in. "Isn't it a little dark in here?"

Abby glanced up, only now noticing exactly how dark the room had gotten since she'd sat down. But did it really matter? The only thing she needed light for was to see what she was eating, and she'd just been shoveling fistfuls into her mouth anyway. She'd no doubt find some stowaways tucked in her tank top—the bra had come off long ago—but she wasn't going to focus on that now. "I don't need the light on. It's better to watch TV this way." And if the darkness just so happened to hide any lingering tears, well, all the better.

Without asking if Abby wanted company, Hilde

settled in on the couch next to her before reaching in to the near-empty bowl of popcorn and grabbing a handful. "Did you have a good day?"

Abby furrowed her brows, shooting her grandma a look out of the corner of her eye. This was bordering on subtle, and Hilde did not do subtle. "It was all right," Abby replied tentatively. "Yours?"

She shrugged as she gathered another handful of popcorn. "Fine. I met Mabel out at that antiques farm on Highway 101 earlier today."

"Oh yeah? She find anything she likes?"

Hilde snorted. "Do you mean of the furniture or human variety?"

Abby's eyebrows hit her hairline as she regarded her grandma fully now. "She's buying humans?"

Hilde cackled loudly, slapping a hand to her knee. "Well, I can't say she wouldn't be the first in line if they'd offer him for sale. But no, she just has a thing for Edward, the owner of the farm. He's a little young—only in his late fifties—but I don't see what the big deal is. Instead of just asking him out like a normal person, she harasses him every chance she gets. When I left her, the two of them had been arguing for fifteen minutes over the price of an antique typewriter."

"What does she need a typewriter for?"

"She doesn't. That's the whole point."

"Seems a lot more complicated than it's worth."

"That's often the way with love, isn't it?" Her grandma was quiet for several long moments—a heavy, weighted silence, where Abby could feel something more coming. "I saw Carter on my way back."

In response to that, Abby's head jerked up automatically, her reflexes too ingrained to be able to school herself into any sort of nonchalance. "He was heading out of town?"

Hilde nodded. "Can't be sure where exactly he was going, but he was headed north."

So that was it, then. He really was leaving. She'd known he was. He'd told her so, and she'd heard it reiterated from Becca just yesterday. But hearing firsthand the evidence of his departure was hitting her harder than she'd anticipated.

"Well, then. I suppose things can get back to normal around here," Abby said, her voice watery as she suited up in her coat of armor, attempting to put on a brave face.

She had no idea how long it was going to feel like this...like a vise was squeezing her heart. But it had to get better at some point, didn't it? She knew firsthand that the heartbreak wouldn't last forever. And anyway, maybe now that he was actually gone...that she didn't have to worry about running into him around town or seeing him when he picked up Sofia from the Sunshine Corner, she could get on with her life, in whatever fashion that shook out to be.

And even though he wasn't there, even though he hadn't chosen her in the end, she could never regret their time together. It'd taught her so much. Had taught her not to take the things, or people, she loved for granted. Had taught her that though her life may not have been what she'd originally planned it to be, that didn't mean it wasn't fulfilling. She was grateful for her life. For the close friendships that she'd cultivated. For the love of her grandma who'd practically raised her. And for her family at the Sunshine Corner.

If that was all she ended up with for the rest of her life, she could be content with that. She could be content without kids of her own or Carter in her life, knowing she'd felt his love, not once but twice. He may not have been hers to keep, but he *had* been hers. How much luckier could she be?

It wasn't until Hilde handed her a tissue that she even realized she was crying. Thankfully, it hadn't been the soul-crushing exhaustive cry of the night before. The one she'd done under the veil of her shower, not wanting her grandma to hear her sobs. The one that had wrung her so dry she'd fallen into bed straight from her shower and hadn't so much as dreamed.

"Thanks," she murmured, accepting the tissue and blotting her face before wiping her nose.

Her grandma rested her hand on Abby's knee and squeezed lightly. "You know what I think we need?"

"More popcorn and maybe some margaritas?"

Hilde laughed and shook her head. "No. Well, I mean, yes, always. But that's not what I was referring to at this particular moment. I was thinking maybe we should take our girls' trip down the coast a little early this year."

For as long as Abby could remember, she and her grandma had taken a vacation, just the two of them, staying in a little beach house on the coast for a week at the end of every summer. Her earliest memories of it had been when she was seven. They'd built sand castles and splashed in the ocean and camped out under the stars, eating too much junk food and laughing until their stomachs hurt. They hadn't missed a single year in the time since.

Honestly, a week away with her grandma in a town that didn't remind her of Carter sounded like *exactly* what she needed.

She frowned as longing filled her chest. "I'd love to but we haven't rented a place yet. Plus, I don't have anything lined up for the Sunshine Corner, and I'd hate to—"

Hilde cut her off with a wave of her hand. "You leave that all to me. If I can get things set up, would you want to escape for a little while?"

Truly, Abby could think of nothing better than getting away from the town that had been revitalized, once again, with memories of Carter. She saw him everywhere she went—even her own bedroom—and she knew that wouldn't abate anytime soon.

Smiling, she nodded. "If you can figure out a way to make it happen, I'd love to escape with you."

Chapter Twenty-Seven

✳

Abby had no idea how her grandma had managed to pull together a weeklong vacation on the beach with less than twenty-four hours' notice. But then again, Hilde had always had a way with things like that. If she wanted something, it seemed she could make it happen simply by manifesting it. Abby didn't care how her grandma had managed to do it. She was just grateful that she had.

They'd traveled down to Florence and rented a small cottage just steps from the beach. They'd spent their days camped out in the sand, books in hand and margaritas on tap, soaking in the sun. Each night, they'd stay up until the wee hours of the morning talking about everything and nothing before the crashing waves against the shore sang her to sleep. She'd lived on the ocean her whole life, but she'd never gotten tired of its all-consuming beauty or its gentle lullaby. Even though they'd only gone a few hours from home, it had felt like a different universe.

"I do believe our little vacation worked," Hilde said as Abby pulled into their driveway just as the sun was setting.

She put the car in park and turned to her grandma with a smile—one that was mostly genuine. The "mostly" part was courtesy of this getaway, and she knew the rest would come with time. "I think you're right." She reached over the center console and pulled her grandma to her, enveloping her in a hug as she breathed in the familiar scent of lavender and cloves. "Thank you for this." Abby's voice shook with emotion, the bone-deep gratitude she felt for her grandma nearly overwhelming.

If she didn't have this amazing, strong, fiercely protective woman in her life, she didn't know what she'd do. And that Hilde had always been there, through every hill and valley in Abby's life, was something she could never repay. It was also something she'd never wished for with anyone else, despite spending years desperate for parents—or at least a mom—to be as invested in her life as her grandma was.

Abby's mom would call at some point, filling the entire phone call with her latest dating woes. That was a guaranteed filler and one Abby could count on. Something else she could bet on was that her mom would never ask about Abby, and she'd learned over the years not to bother volunteering any information. It didn't matter anyway—her mom would forget everything she'd mentioned by their next phone call. At one point, Abby had craved some sort of reciprocal relationship with her mom. But she was beyond that now. She knew her mom just simply wasn't capable of it, and Abby was finally at peace with it.

Hilde patted Abby on the back, rubbing soothing circles. "A little beach time is always good for the soul."

Abby felt tears prick the backs of her eyes at all her grandma wasn't saying. She'd been there for Abby over the week, giving her space when she'd needed it and filling her time when she didn't want to think. And through it all, she'd never once pressed.

Their family home was something to behold, a piece of her history that she loved with all her heart. But she couldn't deny how the weight of the future of the Sunshine Corner settled heavily on her shoulders the moment she walked through the back door.

She'd spent a week away digesting the ending of her relationship with Carter and of his leaving, and accepting the new path her life would take. She hadn't had the mental bandwidth to also think about her troubles with the preschool. That would be on the top of her to-do list this week. She had to call all of the parents who had put their child's name down on the waiting list and inform them that they'd need to find another preschool in the area for their child. She wasn't sure how she'd make it through those conversations without tears, but she'd force herself. The parents would have enough to worry over and didn't need to concern themselves with her problems, too.

She also needed to contact the individuals who'd purchased items at the fundraiser, as well as the businesses who'd donated, and make them aware of the situation. Even though she'd have to borrow against the home equity loan she'd taken out as a safety net, she'd pay each and every one of them back.

Her grandma was already at the bottom of the stairs, her suitcase in hand, no doubt intent on hefting it up the steep steps.

"Hey!" Abby snapped. "What do you think you're doing?"

Hilde heaved a sigh. "I'm tired, Abby. I want to go and get into my nightgown. And then I'm going to get a glass of scotch, and I'm going to sit in my chair and watch the stories that I missed all week."

Abby grinned. While they'd been gone, she'd had to listen to her grandma bemoan the fact that their cottage didn't have cable, and thus she couldn't watch the soap operas she was addicted to. "Fine. That sounds like a wonderful evening, but you know you're not supposed to carry heavy things up the steps. Dr. Gerandy told you that."

Hilde scowled. "Simon's only interested in ruining my fun. All because I turned him down when he asked me out in 1972."

Abby rolled her eyes, having heard this particular gripe approximately three thousand times. "*Dr. Gerandy*," Abby emphasized, "is only interested in your health. He's a good doctor."

Her grandma snorted. "He's the *only* doctor in Heart's Hope Bay, so we're stuck with the old geezer."

"Didn't you two graduate together?"

"Age isn't a number, Abby. How many times do I have to tell you that? Age is a *feeling*. And he feels like a geezer. I, on the other hand, feel like I'm twenty-two."

"Yeah, well, you're not and neither is your back, so I'm going to carry this up for you." Abby yanked the suitcase from her grandma and trudged up the stairs. "I don't know why you have to be so stubborn all the time. Just let people help you once in a while."

"You're a fine one to give that advice. You don't like to take help from anyone."

"That's not true. I took help from Carter for the preschool, didn't I?"

"And that was only because Becca strong-armed him *and* you into it."

Abby shrugged. "Well, I accepted it all the same."

"And what if all your friends showed up here and said they wanted to help you get the preschool done in time?"

Abby stopped short, unsure what she'd do if that actually happened. She'd...what? Put them to work? Ha! *Never.* No, more likely she'd brush them off and wave them away. Tell them not to worry about it because it was her problem. That it wasn't a big deal. She'd gotten herself into this mess, and she could get herself out.

"That's what I thought," her grandma said, smugness ringing in her tone.

"Everyone has their own lives that they need to deal with, Grandma. I don't want to ask them to worry about mine, too."

Once at the top of the stairs, Abby flipped on the light for the hallway and froze, blinking in confusion over what she saw. The drop cloths and various tools were no longer strewn across the faded, scratched floor, and in their place was nothing but gleaming hardwood. The walls were painted a bright, crisp yellow, the white trim work making the color pop. What had once been tiny, closed off rooms were now open and inviting. The cubbies she'd built with Carter stood along the far wall, filled with a rainbow array of bins. Small round tables edged the main room, a large circle rug filling up the center.

Abby stepped into the space, her hands covering her mouth as she looked at her dream come to life. A mural was painted on one wall, depicting a bright sunny day and a replica of their family home right in the center with smaller scenes drawn all around it. And arching above it all was the Sunshine Corner's logo.

Tears pricked Abby's eyes as she examined the beautiful piece, picking out details from her life's work in each of the scenes. Art class, cooking with Hilde, science experiments, and even puppy day with Ollie taking the lead. And right in the middle of it all, in front of her family home, stood Abby with Hilde next to her, surrounded by the people who were her family in every sense of the word.

Giddy but apprehensive, Abby walked toward the two spaces they'd created for the classrooms where the children would spend a designated amount of time each day on their curriculum. She peeked into the three year old room, smiling at the semicircle tables, the backs of the chairs marked with a nameplate for each child already enrolled.

Heart pounding, she hurried to the four-year-old room, flipped on the light, and gasped. Her gaze bounced rapidly over her friends and her extended family from the Sunshine Corner, everyone beaming at her.

And there, amid all her loved ones, stood Carter, a grin stretching his face, hands tucked into his pockets.

"Surprise," he said, as smooth and as calm as could be. Like her heart hadn't leaped into her throat, its beat thrumming wildly.

"Carter, what—" She shook her head and glanced back at her grandma, who stood in the doorway, a smug, knowing smirk on her face. Narrowing her eyes, Abby pointed an accusatory finger in her direction. "You...You did this!" she accused.

Of course her grandma would put this together for her, and of course Carter would have felt obligated to stick around and help, despite his need to leave. The heart that had leaped into her throat suddenly plummeted, her hopes sinking right along with it. She would never admit this aloud, but for a brief moment, she'd hoped that Carter had changed his mind. That he'd come back for her. That he was back in Heart's Hope Bay, not out of obligation, but out of a desire to be there.

She'd take that misassumption to her grave. There was no way she'd tell even Savannah or Gia, having no desire to relive that brief humiliation.

"Actually, it was his idea," Hilde said, lifting her chin toward Carter.

Abby turned back to him, only to find he'd stepped closer. So close, her body reacted to his nearness just the same as it always did. Apparently all the parts of her that Carter had showered so much loving attention on hadn't gotten the message that he was no longer theirs.

"I know it's probably the gentlemanly thing to do to let your grandma take credit for all this, but I kind of need that in order to pull off this whole grand gesture thing."

Abby furrowed her brow. "A grand gesture...for what?"

He breathed out a laugh. "For you, sweet girl. I'm hoping you'll forgive me."

She swallowed down her hope, refusing to get lost in daydreams again. "For what?"

He reached out and cupped her face, brushing his thumbs against her cheeks. "For leaving you. It was the dumbest thing I've ever done—and I've done a lot of dumb things. I wish I could go back in time and knock some sense into myself."

"Just so you know," Savannah called from behind him, "you're on your own the next time you're an idiot."

Abby breathed out a laugh as Carter rolled his eyes, but she didn't dare look away from him. Not when he was staring at her like he was. As if she were his whole world.

"I don't intend on being an idiot again," he said. "Or *much*, anyway. But now that I'm back for good, there's a high probability that it's going to happen."

"What do you mean you're back for good?" Abby asked, shaking her head. "What about your meeting? What about your firm?"

Carter pulled her closer, pressing his forehead to hers. "None of it means anything without you, Abby," he whispered, low enough that it was just for her. He pulled back and looked down into her eyes. "I want to be with you. And if that means Heart's Hope Bay, or that means Yemen or Liberia or wherever, that's where I'm going to be."

"But... you can't ever have your own firm here. And I—" She broke off, glancing over Carter's shoulder at the people who stood there, grins splitting their faces. Savannah, Gia and Marco, Jenn and Jenn's wife Lori... Becca, Norah, and half a dozen other parents.

And though she couldn't see Hilde, Abby could feel her grandma standing behind her, the unwavering support that had been present her entire life as solid as a brick wall. "And I can't leave," she said.

"I don't want you to. I want to stay here. With you. In this town I love, with the woman I love."

Abby ignored the roller coaster of emotions swirling inside her. She desperately wanted to soak in his words. Wanted to pull him to her and kiss him, tell him she loved him, too. But she'd already made the mistake of not listening to him before. Of not concerning herself with his needs. Of plowing on with only her own in mind, and she wasn't going to make that mistake again.

"Even if that means being close to your dad?" she whispered, quiet enough that the roomful of observers couldn't hear.

Carter shrugged. "I'm tired of running from him. I thought I was being brave by branching out on my own and making something of myself in a new town where I started out with no one knowing my name. But I never admitted to myself just how much of a coward I was being. I was running. Plain and simple. I put roots down in Vegas, but I was running all the same. I'm done with all that, Abby. I'm done running from a chance at happiness and a family of my own. With you. If you'll still have me."

At her bright smile, he lifted her face, pressing his lips to hers in a soft kiss that started off slow and sweet but quickly turned into something more. Something that had her gasping for breath by the time he pulled away, heat flooding her body as if a switch had been flipped.

Abby didn't know what to say. Couldn't reconcile how she'd accepted the fact that he was gone from her life with his words now.

She gripped his waist and tugged him even closer, staring up into his eyes. So filled with love it took her breath away. "You're really back in Heart's Hope Bay? To stay?"

"No, Abby." He kissed a path along her jaw, pressing his lips into the sensitive skin below her ear. Quietly, he whispered, "I'm really back with *you*. To stay."

Epilogue

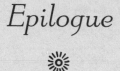

Abby couldn't believe this was actually her life. She'd had five months to get used to it, but it still felt surreal most of the time. They were two weeks into the school year, which meant they were two weeks into ironing out the kinks of their brand-new preschool program, and Abby was surprised at just how smoothly it had gone. She'd known she'd made the right choice when she'd asked Savannah to be the lead four-year-old teacher. The only person who loved these kids more than Abby did was Savannah, and that showed in every interaction with the kids and their parents.

Well, all the parents except one. There was the small issue of the volatile nature of Savannah's relationship with a preschooler's dad...Noah, her brother's best friend. Their relationship had been volatile for as long as Abby had known Savannah, which meant they had about twenty-odd years' worth of animosity built up. She wondered if maybe it was just par for the course with older brothers and their annoying friends, but Savannah got along great with everyone else.

As Savannah's best friend, it was Abby's job to side with her at all times. And she did...or tried to. That said, she'd be an idiot not to see the sexual tension sparking between those two. Sexual tension that Savannah was all too willing to ignore.

"Do I need to put you in a separate room when Noah comes to pick up Rosie?" Abby asked.

Savannah scoffed and rolled her eyes. "I think a better use of your time would be to tell him to keep his mouth shut and his judgmental eyes focused on his own lane."

Abby laughed, waving from the front window as the last parents backed out of the driveway. "Uh-huh. And you don't think any of this hostility has anything to do with the unresolved sexual tension just hovering around you?"

Savannah shot her a look of disgust that might have fooled anyone else. But Abby wasn't *just* anyone. She'd been Savannah's best friend for twenty-five years. She knew her facial expressions and reactions nearly as well as she knew her own. And Savannah's disgust might be genuine, but it was more probable that it was disgust directed at herself that she'd been so obvious.

"You're out of your mind, Abby, you know that?" Savannah gathered her bag and car keys and the two of them strode toward the back door just as it opened and Carter stepped through.

Abby ignored the butterflies that took flight in her stomach when their gazes met and held.

"Good, you're here," Savannah said, clapping a hand on his back. "You can keep an eye on your girlfriend because she's clearly lost her damn mind."

"Keep telling yourself that!" Abby called after Savannah before turning her attention to Carter.

He shrugged off his messenger bag and set it on the hook by the back door. "What was that all about?" he asked as he wrapped his arms around her, his fingertips dancing along the swell of her bottom.

She rested her hands on his shoulders and shook her head. "Denial at its finest."

Carter raised an eyebrow in question. "Am I supposed to know what that means?"

Abby shook her head. "Nope."

"Okay, then. Let me get to the good stuff," he said before lowering his mouth to hers.

This had been their greeting every day since he'd moved in, and she hadn't gotten sick of it yet. He'd stayed with Becca for the first couple weeks after he'd officially moved back, trying in vain to find a rental property. But the size of Heart's Hope Bay meant that rental properties weren't exactly readily available. He and Abby had decided they'd wasted enough time and weren't interested in wasting any more. After discussing it with her grandma and making sure she was okay with it, Abby had asked Carter to move in. His only answer had been a kiss that had turned explicit in a blink and ended with the two of them panting and sweaty.

"Hi," he said, minutes or hours later—Abby wasn't sure which—when he pulled back and gazed down at her.

She sank into him, glad his arms were around her holding her up because he always managed to kiss her stupid. "Hi, yourself. Just out of curiosity, when are you planning to stop greeting me like that?"

Carter lifted both eyebrows. "I'm actually glad you asked."

He stepped away from her and strode toward the record player as she watched with furrowed brow, having no idea what he was doing.

"Are you going to answer me?"

"One sec." He shot her a grin over his shoulder, before he lifted the needle and put on the song they'd danced to back in March. As the melodic strains flowed through the air around them, Carter walked back to her, holding out a hand and beckoning her closer.

Without question, she walked to him. Knowing she'd walk anywhere for him. He held her close, the two of them swaying silently for long moments, Carter's hand a firm but gentle presence on her back, holding her close. Though he wouldn't have to. Now that she had him, she didn't intend to let him go.

Abby delved her fingers into the hair at his nape, gliding her short nails against his scalp like he loved.

He groaned and glanced down at her as she bit her lip, knowing exactly what this was doing to him. She could feel the evidence of his arousal pressing into her stomach, and she wasn't sorry in the least for eliciting that reaction. After all, she was desperate for him nearly every minute of the day. It was only fair he was a captive to her all the same.

Grinning, she stared up at him, into the eyes of the only man she'd ever loved. The one she'd fallen for at sixteen and again at twenty-nine. The only one who saw her for who she truly was and who loved her, not in spite of her flaws, but because of them.

"So...about that question..."

Abby furrowed her brow, wondering how long she'd been trapped under the spell of Carter's mesmerizing green eyes that she no longer recalled a question at all. "I asked...What?"

Carter grinned down at her with the playful smile that tugged one side of his mouth higher than the other, and she felt an answering pull in her heart. "You asked how long I intend to greet you like this."

She breathed out a laugh. "Oh, right. So, what are you thinking? The next month or two? I figure we've got a year, tops."

"Actually, I was thinking a little longer than that." Carter stepped back, reached into his pocket, and dropped to one knee. He opened a small black velvet box and held it up to her like an offering, the center stone sparkling off the lights in the kitchen.

Abby gasped and covered her mouth with her hands, her eyes already filling. "Carter..."

"I wasted a lot of time chasing after dreams that I thought made me the person I needed to be. But I was wrong. I shouldn't have been running away. Not when everything I could ever want is right here, with you. I don't want to wait another minute to be able to tell everyone you're mine. My forever. So what do you say, Abby? Can I be your forever, too?"

She breathed out a watery laugh and nodded. "Yes," she said, breathless, her throat already clogged with emotion.

He beamed up at her, pulling the ring from the box and slipping it on her left hand. Then he stood, gathering her close as he held her and crushed their mouths together. "You said yes," he repeated over and over again, his lips brushing hers with every awed word.

Abby had long since given up the fight to keep her tears at bay, and they ran unchecked down her cheeks as a grin split her face. "Did you have any doubts?"

"You have no idea...Luckily, I had someone reassuring me along the way."

Before she could ask him who he meant, Hilde strolled into the kitchen and tsked. "I thought we came to an agreement that you two wouldn't do that down here anymore after the last time."

Abby choked out a laugh and buried her face in Carter's neck, her cheeks already flaming. Her grandma took absolutely every opportunity to bring up the one time she'd caught them in the act. "We're celebrating," she mumbled against his skin.

"I can see that," Hilde said wryly. "What, exactly, are we celebrating tonight?"

Abby glanced at Carter, one brow raised in question. At his short nod, she spun back to her grandma and held up her left hand directly in Hilde's line of sight. "We're engaged!"

"Well, hot damn!" Hilde said, smiling as she enveloped both Abby and Carter in a group hug. "It's about time you asked her. If you'd have waited much longer, there were bound to be whispers around town. People will already be counting back the months..."

"You knew he was—Wait, what?" Abby asked as the rest of Hilde's words finally registered. Her eyes grew wide as she lowered her hands to her stomach and stared up at Carter, worry and apprehension weighing her down. It was one thing for him to *say* he was all in with her and for him to propose. It was another thing entirely to be faced with the possibility of a child so soon.

But instead of running away like she feared he would, instead of turning in on himself or lashing out, he grinned down at her and lowered his face until their lips were a mere breath apart. Against them, he whispered, "Now or later, I can't wait."

See what happens when sparks fly between Savannah and Noah in the next Sunshine Corner story

A Wedding on Sunshine Corner

Available Spring 2022

About the Author

Phoebe Mills lives near the Great Lakes and loves her family, coffee, and binge watching, in that order. During the day she wrangles kids and by night she conjures up strong women, dreamy men, and ways to wreak havoc on their lives—before giving them a happy ending, of course! It's a tough job, but there's nothing else she'd rather do.

You can learn more at:
  http://authorphoebemills.com/
  Twitter @phoebe_writes
  Facebook.com/authorphoebemills
  Instagram.com/authorphoebemills/

Keep reading for a special sneak peek from another story you may love!

ONLY FOR YOU
by Barb Curtis

Will a fake relationship between two friends lead to true love?

After having his heart broken on national television, Tim Fraser knows only one way to stop the gossip about his love life—a new girlfriend. The problem is, he's done with romance forever. A fake relationship with his friend and Sapphire Spring's sweetest baker, Emily Holland, seems the perfect solution to getting rid of his newfound fame, but their fleeting *faux*mance is stirring up the kinds of feelings Tim has sworn off for good.

Emily has secretly lusted after Tim for years, but pretending her feelings are all for show never factored into her fantasy. Still, her decades-long crush makes it impossible to say no to Tim's proposal. But with each date, the lines between pretend and reality blur, giving Tim and Emily a tantalizing taste of life outside the friend zone...if they can find the courage to give *real* love a real chance.

Chapter One

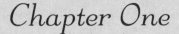

Emily Holland had two simple New Year's resolutions.

The first, reorganizing her life. She'd kick-started the day—and year—by cleaning her apartment and purging her closet of two bags of clothes for Goodwill. Then she'd monopolized both sets of washers and dryers in her building's laundry room down the hall, which was the reason for the cut-off jean shorts and threadbare NSYNC tank top she currently wore.

With the holidays officially over and fad diets in full force, Tesoro, her patisserie in the strip of storefronts downstairs, would see a lull in walk-in traffic until business picked up again before Valentine's Day. She could use the break to organize her work life, too.

Her second resolution? Well, he lit up her phone with his third text in an hour.

Tim Fraser—friend since high school, upstairs neighbor, fellow town council member, and secret object of her affection for longer than she cared to admit.

As recently elected town councilors, she and Tim had spent the last six weeks on the volunteer committee for Sapphire Springs' Christmas festivities. They'd also collaborated on last night's New Year's Eve party, which Emily had secretly hoped would end with a lightbulb flickering on in his ridiculously gorgeous head, when he finally realized they were both single now and a perfect match. He'd kiss her at midnight on the rooftop of town hall, fireworks blasting behind them, and the rest would be history.

Too bad he'd bailed at ten p.m. without even saying goodbye. It had been the final straw, prompting her New Year's resolution to kick her secret crush to the curb once and for all. All she had to do was stop hanging out with Tim all the time. From now on she'd put herself out there, meet other guys, and find the real Mr. Right—somebody who could look past the friend zone and see her as more than "the girl downstairs."

With a nagging buzz, her phone announced another text.

Someone's being persistent today.

Curiosity tempted her to read his texts and see what had prompted so many, but she knew she would then feel compelled to respond, and that would inevitably lead into one of their back-and-forth conversations that lasted an entire evening, until one of them either invited the other over to hang out or said they were going to bed.

Not today, Fraser. No way would she blow her resolution on day one. The clock was ticking, and watching her best friend, Leyna, fall in love with her soul mate and plan their wedding had Emily wondering if she'd ever get her own happily-ever-after. Determined to ignore him, she propped her bare feet on the coffee table and flicked on the television to channel surf as her phone vibrated again.

They'd established a routine back in the fall, watching TV together, or more often than not, watching the same show separately and texting each other the entire time. It had begun with a bunch of nineties teen flicks, like *Clueless* and *She's All That* (her choices), then they'd spent a day on John Hughes classics and another bingeing Adam Sandler movies. Then the Christmas movies had begun. Emily loved the cheesy romances—in fact the cheesier, the better. Tim mostly teased her about it and always got even with a Tarantino flick or two.

In these last few months he'd really leaned on her. They'd gotten close—well, they'd always been sort of close, but now she'd kind of become his "person," which both thrilled her and ignited an ache in her heart that she'd never survive if she kept squashing her emotions. She couldn't do it anymore. It was like the tighter their bond, the further the possibility of them ever being more became.

A chill danced across her shoulders as the clicking of her thumb slowed. On a long sigh, Emily reached for the fluffy mauve blanket draped over the back of the couch and pulled it around her. She lowered the remote to the arm of the couch. *Behind Closed Doors* was airing a mid-season marathon.

The reality TV show revolved around four men and four women in their thirties sharing a mansion in L.A., and it starred Tim's ex, Melissa. After three years together, not only had she cheated on him with one of her roommates, but she'd come to Sapphire Springs back in early September, flanked by her entourage, and dumped him while the cameras rolled.

Her phone lit up again.

Shit.

It was literally the only thing on TV right now, and she'd bet that Tim needed a distraction to stave off the temptation to watch. Emily tipped her head back, resting it on the couch, to stare at the ceiling medallion encircling the light fixture, willing the tiny bulbs to help her decide how to play this.

If the roles were reversed, she could count on him, no question. Take Todd, the hunky police officer she'd dated back in the summer. When Emily dumped him, Tim had shown up with a chocolate cake that had CON-GRATULATIONS piped across it in pink frosting. They'd spent an entire Sunday watching reruns of *Friends*. She laughed even harder during the commercial breaks than she did during the show.

Tim was such a great guy. He hadn't deserved to have his heart ripped out.

The ache in her heart throbbed a little harder.

Ugh. This was exactly the kind of thing that had gotten her into this mess in the first place. She plucked her phone off the coffee table.

Six messages.

Happy New Year!

Mel's show is on all day for the second day in a row. I keep landing on it and getting caught up, like an idiot.

Maybe I'll go for a run.

And then the three most recent messages:

I'm back. What're you up to?

There's a "potty putter" infomercial coming on 😂.

Have you had dinner? I could throw something together.

Emily's gaze rolled toward the kitchen, where a stainless steel pot of turkey soup simmered on the back burner. Damn it. She pushed off the couch and paused in front of the mirror over the fireplace to smooth a hand over her blond hair and rub away the remnants of last night's smoky eyes. He'd seen her looking worse. Ugh, was she really caving on her resolution already?

But he needed her.

Her not-even-twelve-hours-old New Year's resolution practically went adrift then and there, leaving her stranded on the shore. *Just this one time*, she vowed to herself.

Her thumbs tapped out a response.

I actually have a big pot of soup on the stove. Why don't you come down?

He responded right away, and Emily changed the channel to the toilet golf infomercial. Then she went to the kitchen to busy herself until he knocked at the door.

"It's open."

When she glanced over her shoulder, six feet of lean muscle hidden by a faded Red Hot Chili Peppers T-shirt paused in the doorway, blocking the light from the hall. His shaggy blond hair curled on the ends, still damp from his shower.

"Hey, Shorty."

"Hey."

His blue eyes darted around the spotless kitchen as he closed the door behind him. "You cleaned. I cleaned my whole apartment today, too, like I haven't cleaned since the Naval Academy." His eyes fluttered as he drew a deep breath in through his nose. "That soup smells amazing."

She got a couple of bowls out of the upper cabinet and rooted in the drawer for spoons. "It's been simmering all afternoon, so it's ready whenever you feel like eating."

He crossed the kitchen and leaned on the counter, his triceps dipping in a mouth-watering little flex. "Did you have fun last night at the New Year's bash?"

"Yeah, it was a great time," she lied, placing a couple of napkins on the table. "What about you?"

He shrugged. "I got out of there pretty early, actually. Just wasn't feeling it."

His words weighed on her. She wanted to ask if he was okay, but instead she feigned surprise, like she'd been too busy being fabulous to notice him toss back his drink and head for the exit while the night was still young.

Quiet for a couple of seconds, he rubbed at the day-old scruff on his chin. "I know it's completely toxic, but I could not stop pausing on that damn show all day yesterday and today."

Tim had gone under the radar for a few weeks after the breakup, embarrassed and, though he'd never admit it, heartbroken. People whispered about how lost he'd seemed, but he'd perked up during the Christmas festivities, and everyone assumed he was doing better. She chewed the inside of her cheek before broaching the looming question. "Has the breakup episode aired?"

His shoulders rounded when he blew out a breath. "Tonight. This mid-season marathon is all building up to the new episode. Mel called this afternoon to warn me."

The ladle Emily started to dip into the soup came to a halt. "Melissa's *still* contacting you?" She forced a relaxed tone and resumed serving the soup. "This is new information."

He took the bowl she passed him and carried it to the small kitchen table. "Until this morning, she hadn't made any attempts in months, but I guess she wanted to give me a head's-up or something. I should just block her."

"Damn right, you should."

His mouth parted into a grin as he sunk onto the chair—the first sign of humor since he'd arrived. "Ooh, Shorty. You've got a feisty streak."

Emily chose the chair opposite him. "Do *not* watch it. There's no good reason to put yourself through that." She pointed a finger at him. "And stay off social media, too. Seriously." The show had a big following. There was even a ribbon running across the bottom of the screen with live commentary from social media followers.

He removed his ball cap and hung it on the corner of his chair. "I won't. From here on out I'm all about self-preservation. So anyway…" He stirred his spoon around the bowl, unleashing a cloud of steam. "Any New Year's resolutions?"

"Two, actually." She pulled apart a dinner roll and smeared butter on it while explaining her goal to get organized. "I've already started. My bills are all paid ahead of schedule, meals are prepped for the week. I bought a super-cute planner before the holidays, and I'm going to schedule every aspect of my life."

"That's great. I survive on scheduling and to-do lists." He paused to taste the soup, and his lips drew into a smile. "Mmmm. *This* is exactly the soul food I needed today."

The compliment warmed her like a hug. At least her cooking could brighten his day. "After it cools, I'll fix you up with a container for lunch tomorrow."

"You're the best, Shorty." He plucked a roll from the bowl sitting between them. "So what's your other resolution?"

She should've known that question was coming. Why hadn't she just kept her mouth shut? To stall, she went to the fridge to fetch them each a can of carbonated water. "I've only got plain—no lime—you good with that?"

"Sure." He cracked open the can she passed him. "So what's resolution number two?"

Damn it. She opened her can and gulped. "Um, well...to find the perfect guy."

"Ah, come on, really?" Tim set his can down and peered at her. "That's a lot of pressure. You know there's no such thing as the perfect guy, right?"

Maybe not perfect, but Tim Fraser came pretty

damn close. The only thing he lacked was actually clueing in to how great they were together. "Okay, *correction*, the perfect guy for *me*. I fully believe somebody is going to come along who will check off all the boxes."

He peered at her across the table. "You've mentioned these boxes before. Elaborate, please."

She braced her feet on the rung around the bottom of her chair. "Well, for one, he needs to be self-sufficient, because *this* girl is not looking after anyone."

Tim snorted, amusement lighting up his eyes. "Valid. Go on."

"Two, he has to be family oriented and ready to settle down." She put her spoon down and reached for her water.

"And three?" he prompted.

Emily let the cool liquid buzz around her mouth, considering. "Romantic, fun, spontaneous..." Too bad she wanted these things with the one person she couldn't have.

He wiggled the tab on the top of his can back and forth until it snapped off. "Take it from me, the more perfect you think someone is, the greater their ability to hurt and disappoint you in the end."

"Pfft...Not true," she countered, furrowing her brows and shaking her head.

"It *is* true. Truer words have never been spoken."

She blinked rapidly and beckoned with her fingers. "Gimme back the soup."

"What?" His spoon paused halfway to his mouth. "I've already eaten half of it."

"Gimme."

"No." Without breaking eye contact, he guarded the bowl with his arm and shoveled soup into his mouth a little faster.

Emily's gaze fell on his US Navy tattoo, the arm of the anchor drawing her eyes down his forearm. She gulped her water again.

Tim ate his last bite and pushed his bowl away. "I think we all need to stop looking for *the one*, the *happily-ever-after*, and just enjoy the here and now. Real life does not breed happy endings. People will just end up hurting you if you let them get too close."

"You're just jaded right now."

"I've come to my senses."

She shrugged. "I don't buy it. Obviously you've just never met the right person."

"You can say that again. And I'm not planning to, either. I am so done with relationships."

A declaration she'd heard about thirty-seven times in the past four months. "Right. Because they're not a part of your rules." If she had a dollar for every time he brought up his damn rules.

"Exactly." Oblivious to her disinterest, he held up a finger. "Casual dating only..."

She tuned him out as he ticked off rule numbers two and three. *No opening up, no getting close.* Blah, blah, blah. She could list them in her sleep.

"And most important of all," he was saying, "no developing feelings."

Emily waited a few seconds to make sure he hadn't added anything else. It was a growing list, after all. "Rules are overrated."

Tim shook his head and grinned. "Not my rules."

When he didn't say anything more, she leaned back in her chair and stretched. "So any resolutions for you?"

"Nah, you know me. I don't like to make those kinds of commitments." His eyes fell on a stack of broken-down boxes, propped up against the door of the coat closet. "When is the move into the new apartment?"

The guy at the end of the hall was finally moving out. For years, Emily had been on a waiting list for one of those apartments. They spanned the whole width of the building, getting the morning sun from the harbor and the afternoon light coming across town square. She picked at a thread on her jean shorts. "He should be out by the end of the month. I'm going to get a head start packing things I never use. New Year's resolution, and all that." She winked.

"If you need help moving some of your heavy stuff, I'll give you a hand. Just say the word." His phone chimed, but he ignored it. "And I'll have plenty of boxes at the shop, if you need more."

"Sure, that would be great. I don't have much stuff, but I'll keep you posted."

He flashed his teeth, and they practically sparkled

like a 1950s toothpaste commercial. He held her gaze a second, then cleared his throat. "What do you think Fuzzy has in store for us at next week's council meeting?"

"Holiday recap and spring event planning, probably, which I hope he spares me on. I'm exhausted from the Christmas events, and I could use the break to prep for wedding season. I've already gotten ten cake orders, including Leyna and Jay's."

Because her life wasn't complicated enough already, she and Tim were none other than maid of honor and best man at their friends' upcoming wedding in May.

His phone chimed again and he pulled it out of his pocket. "My mom. She wants me to come over and put an Ikea cabinet together." He got up and gathered their dishes. "Cute shirt, by the way." He pointed to a young Justin Timberlake before carrying the dishes to the sink. "I tried frosted tips back in the day."

"Yeah, I remember." Shit. Did she just say that out loud? Why not admit she remembered the exact brand of jeans he wore back then too. *Gap.*

Her phone rang, thank God. "I, um…It's Nana," she stammered.

He put his ball cap back on and backed toward the door. "I've gotta get going anyway. Thanks for the soup. And for distracting me."

With her thumb hovering over the Answer button,

she stuck her head out the door as Tim retreated down the dim carpeted hallway. "*Don't* watch the show."

He spun back around. "I won't, Shorty. Bye bye bye."

As the door clicked shut, Emily answered the call, mustering her most bubbly voice. Her grandmother hadn't been herself through the holidays. She'd been quiet and mopey—a rough contrast to her usual energetic self.

"Happy New Year, Nana."

"Happy New Year, Emmy. How was the party last night?"

Pinching her lip, she turned her head toward the window, where soft flurries collected on the fire escape. "All right." *But I left at eleven thirty so I didn't have to bear the humiliation of having no one to kiss at midnight. Again.*

"Well, I've been thinking about my birthday party. We should book soon."

"Nana, your birthday is five months away." Not that she was judging. Emily had planned her last birthday party six months in advance.

"Damn straight. It's not every day a gal turns eighty-three."

That's right, eighty-three. Not a particularly celebratory number like eighty, or eighty-five. Reserving a few tables for her grandmother's birthday wouldn't be a problem, though. Not when her best friend Leyna owned the most popular restaurant in town. "What did you have in mind?"

From the rattling in the background, Emily knew Nana was digging into her trusty bag of pink peppermints. She'd been hooked on them for years.

"I want a classy little soirée on a boat, beginning at sunset and lasting until after dark, with warm little lights strung everywhere. I'm thinking smoked salmon for an appetizer and sparkling wine. Mini cheesecakes for dessert. I'm sure it'll be no problem for you to pull together something great with Leyna for the food and Tim for the boat tour."

The woman had it all figured out. Emily put her phone on speaker and padded into the living room to relax on the couch. She picked up the remote to scroll through the guide. "Why a boat, though? The new rooftop patio at town hall is pretty swanky, if you want a change of scenery from Rosalia's." And it didn't involve coordinating with the guy she'd just sworn off.

"Uh-uh. At my age, who knows how many parties I have left. I want a nice little boat cruise, like when your grandfather and I got married. That was the most romantic night of my life, you know."

Well, shit. How could any other option compete with that? "Okay, leave it all to me. Just don't forget I have to help organize Leyna and Jay's wedding, too, which is the week after your birthday." Priorities and all that.

Nana continued to chat, changing the topic to the new book she'd started. Half listening, Emily selected the channel airing *Behind Closed Doors* and lowered the volume. She may have told Tim not to watch tonight's episode, but she damn well would.

She picked her nail file off the coffee table and ran it along her thumbnail. The live feed already ran across the bottom of the screen with commentary. The show reminded Emily of a real-life soap opera, with cattier fights and real booze flowing freely. Viewers seemed to embrace Melissa and Dak, and to be glad she'd decided to break up with her boyfriend.

When a glammed-up Melissa drove by the WELCOME TO SAPPHIRE SPRINGS sign, the lake beyond glistening in the September sun, Emily tossed the nail file and tapped her phone off speaker. She interrupted midway through her grandmother's latest book club gossip. "I have to let you go, Nana. Sorry. I'll keep you posted about the party planning."

Her hand trembled as she ended the call. Why was she so nervous? She already knew, more or less, how the episode played out.

Emily's breath hitched when the camera panned the boats bobbing along the dock and then moved along to the group of bold-colored clapboard buildings nicknamed Crayola Row before framing in on Tim's shop. She and Leyna had been in the kitchen at Tesoro the day the footage was shot, and they'd spied through the window as it all went down. It was innocent enough at the time, but this... This felt almost voyeuristic, somehow.

Had Melissa really needed to break up with him at

work, so the whole world could google him and the town where he lived?

There on her TV screen, Tim stepped out of the shop and closed the door behind him. He looked amazing—still tanned from the summer, wearing faded jeans and a dark green shirt with the sleeves rolled up to the elbows. He flashed a big, genuine smile before hesitating at the sight of the cameras. Then he hugged Melissa, his greeting muffled by the microphone on her denim jacket.

As always, Melissa looked gorgeous, her caramel-colored hair falling in long waves. Just seeing her again made Emily feel out of Tim's league.

The comments on the bottom caught Emily's eye. *Abort mission, this guy is hot!!!*

Emily's jaw turned to stone.

Tim clasped hands with Melissa and glanced over her shoulder at the camera and then back at her. "This is a nice surprise. I'm so glad you're here. How are you?"

She mumbled something about how she'd been better.

"Can you come inside, away from these guys?"

When it cut to Melissa, she was shaking her head. "I can't. What I came to say won't take long, anyway."

He let go of her hands.

Melissa made a show of wiping a tear and breaking eye contact with him before launching into a confession about falling for this guy, Dak.

The camera zeroed in on Tim's face, his eyes filled

with comprehension and betrayal. His Adam's apple bobbed as he swallowed, struggling to hold back his emotions in front of the cameras.

Emily gripped the TV remote so hard she had to relax her hand when it cramped. The live feed rushed across the bottom of the screen so fast it was almost impossible to make out the comments.

Tim's brows were drawn in, like he was trying to make sense of her words. When he spoke, his voice was barely above a whisper. "Did you sleep with him?"

Chin quivering, Melissa confirmed it with a nod before rushing to explain. "You and I have barely been able to talk to each other since the show started filming, and we haven't seen each other in months. And Dak... He's just like *been* there."

Tim's lip trembled slightly. He glanced out at the lake and then back at her, his eyes tortured and his jaw rigid. "So this is how you launch your acting career?" He tipped his head back in a laugh that sounded forced—a sure effort to save face rather than break down in front of the camera. "This is so"—here the producers inserted a *bleep*—"clichéd."

The camera zoomed closer. "Get away from me," he muttered, and then his hand masked the lens. The footage shook for a few seconds and then stabilized in time to show Tim storming into the shop and slamming the door hard enough that the OPEN sign crashed to the ground.

The image faded and a sappy song kicked in, cutting

to Melissa, in the back seat of the car, crying in some sort of "confessional" interview. But it was the bottom of the screen that grabbed Emily's attention. Fans were suddenly turning on Melissa and Dak.

> *How could she hurt her boyfriend like that?*
> *He's gorgeous.*
> *#Tim4Season2*

Within seconds, the hashtag appeared across the screen easily a dozen more times.

Her phone rang and Emily jolted halfway off the couch. Tim.

"Hello?"

"Em, what the hell is happening?" Tim's voice was frantic. "My Instagram is blowing up."

She could hear his phone buzzing continuously with notifications. "The episode just ended. Viewers seem to be smitten with you—they're going ballistic."

"Why?" He sounded horrified.

Um, because you're sexy as hell? "They think it's awful, what she did to you."

"I thought everyone wanted her to hook up with Dak. Christ, I feel ridiculous even saying this shit out loud."

She heard a door slam in the background. "They did, but now… They seem to be siding with you. There's even a hashtag. Tim for season two."

"Jesus," he muttered. "Just what I freaking need." He

cursed again and said he had to go. He was still trying to assemble the cabinet for his mother.

When the call ended Emily went straight to Twitter and searched the hashtag.

Tim was going to lose his shit.

He was trending.

Want more charming small towns?
Fall in love with these
Forever contemporary romances!

THE SUMMER COTTAGE
by Annie Rains

Somerset Lake is the perfect place for Trisha Langly and her son to start over. As the new manager for the Somerset Cottages, she's instantly charmed by her firecracker of a boss, Vi—but less enchanted by Vi's protective grandson, attorney Jake Fletcher. If Jake discovers her past, she'll lose this perfect second chance. However, as they spend summer days renovating the property and nights enjoying the town's charm, Trisha may realize she must trust Jake with her secrets...and her heart. Includes a bonus story!

FALLING IN LOVE
ON WILLOW CREEK
by Debbie Mason

FBI agent Chase Roberts has come to Highland Falls to work undercover as a park ranger to track down an on-the-run informant. But when he befriends the suspect's sister to get nearer to his target, Chase finds that he's growing closer to the warm-hearted, beautiful Sadie Gray and her little girl. When he arrests her brother, Elijah, Chase risks losing Sadie forever. Can he convince her that the feelings between them are real once Sadie discovers the truth? Includes a bonus story!

A WEDDING ON LILAC LANE
by Hope Ramsay

After returning home from her country music career, Ella McMillan is shocked to find her mother is engaged. Worse, she asks Ella to plan the event with her fiancé's straitlaced son, Dr. Dylan Killough. While Ella wants to create the perfect day, Dylan is determined the two shouldn't get married at all. Somehow amid all their arguing, sparks start flying. And soon everyone in Magnolia Harbor is wondering if Dylan and Ella will be joining their parents in a trip down the aisle.

FRIENDS LIKE US
by Sarah Mackenzie

When a cancer scare compels Bree Robinson to form an *anti*-bucket list, she decides to start with a steamy fling. Only her one-night stand is Chance Elliston, the architect she's just hired to renovate her house. Bree agrees to a friends-with-benefits relationship with Chance before he returns to the city at the end of the summer. But as their feelings for each other grow, can she convince him to risk it all on a new life together?

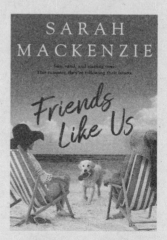